MRS. MORRIS AND THE MERMAID

Charlene continued down the hall to the last room. The door was ajar. Could this be the one? She knocked. "Trinity? I'm Charlene . . . Brandy sent me to check on you."

The door inched open. No answer.

Alarmed, she pushed the door further and saw the fingers of a pale hand curled.

"Trinity?"

Nothing.

"I'm coming in." Charlene hurried to the woman on her back, dressed in the iconic *Sirena* skirt/tail and a clam shell bralette top . . .

Books by Traci Wilton

MRS. MORRIS AND THE GHOST
MRS. MORRIS AND THE WITCH
MRS. MORRIS AND THE GHOST OF
CHRISTMAS PAST
MRS. MORRIS AND THE SORCERESS
MRS. MORRIS AND THE VAMPIRE
MRS. MORRIS AND THE POT OF GOLD
MRS. MORRIS AND THE WOLFMAN
MRS. MORRIS AND THE MERMAID

And writing as Traci Hall

MURDER IN A SCOTTISH SHIRE
MURDER IN A SCOTTISH GARDEN
MURDER AT A SCOTTISH SOCIAL
MURDER AT A SCOTTISH WEDDING
MURDER AT A SCOTTISH CASTLE

Published by Kensington Publishing Corp.

MRS. MORRIS AND THE MERMAID

TRACI WILTON

Kensington Publishing Corp.
www.kensingtonbooks.com

All Kensington titles, imprints, and distributed lines are available at special quantity discounts for bulk purchases for sales promotion, premiums, fund-raising, educational, or institutional use.

Special book excerpts or customized printings can also be created to fit specific needs. For details, write or phone the office of the Kensington Sales Manager: Attn.: Sales Department. Kensington Publishing Corp., 119 West 40th Street, New York, NY 10018. Phone: 1-800-221-2647.

KENSINGTON and the KENSINGTON COZIES teapot logo Reg US Pat. & TM Off.

First Printing: March 2024
ISBN: 978-1-4967-4193-4

ISBN: 978-1-4967-4140-0 (ebook)

10 9 8 7 6 5 4 3 2 1

Printed in the United States of America

I had a lot of fun researching mermaids and the mermaid lifestyle for this particular story. I love how unique people are and was just a little envious of Charlene's B & B.

I'd like to dedicate *Mrs. Morris and the Mermaid* to all of the readers out there who enjoy diversity through books. You all rock!

ACKNOWLEDGMENTS

My immense gratitude to John Scognamiglio for his support of the Salem B & B series. To the team at Kensington who really make each book shine, from the cover to the copyedits. As always, my thanks to my agent, Evan Marshall, who makes the magic happen behind the scenes.

CHAPTER 1

Friday afternoon, two days before the inaugural Mermaid Parade on the first Sunday of September, Charlene Morris was in her element, directing guests and bags from the foyer of her bed-and-breakfast. It was organized chaos, as her previous guests had checked out at eleven thirty and this wave all wanted to check in at one with mounds of luggage. The atmosphere was holiday festive as the guests conversed.

Three of the four suites would be occupied by those in the parade, except for the Bonets, Dirk and Rose, from Washington State. The young couple was thrilled by the lucky happenstance.

Natalie Southern, mermaid name Tida Wave, whose pink hair matched her pink shirt, offered to help the Bonets with costumes if they wanted to walk the route. She was a seamstress and had packed extra fabric, which explained all four trunks. Natalie's husband, Linc, had a hand on each of his twin girls' shoulders—blond cherubs named Aqua and Jewel—according to the front of their T-shirts.

Dr. Jack Strathmore, her resident ghost, watched from the kitchen hall, arms crossed as he observed the newcomers. Silva peered down from the second-floor landing, the Persian cat safely tucked between the rails, queen of all she surveyed as she flicked her thick, fluffy tail.

Andrew and Barb Martin had multiple suitcases. "You don't have an elevator?" Barb asked with an eye at the central staircase.

"No elevator. If something is too heavy, I'm happy to help so we don't ding the stairs," Charlene said. The carpet runner on the steps did its best as folks lugged bags and cases without a thought to the wood beneath.

"I can lift them." Andrew grinned and curled his arm to flex his biceps. He had a trim physique, average height, brown hair and eyes. He and Barb, his wife, a petite, attractive woman with light brown hair, were in their mid-thirties.

Minnie Johnson, the housekeeper at Charlene's, walked through Jack with a shiver as she read from a clipboard. "The Martins are in the blue room, the Bonets in the gold, the Southerns are in the pink, and the Wheatons in the green. Look for the colored anchor on the door. Inside your suite you'll find a list of restaurants and activities. See me for your key."

The Wheatons stepped forward, a harried couple in their forties with a ten-year-old son who had a pinched mouth. "The green, you said?" Terry brought his wife, Lottie, to his side as he waited for Minnie's confirmation.

"Yes. Here you go." Minnie gave him the key and the trio hurried toward the stairs.

"There will be a bathroom in the suite, Dillon," Lottie said to their son, which explained his nervous expression.

Within fifteen minutes, the guests had all gone upstairs—except for the Sanchos brothers, who wouldn't arrive until after four. They had two of the singles on the third floor.

"We're getting the hang of handling a crowd," Charlene told Minnie with appreciation. "The colored anchors on the doors and the matching key fobs really simplified things."

"Your idea, and a good one." Minnie read the list on her clipboard and put a check mark next to the names of those already there.

Check-in was usually more staggered, but because of the parade, everyone wanted to be in as early as possible. "I can't wait to see the mermaid costumes," Charlene said. "I had no idea people still traveled with trunks. That must cost a fortune."

Jack, dressed in golf shorts and a polo the same turquoise as his eyes, stared upward at the second-floor gallery. "What a unique event! I've never met a mermaid before and now we'll have a house full."

Silva loped her way gracefully down the stairs now that the crowd was gone. Charlene had noticed the cat liked to observe the new guests just as much as Charlene, Jack, and Minnie did.

"Too bad Avery couldn't come home this weekend." Minnie stuck the pen behind her ear. "She'd enjoy the parade too."

It was Avery's first official week at college, only forty minutes away in Boston, but she lived in a dorm so she could be independent. They texted every few days.

Charlene missed the teenager terribly yet understood that Avery needed to spread her wings. She'd learned from her parents and didn't want to smother Avery, who hadn't been away from Salem before now. "She'll be home on Friday." She couldn't wait.

"Yay!" Minnie smiled. "I'll make her favorites. All of them."

"Avery loves everything you create, Minnie, so you'll be busy."

The plump housekeeper/cook/friend blushed as she gave her gray curls a sassy pat. "I've got a shrimp and bacon recipe I want to try today for happy hour that I need to get the marinade started for. I added orange zest cookies to the welcome baskets in the rooms that are new, too, so I hope to get some feedback."

Charlene's goal when she landed in Salem and bought this historic mansion sight unseen had been to create a classy bed-and-breakfast in a town known for its witches and paranormal activity.

She hadn't believed in ghosts, and yet Dr. Jack Strathmore haunted this mansion and still resided in it.

Each suite had deluxe sheets and comforters, down mattresses, and an attached bathroom so that the guests would feel pampered. She offered a daily happy hour and full breakfasts on the weekend, with lighter fare during the week.

It would be two years this month since her arrival in Salem from Chicago after the death of her husband and she was moving forward. Thanks to Jack and Detective Sam Holden, who she'd gone on four actual dates with, Charlene was at peace with her past.

"I'll let you know what I hear about the cookies, but I'm sure they'll get high praise." Her secret weapon for the fabulous reviews online was Minnie. The woman turned average into gourmet, and the guests could tell the food was seasoned with love.

"Thank you." Minnie inched toward the kitchen with the clipboard to her chest. "And what are you going to do?"

Charlene gave Minnie an embarrassed smile. "I hate to admit this, but I haven't seen *Sirena*."

Jack had suggested they watch the movie so Charlene wouldn't be clueless about the pop culture references from twenty-five years earlier during the Mermaid Parade weekend. She'd meant to do so before now but had been too busy juggling her business, her mom threatening to move to Salem, and Avery going to college. Dates on the quiet with Sam were a bonus, though he'd been traveling quite a bit to New York for work.

Minnie's eyes widened at Charlene's confession. "It was so popular! Well, maybe it was a bigger deal in Salem because Trinity Powers, the star, is from here. You've seen the remake? My grandkids are all about it."

"No." Charlene shrugged. "It's on the agenda to watch them both today."

Minnie clicked her tongue against her teeth in mock shame. "What on earth? It's not like you're running a bed-and-breakfast or anything. Unless you have something against mermaids?"

Charlene liked mermaids just fine, but they weren't something she went out of her way for. "I saw *Splash*."

"Well *Sirena* came out after that," Minnie said. "It wasn't a romantic comedy but more of a drama. Trinity Powers was a lovely water ballet artist and very graceful. Her presence on screen was mesmerizing. The remake came out three months ago and my grandkids have seen it several times. I don't know the name of the actress. How could she be as good?"

"I'll watch the first one at least." The parade would feature Trinity Powers in the lead float to celebrate the twenty-fifth anniversary of the original movie.

"Charlene?" Natalie Southern hurried down the stairs with a friendly laugh. She exuded good vibes as she reached the foyer where she and Minnie, and Jack, stood.

"Natalie!" Charlene turned toward their pink-haired guest. Avery used to color her hair in fun ways too. "Is everything all right?"

"The rooms are perfect!" Natalie enthused. "I overheard you about the movies. Do you have a TV in a common area to play them on? I'm sure the girls would love to see both. They have the remake memorized, but I don't think they've seen the original. I have some last-minute costume adjustments to make, and I could use space to spread out."

"Sure—why not come into the living room? We can set you up." She glanced at Jack, who nodded.

They wouldn't view it together in her suite, but he could still watch it with her out here. In business, she'd learned that one had to be flexible.

Jack could comment all he liked, but she'd have to be careful not to reply or look like an idiot. He liked to trick her into giving herself away. She was the only human so far who could see Jack, though Silva could too.

The cat had figured out by trial and error that she couldn't touch Jack, who often teased her. Hard to believe that when Charlene met Jack, he'd been so grumpy because he was very lighthearted now.

Charlene smiled at Natalie and checked her watch. One thirty. "Give me a few minutes and I'll meet you in the living room. I'll ask if some of the other guests want to watch the movie too. Shall we start with the old or the new?"

"I love Alannah's version—it's modern and hip while staying true to the storyline," Natalie said. "Cute guy falls overboard, mermaid saves him, they fall in love. Mermaid captured, but cute guy saves her."

Nice summary, Charlene thought.

"You should probably watch the original first, to compare," Jack said. "Trinity Powers was magnetic on screen."

Minnie unknowingly echoed Jack's sentiment. "I think you should start with the classic and then the remake, to understand the differences."

Natalie brushed back her bangs, her eyes glinting with lighthearted mischief. "Minnie, are you Team Trinity?"

"Maybe." Minnie lowered her clipboard suspiciously. "What does that mean?"

"There's a big feud going on right now between Trinity's fans, who like the original, and Alannah's fans, who prefer the modern." Natalie leaned closer to murmur, "It's all over the internet that Alannah called Trinity a has-been and a nobody."

"That's not nice." Minnie frowned.

"It's not personal," Natalie said, blowing the comments off.

"How couldn't it be personal?" Jack asked.

"Of course it's personal," Minnie replied. "How would you like to be called a nobody?"

Natalie's cheeks turned darker than her pink hair. "You're right. I guess because of social media the insults seem disconnected from the actual actresses. There has to be more to the story of why Alannah would say that, don't you think? Our girls idolize her! I can't wait to find out. I heard that Trinity is practically a recluse in LA. That's where Alannah lives too. To meet them both?" She clasped her hands over her heart and sighed.

Charlene had more than an average curiosity and now she also wanted to know what was going on behind the scenes between the stars.

Brandy Flint, president of New Business, had reached out to Trinity because they'd attended elementary school together, to celebrate the twenty-fifth anniversary of *Sirena* with the debut of the Mermaid Parade. Her daughter, Serenity, had suggested the parade to raise money for Clean Oceans of Salem, a project focused on clearing plastics from the sea.

Serenity had gone several years in a row to

"It was filmed in the Bahamas," Jack said.

"Yeah!" Linc sat on the floor by his daughters, cross-legged. "Never saw the original either. It'll be hard to beat Alannah Gomez though. That woman can swim."

"She's a mermaid, Dad." Aqua giggled.

"Yeah, Dad," Jewel said in a serious tone. "Mermaids have to swim."

"You're right, girls." Linc smacked a palm to his forehead. His hair was brown, his manner as friendly as Natalie's.

"Cute." Jack bestowed a fatherly smile at them.

Charlene sat on the yellow brocade chair and was swept away by the magic of the film. Josh, a handsome yet arrogant young man, was partying with friends on a cruise ship. He fell overboard during a dance scene. Sirena, a mermaid, saved his life, bringing him to a deserted island and feeding him coconuts to survive. Lots of coconuts.

Trinity Powers was true grace as she swam in the ocean, her movements fluid and hypnotic. Her large violet eyes compelled the viewer to fall in love; her hair, long and dark chestnut, the hint of breasts peeping between the soft, waist-length curls in a teasing game of peekaboo. Nothing too risqué.

The near-death experience caused Josh to realize the error of his ways. He spent a month with Sirena, making love during the moonlight, when she came ashore and gained legs, only to be back in the water again at dawn or risk death. Again, made for a PG audience.

Toward the end of the movie, Josh was bit by a scorpion and almost died. The emotion in Sirena's violet eyes transcended the twenty-five years since the film was made. No wonder it was a cult classic!

Charlene glanced at her guests—Natalie was as enthralled as her girls and husband, her needle poised over a scrap of fabric. They were all afraid when Sirena was captured by the cruel government for testing and experiments, and they cried when Josh rescued her at great risk to himself. They cried more when the pair accepted their doomed love. Sirena swam away and Josh spent the rest of his life pining for her.

The credits rolled. Through her tears, Charlene read that Trinity Powers starred as Sirena, Mickey Bee as Josh. Natalie cried big tears and Charlene offered her the box of tissues from the side table after swiping one for herself. She sucked in a quivering breath.

"That is tragic and romantic and beautiful." Charlene dabbed her damp cheeks. "Why didn't they do more?"

"I had no idea it would be so good," Linc said, awe in his voice.

Jack cleared his throat, a human affectation as ghosts didn't actually need to do such a thing. "Trinity sure could act. Shame she never went anywhere after this."

The girls were glued to their dad's side. "That was too sad, but I want to see it again," Jewel said, her lower lip pouting.

"A romantic at heart, like me." Linc gave a low chuckle.

Aqua stood and leaned against Natalie's knee. She was over it. "Now can we see the good one?"

Natalie snugged an arm around her daughter. "You like the new version better?"

"That was all right, but I like the music and songs. And the dancing." Aqua bounced up down and twirled, knocking into Jewel.

"Hey!" Jewel crossed her arms and glared at her sister.

"It was an accident," Aqua said. "Soooorreee."

Charlene intervened and lifted the remote control to switch films. It made sense for the younger generation to be into a happier version. "I'm ready when you are."

Minnie arrived with a snack tray loaded with juices and cookies.

"Thank you, Minnie," everyone said as she passed the treats out. She placed the empty tray on the sideboard.

"Welcome! I might stay and watch the second one; I haven't seen it either." Minnie pulled up a vacant chair. "Find out why the grandkids are obsessed with it."

Charlene started the movie once everyone settled down. Right away, this film had a different flavor. The music was upbeat and Alannah as Sirena was not as serene, or as compelling. Alannah had dark hair and dark eyes; her swimming was good but not as fluid as Trinity's. Still lovely, but in a different way. Josh, played by Dom Preston, held his own as a heartthrob rather than taking a back seat.

The plot was the same but modernized. The time on the island was shortened, and they'd given Alannah two attractive sisters to swim with. Barb and Andrew joined them near the end of the film, finding places to sit on the floor. In this version, the pair also accepted their doomed love. Josh went on to be an oceanographer, while Sirena and her sisters moved islands to avoid future capture.

Charlene's cheeks were dry when this one was over, though her feet had tapped along to the music.

"What's your favorite?" Natalie asked Minnie and Charlene when the remake was over.

"I like them both," Charlene said. "For different reasons. Just maybe Alannah has an edge for me because it's not as sad." She'd cried so much after Jared's death that she didn't need to be reminded of tragedy.

Aqua spun around and tried to move her body as if she was swimming with a tail. "I love Alannah Sirena!"

Minnie laughed at the little girl's antics. "I can see the appeal for this one, but I prefer Trinity Powers to Alannah Gomez. So yes, I guess I am Team Trinity."

"Welcome to the club, Minnie," Andrew said. "If you'll be at the parade on Sunday, I'll introduce you to the fan club president, Ariel Glitter. She's organizing a party tomorrow night for Trinity's fans if you want to come to that too."

Minne stood and clasped her hands before her. "That's thoughtful, but I hadn't planned on going to the parade. My husband, Will, and I have a matinee theater date. First Sunday of every month there's a new show."

"Aqua, come here, hon, let's see how this fits." Natalie held up the soft fabric Charlene assumed would be a bodice with scalloped frills.

"Where's the tail?" The little girl sounded frantic.

"Relax, Aqua. I'll attach it later. It's easier to do this in sections." Natalie seemed pleased and lowered the bodice to her lap. "I found a new pattern this year that allows easier movement for walking."

"I'd love to see it!" Barb said. "Will you all be wearing costumes?" Silva stalked and pounced on a fabric scrap.

"Yep. Even me," Linc said. "I've got a staff with Neptune as the handle. Found it at a mermaid festival in Southern Cali."

"That sounds great," Andrew said. "Is that festival any good? We've been sticking to the East Coast."

"It was so much fun." Natalie used tiny scissors to snip a thread. "Two hundred people in the parade. We were part of a float to raise awareness for water safety."

"That's a lot!" Barb said. "The Coney Island parade only averages a hundred entrants."

A hundred was what they were at already. Charlene glanced toward Jack, who grinned at her as he said, "Mermaids. Who knew?"

Linc stood and stretched his body from his cramped sitting position. "It's been around for ten years now. I'll give you the registration information if you like. How many festivals do you hit up each year?"

"One." Barb rested her fingers on her husband's arm. "Andrew would like to do more, but it will have to wait until we retire, right, babe?"

"Right. It's expensive to travel, but it's our thing

to do together." Andrew rested his shoulder against Barb's. "We work full time in the tech industry."

"The festivals and parades are a way of life for us." Natalie smiled fondly at her family. "We have a merfolk website, Tida Wave's Creations, where we sell bespoke tails and costumes. We participate in the festivals with vendor opportunities. It allows us to do what we love."

Jack teased Silva with a piece of cloth behind Charlene's armchair, causing the cat to sit back on her haunches before she leaped at the chair leg. Jewel laughed. "Silly kitty!"

"What about the girls?" Barb asked. "Aren't they in school?"

"We homeschool." Natalie took a pin from the bodice fabric and stuck it in her wristlet. It had a magnet that made the pins stick if she missed. "We live in New Jersey."

"So, you've probably been to the Coney Island parade lots of times," Andrew said.

"Oh yeah." Linc bent to retrieve a lace scrap from Silva, accidentally getting close to Jack. He rubbed his arm as if chilled. "That's where Natalie and I fell in love. Folks go all out for the parade. It's the start of the tourist season for them."

"We've been once." Barb held Andrew's hand. "It was so fun. We met Deborah Harry."

"The year she was Queen?" Linc asked.

"No," Andrew said. "I forget who won the crowns—we were so overwhelmed by everything. Still, she was nice. We've met other celebrities who weren't as chill."

Charlene enjoyed Deborah Harry's acting and music. So much talent in one woman.

Barb looked at the girls, and whatever she'd been about to say, she changed her mind. "It was a *wild* weekend."

Jack laughed. "Now *that* I'd like to know more about."

"We can't wait to meet Trinity." Andrew freed his hand to brush his hair back off his forehead. "I hope she's cool too. I'd love to get an autograph or a picture with her."

"She hasn't been on the scene for twenty years," Barb confirmed what Natalie had told them earlier. "It's like she disappeared! Trinity is why we're in Salem."

"I want to meet Alannah," Aqua declared.

"And Trinity," Jewel said. "Both."

"You will," Linc promised. He straightened and nodded at the Martins.

"You guys are great," Andrew said. "Even if you aren't Team Trinity."

Natalie grinned. "We're Alannah all the way. But you both are awesome too. We shouldn't let a silly feud get in the way of the Mermaid Parade!"

"Hear, hear!" Charlene clapped her hands. Everyone in the room cheered.

CHAPTER 2

Sunday morning, Charlene prepared to be down-town by nine. She wore a Salem Mermaid Parade T-shirt in bright, tie-dyed colors with Trinity as Sirena on the front for the twenty-fifth-anniversary bash. *Splash* came out in 1984 and still held a cult status for mermaid movies. *Sirena* was just as popular.

"Great shirt," Jack said.

"Thanks." Charlene smiled at him as she tucked it in, then pulled it out, finally settling on tucking in just a portion. She loved the colors. "Okay?"

"Gorgeous." Jack fluttered her long hair, which she'd smoothed into a high ponytail.

Sunglasses, check, cell phone charged, and an over-the-body small purse just big enough to hold her ID, credit card, and phone so she could be hands-free.

"Have fun, Charlene. Take lots of pictures!"

"I'll try. Bye!" Charlene left her suite and headed

to the dining room. She'd agreed to be Brandy's assistant/minion to alleviate the pressure of parade day. Brandy wanted everything to be perfect. Not only would this supply funds for Clean Oceans of Salem but it would also bring positive media attention—always a plus.

Brandy was secretly dating a city councilman who was well aware that she was a witch. Tony Cortes had requested that they keep their relationship out of the spotlight. If anything went wrong today, it might reflect poorly on him, and he was up for reelection. Brandy had an allure that her age didn't diminish. At just over fifty, she claimed to be more powerful now than ever.

Charlene stepped into the dining room and clasped her hands together. Her guests were in varying stages of preparation for the big day and the kids—even Dillon—were brimming with excitement.

"Great costumes." She could see why the twins had won in prior contests because of the intricate beadwork.

Aqua and Jewel were in blue and green bodices and tails. Aqua's hair was dyed blue to match and Jewel's was dyed green. The tails were propped against the wall to keep them clean as the twins finished breakfast.

"Thank you!" Natalie was finishing some eggs and toast, with coffee and juice. "I'll get dressed when I'm done here. Linc has to help me with the coconut shells."

Linc, his bare chest painted blue, winked. "My pleasure."

Barb and Andrew were in street clothes as they ate. "I have a new clamshell top that I bought to wear with a skirt that ripples like water."

"It'll be really pretty," Andrew said. "But let's get Natalie's email and maybe we can buy you a custom tail for next year."

"That would be nice!" Barb said. "How much are they?"

Linc sipped coffee. "Anywhere from five hundred to ten thousand. Check out Tida Wave's Creations."

Charlene swallowed her surprise. That seemed expensive, but Natalie's work was first-rate. That explained how they could afford to travel.

Andrew didn't blink at the cost. "Thanks. We will."

Natalie shifted toward Charlene. "Registration starts at ten, right?"

"Yes." Charlene bestowed an encouraging smile at each of them, her keys to the Pilot in her palm. "I'll see you there, so be sure to say hello." Brandy had rented metal stands for observers, though people were welcome to bring their own chairs to watch from the sidewalks or their lawns. "Parade begins at noon. There will be food trucks all day. The King and Queen Neptune will be announced at six. At eight we'll start *Sirena* to celebrate the twenty-fifth anniversary of the movie at the Common."

Natalie gestured to Charlene's shirt. "Is that the T-shirt for registration? It's very cool. Too bad there wasn't one with Alannah Gomez on it. The new Sirena."

Charlene hadn't realized this would be such a

point of contention, but after hearing Andrew and Natalie discuss it on Friday, she and Jack had looked up the feud online. Fans were vicious in their defense of their chosen mermaid. Trinity fans claimed that Alannah needed support from her other actors because she wasn't as graceful in the water, and Alannah fans said that Trinity was boring.

"Trinity is classic," Andrew said. His tone today wasn't as friendly as it was on Friday. She wondered if it had anything to do with the party at Ariel Glitter's house last night. Jack had told her that the Martins had come in after midnight.

The Bonets wore T-shirts with Daryl Hannah from *Splash* on the front—nice, neutral ground at the dining table. The Sanchos brothers had on tight, silver T-shirts that would be paired with their tails later but, for now, wore jeans. Dean was older by a few years than Steve.

"We are Team Alannah too," Lottie said. "Dillon knows all the songs."

Dillon, hair dyed dark blue, wore a navy shirt and shorts with painted scales. His parents were in matching shimmering shirts—jeans for Terry, but Lottie wore a skirt.

"I heard there might be trouble at the parade," Dean Sanchos said to Charlene.

"What kind of trouble?" Charlene hid her dismay behind a cool façade. She hoped to nip the problem in the bud.

Steve plonked his elbow next to his plate with a sigh. "At Ariel Glitter's party, there was talk of a possible showdown. Trinity's people want Alannah to apologize in person for all that she's said."

"What?" Terry asked, confused. "We don't know anything about that."

Andrew slammed his coffee cup onto the table. "Team Trinity will defend their queen."

"When?" Charlene asked. She'd need to tell Brandy.

Barb waved her hand. "That was just a bunch of people blowing off steam after too much beer. Ariel probably won't remember anyway. Nothing will happen."

"Don't know a time." Dean glanced around the table. "Me and Steve want a chance at the prize money for the best costume. We created an animated Triton. It'd be cool to meet Trinity, but we don't care about fighting."

Charlene cleared her throat to get their attention. "I declare this B-and-B Switzerland." Her guests laughed and she relaxed. "Good luck, everyone!"

She left, concerned now about possible fights breaking out at the parade. It wouldn't be good press for Brandy or the New Business board.

With a goodbye wave to Jack on the front porch, Charlene drove downtown and parked on a side street. Brandy and Serenity, mother and daughter both lovely with auburn hair and magical powers, waited by the bandstand. The metal bleachers had been erected inside the fenced area. Salem Common had been in use for hundreds of years in one capacity or another.

"I want the movie screen over there," Brandy told a worker in an orange vest. "So that folks on the stands as well as the lawn can see it. I want a small stage before it for the announcements of Queen and King Neptune. Got it?"

"Yes, ma'am." The worker doffed his ball cap to her and walked off to his team.

"Mom, do you have to be so bossy?" Serenity rolled her expressive green eyes.

"I do," Brandy said. "That's how you get things done."

"*You* do it that way. I've been nice and polite this whole time and still accomplished what I needed." Serenity sounded exasperated.

"Good morning, ladies," Charlene intervened. The Flints were beautiful and powerful, but there was something about a mother-daughter dynamic that sometimes grated. She knew that because of her own mother. "This looks terrific! Can't believe it's the same park."

The registration booth was just outside the iron fence and vendor booths were lined up for an entire block. Traffic had been diverted from eleven to three to accommodate the parade.

"Floats will start lining up at ten, with the registration," Brandy said. "I had nightmares that it would rain." She and Serenity also wore the parade tees with denim, knee-length shorts.

The sky was summer blue and the weather was expected to be in the high seventies.

"No rain," Serenity said. "I performed a fair weather spell this morning, so just chill, would you?"

Brandy's body relaxed. "Smart young lady. Fine. Charlene, come with me to make sure the registration table is set up."

Serenity shook her head and mouthed, *Bossy*, as they passed by.

Charlene hid a smile but agreed—in her mind only. She had a lot of respect for Brandy, and for

Brandy's temper. She'd learned a while back that there was something genetically different about redheads that caused them to flare. Serenity practiced yoga and being mindful, while Brandy allowed her passionate side free.

Brandy led the way to the booth, where a young man with dark, romantic curls and big brown eyes unloaded boxes marked S, M, L, and XL from the back of a pickup truck next to a long table with pens and stickers to commemorate the event.

"Bobby!" Brandy exclaimed, her nature sunny for the artist she'd chosen to design the parade T-shirt. Each one was hand-dyed by him, the image of the mermaid on a cresting wave hand-painted. They were meant to showcase Bobby's talent and find him a sponsor.

Two chairs were behind the long table. Tina Setzer, the woman in charge of the cashbox for the parade and Clean Oceans representative, hadn't arrived yet. Charlene checked her watch—not even nine thirty.

Bobby's loose poet's shirt was fashionably rumpled and untucked from tight jeans. He gave the top of a box a morose pat. "Trinity hates the design. I showed her a new one and she didn't like that one either." Tears welled in Bobby's dark eyes. Talented, but oh so sensitive.

"Too bad!" Brandy's temper returned. "The design is not up to her—we okayed it, and everyone signed a contract, including her. What are you even talking about?"

"I loved her in *Sirena* and did my best to convey her image while imprinting my own style." Bobby brought his knuckles to his mouth. His fingers were slightly stained with a rainbow of colors.

"You tried to change the design? We ordered one hundred and seventy-five T-shirts. One-of-a-kind design by you, Bobby." Brandy quivered with anger.

"I wanted Trinity to be happy!" the artist exclaimed dramatically. "She's a Salem native, like us. I'm gutted." He pressed his hand to his trim stomach, showing off a silver belt buckle.

"I could care less about her happiness." Brandy opened a box and withdrew a shirt. The artistic rendering was of a silver and gold mermaid on a wave against the tie-dyed fabric. The figure had swirling dark hair and violet beads for the eyes. "We have a deal."

"I love this," Charlene said, touching the mermaid figure on her shirt.

"I'll speak to her." Brandy's tone was layered with controlled fury. "She's at the Hawthorne Hotel. In a nice suite *I'm* paying for."

"No, she's not." Bobby straightened from his slouch over the boxes so fast that a vape fell from his jeans. "She moved to the Waterway."

Brandy's mouth thinned. "Why?"

Bobby stuffed the vape into the back pocket of jeans so tight there wasn't much room. "She didn't say. Could be because of Alannah and her fans. Alannah and Dom are at the Hawthorne, partying and acting like rock stars. I'm sure sweet Trinity doesn't want to be anywhere near them, with the feud and all."

"Feud?" Brandy queried. "What feud?"

Bobby didn't elaborate, so Charlene explained what she knew, including what her guests had mentioned about a possible confrontation today between the actresses.

Brandy pursed her lips but didn't comment, focusing instead on Bobby. "*When* did she move?"

"How should I know?" Bobby ruffled his curls with a slight pout. "Her dad was just here looking for Trinity a second ago. I talked to him about the design, to see if he could reason with her, you know?"

"Grant's here? Of course he is." Brandy answered her own question. "Unless he's moved, but the family used to live practically across the street."

"He'll be back for the parade." Bobby lowered his voice. "He told me they've been estranged and he wants to make amends. I'm sure Trinity has her reasons for shutting her dad out. Being denied her affection is worse than the sun shuttered by a cloud."

Bobby, barely thirty, had painted murals on some of Salem's old brick buildings to bring beauty to ruin—his words. The tall images of love and light over crumbled brick had shown his talent. He had an artist's view of the world and, it seemed, an artistic temperament to match.

Brandy gave a delicate snort. She was certain with the right backing Bobby could get his own studio and sell his art on the harbor rather than share a workspace. "I'll talk with her and find out what's going on."

"Please don't bother Trinity with the T-shirt situation." Bobby pulled out a soft shirt and ran his hand over the stylistic mermaid on the front. "I thought she'd like it, I really did, but she's under a lot of pressure."

Brandy crossed her arms. "Why?"

"She didn't say." Bobby returned the shirt to the box and sucked in his lower lip. "How can we give these out when she doesn't think they're good enough?"

"Don't let her crush you," Brandy said. "I want you to forget about Trinity."

"She's the leader of the parade. On the number-one float! She said my design was rubbish. Rubbish." Bobby sagged against the boxes.

"Get yourself together!" Brandy shook him gently by the shoulders. "Part of your contract was to give out the T-shirts and introduce yourself as the artist. This is how to find a patron. Do you understand?"

Bobby blew out a breath at that directive. "I do. Okay. I–I just need a minute." He shuffled across the sidewalk and climbed into the front seat of his truck, windows down, listening to the soundtrack of the *Sirena* movie—the original score, not the peppy one. Charlene, if she had to pick a side, was more on Alannah's than she was before. Why would Trinity be so cruel to someone only wanting to please her?

"Artists!" Brandy said. "Now, what to do about Trinity?" She glanced toward the waterfront and the Waterway. "I just don't have time to deal with a diva right now. Trinity's been that way since preschool." She turned her back to the hotel and faced the table. "We've got to attach numbers on the floats. Can you do that?"

"Yes." Charlene liked that job assignment because it meant she could see all the parade entries and the costumes. "Happy to!"

Brandy nodded but didn't smile. "Kevin and Kass will be here at eleven to begin judging the costumes and the floats. When the parade starts you can sit with them. We need to alert them to the possible mood of the fans."

"I hope it turns out to be a lot of hot air." Charlene wondered if she should alert the Salem PD. It would be a nice excuse to text Sam.

"You and me both."

Before she could message Sam to give him a heads-up, Tina Setzer arrived, carrying a metal cashbox and a loaded beach bag. The organizer of the cleanup project was a college friend of Serenity's, with long blond braids and a charming smile. Big blue eyes and a bikini top with short shorts.

"Hi Tina," Brandy said. "Bobby is taking a minute in his truck, but he'll be here to help you with registration—you'll accept the money and he will hand out his shirts."

"All right." Tina placed the box on the table, and then the bag. "We're so excited about the parade and the donations for Clean Oceans. Do you mind if I set out information?"

"Not at all," Brandy said. "The state of our ocean is a very hot topic right now, and so important for the fish in our harbor. It's where our restaurants get their fresh catches."

Bobby left the truck when he saw the cute blonde behind the table and came over to introduce himself. "Hi. I'm Bobby Rourke."

"You made the tees?" Tina sounded impressed. "I'll wear one, too! Are they organized by size?"

Bobby patted a box. "Yeah. S, M, L, XL, and XS for kids."

Bobby was in good hands. Brandy happened to look up and said, "There's Grant Powers! Come on, Charlene." She took Charlene's elbow and headed across the Common to the old houses along the side streets. Some had been turned into townhomes a hundred years before.

What had happened between Trinity and her dad that they were estranged? Charlene had had her rough moments with her mother, but they were in a better place now. Even at their worst, they'd still talked. Family was family.

"Hey, Mr. Powers. Grant!" Brandy called to an older man of about seventy with a beard walking beside a heavyset gentleman around fifty, give or take. Was this his son, Trinity's brother? Charlene didn't know very much about the Powers family.

The older man turned and squinted, then grinned. "Brandy Flint!" Grant opened his arms for a hug. "Darling, you're as lovely as ever. I buy your red wine twice a week."

Brandy kissed his cheek. "You are a sweetheart!" They pulled back. "This is my friend, Charlene Morris," Brandy said. "She owns the bed-and-breakfast on the hill."

"Nice to meet you." Grant gestured to the man at his side. "This is Michael Brown—he's writing a biography on Trinity. Twenty-five years ago she was at the pinnacle of her career. Something happened to her, but she won't talk to me. I'd love to know what went wrong and why she gave up acting. Why she won't speak to me. Michael's agreed to help."

"How is Madeline?" Brandy asked softly.

"Died ten years ago. Not that we were close, since she up and took Trinity to Hollywood without my permission. She was only ten. Madeline Powers cared about making Trinity a star, end of story." Grant sighed heavily.

Michael gently patted Grant's back. "You've reached out to her at the Hawthorne. After all this time you finally get to see her, leading the parade."

"She's no longer there," Brandy said. "Moved to the Waterway. Guess the Alannah *Sirena* fans are being a pain over some online feud. I had no idea."

Grant looked at Michael with sadness in his eyes. "I shouldn't get my hopes up."

Charlene blamed her wanting to help nature for squeezing the older man's hand in compassion. "Trinity will be on the first float, and they'll start lining up at eleven thirty, so maybe you could come then? It might offer a chance before things begin."

Grant nodded. "I'll be there. I'm not getting any younger. If it's my fault that she's hidden her light for so long, then I must make it right. It's fate that she's here after all this time."

Brandy gave the man a side hug. "I hope you reconcile, for your sake. Bye, Grant. Michael." She turned around and strode back with Charlene toward the registration table. Brandy whispered, "Once a diva, always a diva."

"She was so young!"

"Her mom spoiled Trinity rotten, but the girl could swim like a beautiful fish. I think Madeline wanted her to be the next *Million Dollar Mermaid*."

"What's that?"

"Charlene." Brandy shook her head. "The biggest swimming star of all time—even better than Trinity. Esther Williams."

"I watched both *Sirena* movies on Friday . . . I find that hard to believe. Trinity is so talented."

"And then kaput. She did two other films after *Sirena*, neither in the water, and her career tanked."

"I wonder why."

"Good luck getting answers." Brandy stopped just before the table and raised a brow at Charlene. "Actually, if anybody could do it, it would be you. I should send you to talk with her, since she didn't even give me the courtesy of letting me know she'd changed hotels."

Compliment or insult? Brandy's mood made it hard to tell. "Thanks?"

"You're relentless when you want to know something."

"I'll try not to be offended," Charlene said, lifting her hands.

"Sorry. It's just that Trinity making Bobby feel bad has me up in arms. That man worked very hard to straddle the artistic and commercial components one must to achieve success—financial success, which he said he wanted."

"That might be difficult."

"Listen, if Bobby wanted to paint sheds on the weekends while earning a living doing something else, I wouldn't have put the time into it—but he's got talent and drive beneath those curls."

Charlene watched Bobby and Tina share jokes and smiles. "I think he's better now." Charlene chuckled.

"I would never date an artist," Brandy said.

No, Charlene thought, Brandy liked her men to be powerful, and usually rich—at least as wealthy as she was.

"How is Tony anyway?"

"Fine." Tony had a thick head of silver hair, brilliant blue eyes, and a charismatic smile that had bowled Brandy over. "He'll be on the fringes today . . . just to say hello to the people."

In other words, he would do no more than nod to Brandy. Charlene couldn't judge, as she and Sam were also on the downlow. She didn't want to upset Jack or her guests by being overly affectionate at the B-&-B, nor did he want that at the department.

Instead, they'd had four dates—the last one in Boston, for a romantic dinner where he'd kissed her until her toes curled, after he'd been away for his job. Relationships were complicated things.

At ten, Charlene stood with Tina as registration opened and handed out numbers to folks for the parade. The costumes ranged from none at all to elaborate. The Sanchos brothers were two parts of an animated King Triton that was very impressive.

Trinity hadn't yet arrived. Her float driver was her fan club president, Ariel Glitter—the woman who'd hosted the party last night for Trinity and her fans. Ariel was a large woman with a wig of blond curls to her waist. Her costume was a rainbow tail of foam and shells that had been strategically placed as a top. Charlene feared the shells might not win the battle over the bosom.

Charlene handed the number one to her. The float was the iconic island scene, complete with palm trees, a rock, and several large conch shells. Coconuts and a scorpion.

"This is great." Charlene nodded toward the float. "Nice to meet you, Ariel."

"And you! The team and I worked real hard on it. Some friends of mine are staying at your B-and-B." Glitter and sparkle had been dusted over Ariel's cheeks, arms, and ample cleavage. "Have you seen Trinity yet?" Ariel paid the hundred-dollar registration fee for the float. Walkers were only fifty bucks. Everyone would get a T-shirt and half of the proceeds would go to the Oceans project. "She didn't stay long at the party last night; claimed to be tired. We were all disappointed but understood. It's a lot for her."

"I haven't," Charlene said. Andrew and Barb hadn't mentioned Trinity leaving early that morning at breakfast.

"T-shirt?" Tina asked with a bright smile.

"Yes, please." Ariel gave her size and accepted both the shirt and the educational material about keeping the ocean plastic free.

As instructed, Bobby introduced himself. "Each shirt was hand-painted by me."

"Thank you!" Ariel admired it and then put it

over her arm. "A keepsake for me, since I don't want to ruin my costume. I'll add it to my Trinity merchandise collection."

Ariel wandered toward the float to put the number on the front as Charlene greeted the next person in line. She saw Grant waiting for Trinity. He greeted Ariel with bowed shoulders.

Fifty floats later, Charlene was bowled over by people's creativity. A hundred walkers had registered. Excitement was palpable, like a carnival. She had no idea who would win the prize for best mermaid costume and was glad she wasn't a judge like Kass and Kevin. There was also a prize for the best float.

Alannah Gomez arrived, surrounded by fans. The actress was a pretty, vivacious young lady with a big smile. "I just talked to Serenity Flint, and she accepted my late admission. My fans surprised me with the idea yesterday and we've been hard at work on the float."

"Oh! Sure." Brandy had made sixty numbers just in case, so Charlene handed Alannah number fifty-one.

Bobby forgot about Tina for a moment as his artist's eye was drawn to vibrant beauty. Alannah wore her costume from *Sirena*, which was hot pink, orange sherbet, and deep green for her tail. Her shells were firmly attached, and she wore a tiara that glittered in her long, dark tresses. Her brown eyes sparkled with mirth, as if life was a party and she was there to celebrate.

"Where is Trinity?" Alannah asked. "I've been by the float numerous times to make up this silly squabble. Yes, I may have said she was a has-been, but it was after too many daiquiris and entirely a jealous comment."

Charlene was taken in . . . until she saw the smirk that suggested the apology was not exactly sincere. "She's not here yet."

"The parade starts at noon?" Alannah shifted toward "Josh," played by a very handsome young man—even more handsome than Bobby. "What time is it, Dom?"

"Ten till." Dom, as Josh, was shirtless and in loose shorts, as he'd been when he was overboard on an island. Charlene pulled her gaze from his muscled chest with difficulty. His body was a work of art, chiseled and toned.

"Hmm. She's probably hiding." Alannah fluttered her fingers and left.

Charlene and Tina exchanged looks.

"I was Team Alannah until just this minute," Tina said. "I don't like mean girls." She kept her shoulder to Bobby, showing that she didn't like boys who liked mean girls either.

At noon, there was still no sign of Trinity. Brandy rushed to them, her cheeks flushed.

"I've tried Trinity's cell phone over and over." Brandy's mouth tightened. "Charlene, will you please go check on the little diva? Try the Waterway. I called, but they won't confirm she's there. Knock on every door if you have to. This is very unprofessional."

"You bet." Her assignment was to make Brandy's life easier.

"I paid her five grand to show up today and her

behind had better be on that float." Brandy shook her head. "You know what? Don't rush. Alannah wins this round as far as I'm concerned. Let the float be empty for all I care."

Charlene didn't much like either mermaid's attitude. "Ariel Glitter is the driver and ready to go. Maybe we can hop on during a lull in traffic. Bobby, what room is Trinity in?"

"I don't know—second floor, though."

Choosing to walk rather than move her car, Charlene hurried to the Waterway. The modern hotel had several spaces for boats, and half a dozen bobbed in the harbor. She reached the parking lot and halted midway as a man who might be one of her guests entered the hotel.

If that was Andrew Martin, Team Trinity, maybe he'd stopped in to see what was keeping the actress or to get an autograph. Charlene pushed open the glass door to the lobby and stopped at the desk. "Trinity Powers, please."

"She's popular today," the clerk said. "And I'll say to you what I did everyone else—we don't give out that information. Don't try to tell me you're her dad either."

Had Grant been here? While Charlene was glad the clerk was professional, it didn't help her bring Trinity to the parade. The clerk turned away to answer the phone. "Waterway!"

Charlene used that opportunity to sneak past the front desk. There were only two stories to this hotel and Bobby had said the second floor, so, while the clerk was occupied, she went down the hall as if going to the coffee shop. A man with glasses, not her guest Andrew, ate a sandwich, and

Trinity wasn't inside. Where had he gone? She had to be mistaken.

She climbed the stairs to the second floor. A brunette maid was just leaving a room to the left with a cleaning cart. "Hi!" Charlene said. "I'm Trinity Powers's escort to the parade. I've forgotten her room number?"

The maid showed a rolled tube among the supplies and gave a wistful smile. "I wish I could be at the parade, but I work until two. Trinity signed a poster for me."

"That's great!" Maybe the reclusive star wasn't always a diva.

The maid nodded to the room on the opposite end of the hall. "At the end."

"Thank you." Charlene felt a teensy bit bad about her white lie. "Find me afterward and I'll give you a *Sirena* T-shirt. I should be around the bandstand."

"I will. Thanks!" The maid opened the door of her next room to clean and disappeared inside.

Charlene continued down the hall to the last room. The door was ajar. Could this be the one? She knocked. "Trinity? I'm Charlene. . . . Brandy sent me to check on you."

The door inched open. No answer.

Alarmed, she pushed the door farther and saw the fingers of a pale hand curled.

"Trinity?" Nothing.

"I'm coming in." Charlene hurried to the woman on her back, dressed in the iconic *Sirena* skirt/tail and a clamshell bralette top. She'd been ready for the parade.

A rainbow T-shirt was jammed in Trinity's mouth.

Her neck was red. Charlene dropped to her knees to check Trinity's pulse, but the vacant stare at the ceiling confirmed that Trinity Powers was dead.

She sucked back a cry, got out her phone, and called Sam. He was the best detective in Salem, and she knew he would find out who was responsible for this tragedy.

Murder.

CHAPTER 3

Detective Sam Holden arrived within minutes as he'd been at the police station, and he didn't berate her for not calling 911 or for using her cell phone to inform him of the crime. They'd been through this situation before, unfortunately, and the rules between them had relaxed.

"Charlene!" Sam, almost six and a half feet tall and solid muscle, dark brown hair, deep brown eyes, and a thick mustache, entered the room. He knew that Charlene wouldn't fall apart or blab to anybody about what she'd seen, and that she could be counted on to give concise details regarding the tragedy.

Two years had created trust between them. They tentatively were trying to move their relationship, but at a turtle's pace. Her stomach gave a little flutter of attraction that was squelched as Sam was followed by Officer Jimenez of the gray-eyed glare.

The woman had it in for Charlene and time

hadn't calmed her down any. Charlene ignored the officer and her bad attitude to nod at Sam.

"What happened?" Sam asked. "Do you know who this is?"

Charlene backed up from Trinity and folded her hands in front of her. She'd surveyed the hotel room from her position for any clues that might help Sam with the case and put Trinity's death in a little box in her head. She'd tried to keep what she'd touched to a minimum. The doorknob, the actress, her phone. A medication bottle was on the nightstand with a glass of water. The label was turned away from Charlene. There was stationery from the Hawthorne Hotel beneath the woman's body, but she couldn't read what the letter said. "Yes. This is Trinity Powers. She's supposed to be the lead mermaid in the Mermaid Parade today."

"Lead mermaid?" Sam pulled his notebook from the pocket of his chinos—dark blue, with a lighter blue polo shirt.

"Trinity was from Salem before she moved to Hollywood as a child to be an actress. She starred in *Sirena* twenty-five years ago, a movie about a mermaid. Minnie and Jack said that could be why she's got a big following here in the Team Trinity competition."

"Can you explain?" Officer Jimenez also took notes but used her phone to record the conversation. Her uniform was navy blue pants and a shirt with a witch emblem on the sleeve, black shoes, and a hat with gold embellishments.

"Alannah Gomez did a remake of *Sirena* three months ago, and the fans are taking sides. Alannah has the edge with the younger crowd because of the music, and I kind of agree, but . . ."

Sam's brow furrowed. "You've seen the movies?"

"Friday afternoon I decided to watch them both because my B-and-B is full of merfolk coming to the parade."

"Merfolk," Jimenez drawled.

Charlene stifled her defensive bristle. "We are supposed to crown a Queen and King Neptune before the movie tonight. This is the twenty-fifth anniversary of the original *Sirena*." What could they do? As part of the board for new business in the city of Salem, Charlene understood the need for positive media, and this—this was Brandy's worst nightmare.

"The star is now dead." Jimenez snapped photos of the woman. "What's in her mouth?"

Charlene tapped her shirt. "A T-shirt. Everyone who participated in the parade was to get one. I guess she didn't like the design and argued with the artist this morning."

Sam and Jimenez alerted like greyhounds. "Who is that?" Jimenez asked.

"Bobby Rourke." She recalled the young man's dramatic despair. How he'd talked to Trinity's father, wanting Trinity to approve his design. Was that the new T-shirt in her mouth, or the original? Did it matter?

"What do you know?" Sam asked. He could read her like a book.

Charlene pulled her phone from her pocket after it dinged. Brandy had texted to see if she was coming. "Brandy had arranged for Trinity to be staying at the Hawthorne Hotel. Bobby thought that because Alannah Gomez was there with her fans, Trinity moved to the Waterway. And Grant Powers, her dad, lives across the Common. Bobby said they were estranged."

Jimenez shifted impatiently, but Sam quieted her with a look that reminded her that he was in charge.

"Bobby seems to know a lot about what's going on," Sam said. "What was he like when you talked with him?"

"Bobby is a huge Trinity Powers fan and was devastated when he discovered that she didn't like the design, which I think is really great. He tracked her here to show her a different design."

"How did he do that?" Sam asked.

"I don't know," Charlene answered, glancing at the T-shirt in Trinity's mouth. It was also tie-dyed. Was it the same? "She didn't like that one either. He was crushed."

"Enough to kill her?" Jimenez asked.

"I don't think so!"

"What time did you see him?" Sam asked. "What was his mood?"

"Dejected! Trinity had just turned down his other design idea. That was nine thirty this morning. Brandy wasn't pleased that he'd done any of those things as she'd contracted him for one hundred and seventy-five T-shirts, hand-painted, to help him launch his career."

"Brandy . . ." Jimenez said.

"Flint. Coordinator of the parade, with her daughter, Serenity Flint. Half of what comes in today will be donated to the Clean Oceans of Salem project. Tina Setzer is heading that up and working with Serenity directly. Once Tina arrived at the registration table he was in a better mood, flirty."

Hardly dangerous. Then again, he'd had to gather himself in his truck. Could he be a killer?

Sam and Jimenez exchanged glances; then Sam said, "I'll call the coroner and let him know we have a homicide on our hands. Jimenez, I want you to escort Charlene back to the parade, find Bobby Rourke, and bring him in for questioning."

"Yes, sir." Jimenez took several more pictures and then murmured something to Sam. He nodded.

"Charlene, before you go, tell me exactly how you happened to be the one to find the deceased?"

Sam's tone suggested it had better be a good reason and all aboveboard. He'd asked her to stay out of trouble, especially after the movie theater fiasco. This was why he was okay with keeping their new relationship out of the public eye. He might be criticized at the station when he was on track to be promoted.

He'd been offered a promotion in Portland, Oregon, and he had to tell them yes or no by the end of the month. If Sam moved, she couldn't go with him—not that he'd asked directly. He'd hinted in broad, hypothetical conversations that she'd quickly shot down.

Salem and her business were her new home. She had Avery to consider as well.

"Charlene?" Up went a thick, brown brow.

She tucked her phone into her pocket, unable

to answer Brandy's text. "I asked for Trinity's room number at the front desk, but the clerk didn't give it to me."

"Doing his job," Jimenez said with approval.

"Didn't Bobby know?" Sam asked. "Since he was here?"

"He didn't recall her room number, just that it was on the second floor. I was to make sure Trinity made it to the parade." Jimenez stared at her, and Charlene swallowed, her mouth dry. "I went upstairs and talked with a maid, who didn't give me the room number either." While giving a direction, it hadn't been the exact room, and she didn't want the maid to be in trouble.

"What was the plan?" Sam asked.

Charlene blushed but didn't look away. "Brandy told me to knock on every door if I had to. There are only ten per side. I started at this end and found this door, well, ajar."

"Did you break in?" Jimenez patted her badge, as if to say she didn't believe a word and Charlene had better tell the truth.

"I did not!" Not really. She couldn't look at Sam. "I knocked, and the door opened slightly. Because Brandy was worried for Trinity, that made me worried too."

"Then?" Jimenez prodded.

"Then I called out for Trinity and warned I was coming in, and that's when I saw her. On the ground. The shirt in her mouth." Charlene gulped and glanced down at the poor woman. "Oh! Her throat—are those bruises?"

Sam ushered her toward the door. "Jimenez,

find Bobby Rourke and I'll meet you at the station. Charlene." He put his finger to his lips.

She nodded. Jimenez kept her hand on Charlene's elbow, like she might run from the officer.

The maid exited the room she'd been cleaning, her eyes wide. "Is everything okay? With Ms. Powers?"

Jimenez was in a bind. Her job was to question people and find criminals. Charlene being there with her was very inconvenient.

"What is your name?" the officer asked the maid.

Charlene guessed that the maid was around twenty-five, with dark eyes and a trembling voice as she answered Jimenez, "Mary Clarkson."

"How much longer are you on shift?"

"I'm off at two." Mary glanced at her watch. "An hour or so."

Jimenez gritted her teeth. There would be no guarantee how long questioning Bobby might take. "When was the last time you saw Trinity Powers?"

"This morning," Mary said. "She signed an old movie poster for me at breakfast in the dining room."

"What time was that?"

"Nine o'clock," Mary said. "I was on my meal break."

So, Trinity was alive at nine. Bobby had been at the parade registration desk at nine thirty after showing Trinity his new shirt.

Jimenez glanced at Charlene and then stared at Mary. "When are you working again?"

"Tomorrow," Mary said. "I work five days a week, six to two. Is Trinity okay?"

"Thank you." Jimenez conveniently didn't answer the question and urged Charlene forward to the stairs. Charlene was glad the woman didn't mention the T-shirt she'd offered and complicate things with Jimenez.

They reached the lobby, the clerk's gaze narrowing at Charlene being upstairs, and then they were out the glass door to the parking lot.

Jimenez released Charlene and stopped to pull her tablet from her pocket, then typed information, probably what Mary had told her.

"Bobby was at the registration table for the parade at nine thirty because Brandy wanted him there to hand out his shirts," Charlene said.

Jimenez made a note on her tablet. "Thanks. Anything else?"

"Grant Powers, Trinity's dad, lives close by. They were estranged, but he wanted to make amends. I think he tried to see Trinity this morning at the Waterway. You should talk to the clerk. He will need to know that she's . . . gone."

After adding that name, Jimenez palmed her tablet. "You don't talk to anybody, got it?" The officer moved from the parking lot to the street.

Charlene glanced at Jimenez as they trekked away from the water toward the Hawthorne Hotel and Salem Common, but the woman behaved as if Charlene and the parade didn't exist. She had a mission to perform and the rest of the world didn't matter.

The music from the floats could be heard a block away. Traffic was jammed with floats and parade participants. The Southern family ambled behind a giant conch shell on wheels with four mermaids on it, waving and cheering. They were float number twenty-five, so this was the middle. Linc and Natalie were as festive in their costumes as the girls, Linc's Neptune staff taller than him.

Alannah Gomez and Dom Preston would bring up the rear.

The floats would complete their cycle by two, arriving back at the registration table. The whole thing was less than a mile, but there were horses and carts, broken wheels, the middle school band, and the ocean cleanup crew, collecting people's empty plastic bottles.

"We have to tell Brandy that Trinity is dead."

"No, we don't," Jimenez said.

"What am I supposed to do? That was the reason I went to the Waterway Hotel in the first place, to bring Trinity to the parade."

Jimenez shook her head. "Right now, I need to find Bobby Rourke for questioning. Where was he last?"

"The registration table in front of the Common." Charlene darted across the parade traffic during a baton-twirling trio in mermaid costumes.

Jimenez strode behind her until they reached the table. Tina sat with Brandy, Serenity, and Bobby, by the remaining T-shirts. There couldn't be many left.

Bobby gave Charlene a lazy smile and stood— then he noticed Officer Jimenez and backed up before quickly walking away. Not running, but not there anymore. Poof.

"That's Bobby Rourke." Charlene pointed to

the young man cruising through the parade viewers, dark curls flowing.

"Hey!" Officer Jimenez called.

Bobby didn't turn around.

Jimenez took off with a "Stay" to Charlene that was more annoying than forbidding. She would go where she wanted if she wanted.

Brandy crossed her slender arms. "What was that all about?"

How was she supposed to be quiet? "I'm not sure."

"Liar," Brandy whispered, tugging Charlene by the elbow, much as the officer had done earlier.

She pulled free. Brandy couldn't send her to jail.

"Sorry," Brandy said when they were five feet from the table, Tina, and Serenity. Both ladies watched them in consternation but couldn't overhear.

"I can't tell you anything, so don't ask." Charlene tried to change the subject. "How is the parade going?"

Brandy jutted out her chin, not put off by Charlene's statement. "Here comes your friend."

Officer Jimenez returned, barely out of breath from her dash after the artist. Her nose flared and she eyed Brandy, then scowled at Charlene.

Not her friend by any stretch of the imagination. "Officer Jimenez, this is Brandy Flint. She's president of New Business for the city of Salem. She and her daughter are cochairing the Mermaid Parade."

"What do you know about Bobby Rourke?" Offi-

:er Jimenez adjusted her hat. "Does he have a :riminal history?"

"Bobby passed a background check before be-ng offered a contract with the city. It's standard procedure." Brandy wasn't affected by Jimenez's :hilly demeanor.

"Can I get his address and phone number?"

"Of course." Brandy glanced from Charlene to the officer. "Now?"

"Yes, now."

Brandy bristled.

Serenity joined them, a beautiful version of Brandy, give or take twenty years. "What's going on?"

"This is my daughter, Serenity, cochair." *As in, she has a reason to be here,* Charlene thought.

"I'd like the contact information for Bobby Rourke," Officer Jimenez said.

"Sure." Serenity whipped out her phone and spoke into it. "Pull up the employment files for Bobby Rourke."

Charlene marveled at how simple she made it seem, with information at her fingertips.

Serenity scanned her phone, then lifted an auburn brow at the officer. "Where would you like it sent? I can airdrop it to you or send it via email."

Brandy exhaled. "Technology."

"You could do it too, Mom," Serenity said.

"I'm fine." Brandy raised her chin.

"Grandma's more savvy than you with her cell phone." She looked at Jimenez. "Gen Xers."

Charlene laughed aloud when Brandy coun-tered, "Millennials."

Even Jimenez unbent enough to allow a smile. "Email, to jimenez@salempd. Appreciate it."

"What happened to Trinity?" Brandy asked.

"What did you tell her?" Jimenez barked at Charlene.

Charlene backed up a step, out of glaring range. "Not a thing."

"I'm not a dumb woman even though I don't like technology. I sent Charlene after Trinity, who was a no-show for the parade. She came back with you, and you chased after my artist, who we know had been to see Trinity this morning."

Jimenez's jaw clenched.

"It's obvious that something happened to her," Brandy deduced. "Since Bobby ran, and she's not here, I'm guessing she was killed."

"No comment," Jimenez said.

Serenity gave her mom a look of respect. "Nice."

Brandy nodded. "Thanks."

Charlene sighed and rubbed her arms. "I can't go around saying 'no comment' to everyone, Officer. What do you want me to do?"

"You, Charlene Morris, are the detective's problem. Thank God. I'm going to track down Bobby and question him, as directed by my supervisor." Jimenez gave them each a curt nod after reading her phone. "Thanks for the information, Serenity."

The officer left and Brandy shivered. "Still hasn't warmed up to you, has she?" Brandy asked.

"She's got confusing auras," Serenity said. "Love and hate. Interesting." She shifted to study Brandy and Charlene. "Does this mean that Trinity is dead?"

Miserable, Charlene tried the no-comment tact, but it didn't fly.

Brandy sighed. "You found her, didn't you?"

"This has to stay between us, but yes. I did."

"Devil take it," Brandy complained. "I didn't like the woman, but I would never wish her dead."

"Of course not!" Serenity gave her mom a side hug. "What did you see, Charlene?"

"I really can't give details, all right? Sam asked me to keep quiet. It's not reasonable for me not to tell you that she is deceased, but no more than that until I get the okay . . . okay?" It would have to be good enough.

Serenity nodded. "Fine. I'll keep my eye out for Bobby and let you know if I see him."

If he was the killer, then that was a bad idea. "Don't approach him—text or call me, and I'll forward the message to Sam."

"You're not buddies with Jimenez?" Serenity teased.

"Funny girl." Charlene tossed her ponytail. "What will you do about the prizes to be awarded this evening? King and Queen Neptune? The show for tonight!"

Serenity paled. "By the Goddess. Trinity didn't participate in the Mermaid Parade. It's tacky to continue with the movie after her death."

"Tacky. Bad taste. So tragic." Brandy paced two feet one way, then two feet another. "This was a mistake."

"Wait!" Charlene had been a marketing major in college and she was very good at spinning things. "Let me think."

"You know what I have on the line here," Brandy said. It was not only the first Mermaid Parade but more income streams for Salem, while

Brandy dated her politician behind the scenes. She couldn't afford bad press and the pressure was on by him to grow the city's coffers. Elections were in November.

Charlene held her chin in thought. Once Sam gave the all clear about telling people Trinity was dead, their decision to show the movie could be construed as a way to honor the actress who'd made *Sirena* famous in the first place.

Serenity and Brandy watched her, both women worried.

"I say we scratch the Neptune ceremony . . . but still give out the prize money for best float and costumes." Charlene wished she had a pen and paper to doodle, which helped her think. "We set up a scholarship in Trinity's name and rename the Mermaid Parade to the Sirena Parade. . . ."

Serenity snapped her fingers. "That could work."

"A scholarship and a name change?" Brandy asked. "What will that cost?"

"Think of it as collateral damage. We want to convey that we're not heartless about continuing the festivities although she died," Charlene said.

"She was *murdered*. Why?" Brandy asked. The pulse at her throat beat fast.

"I don't know." Charlene kept Trinity's death and what she'd seen at the hotel in a tiny box inside her head. She could fall apart later at home, when she discussed things with Jack.

Brandy sighed and shook her hands, as if expelling emotion. Serenity and Charlene both looked at her.

"What is it?" Serenity asked.

"I . . ."

"Yes?" Charlene encouraged, not getting a good feeling.

"This is my fault," Brandy said, her pale forehead drawn.

"Did you kill her?" Charlene whispered. Had she gotten angry at Trinity? No, Brandy might have a temper, but she would never hurt anybody.

"No." Brandy tilted her head. Auburn hair bounced at her shoulders.

"How so, Mom?"

Brandy straightened. "I paid her five thousand dollars to leave her home. She suffers from anxiety, so it took some convincing."

"That's sound business," Charlene said. "Who better to lead Salem's first-ever Mermaid Parade than Trinity Powers, a woman you've known since elementary school?" Anxiety might be the reason that Trinity stayed in LA and didn't travel.

Brandy looked at them with a pained gaze and pinched her fingers together. "I may have used a tiny little spell to get Trinity here."

Serenity's mouth dropped in shock. "Well, no wonder you feel guilty!"

CHAPTER 4

"That doesn't mean your mom killed her!" Charlene said to Serenity in defense of Brandy.

"No . . . but that spell *could* have altered Trinity's free will." Serenity touched a moon charm on her necklace. "Mom is a very powerful witch. Whatever Trinity was anxious about kept her out of the public eye. We've advertised this parade for months. As soon as she leaves LA, she gets murdered?"

Brandy put her fingers to her mouth to stop a gasp. This affected her friend deeply.

"Serenity, if I've learned one thing from your family, it's that you do spells with the caveat that they do no harm," Charlene said. "Isn't that so?"

Serenity nodded. Both women's hiked shoulders relaxed the slightest bit.

"Charlene, you need to help me find out who did this to Trinity so that I can make it right, just in case," Brandy said.

"Sam doesn't want me involved."

Brandy grabbed Charlene by the upper arms, panic in her gaze. "You *are* involved. You found her."

Charlene sighed and bit back the retort that it was on Brandy's request that she'd done so—at this point, it would only make things worse.

"Mom! Let Charlene go. Think happy thoughts. Blue skies, ripe grapes, rich soil . . ."

Brandy released Charlene and stepped back, exhaling. "Sorry."

"I will do what I can." Charlene forgave Brandy for her outburst as it was fueled by fear. "Right now, we need to decide how to continue with the day—do we cancel or go ahead with the program?"

"I like your idea, Charlene," Serenity said. "We could show the movie as a tribute to Trinity Powers, a Salem native. Honor her life."

"Yes," Brandy agreed. "Me too." She glanced at her phone. "Almost two. Let's hustle over to the last float and Alannah Gomez. Do you think she might be in danger too?"

"Are you worried that someone could be out to hurt the mermaids?" Charlene couldn't conceive of a plausible reason to kill another human being.

"I don't think so," Serenity replied. "We would have heard something."

Brandy stepped toward the street where the first float would park at the end of the route. "I've lost track of my favorites, so I hope Kass and Kevin are managing."

"They are!" Serenity jerked her thumb toward

the registration table. "I checked with them a half hour ago. They have their choices for first, second, and third in all categories."

"Good. Thanks. Do you think Bobby's been caught yet?" Brandy asked. "I feel responsible for him."

Charlene scanned the Common, searching the throng for a head with dark brown curls being chased by a woman in a police hat. Nothing. Lots of pinks, purples, and gossamer fabric abounded. No Sam either.

She read her phone. No messages. Hard to believe that an hour and a half had passed since she found Trinity.

Just then, a man with skin painted silver broke through the parade with a shout. He'd been coming from the direction of the harbor. She recognized Dean Sanchos, her guest, and his brother Steve as two parts of a King Triton costume. "Trinity's dead! Sirena is dead!" Dean saw Charlene and raced for her, grabbing her hand in disbelief.

"Dean!" What did he know? "What's wrong?"

He didn't need any prodding as he said in a rush, "Me and Steve were grabbing a beer at the Pirate Bar and saw a body taken out of the Waterway Hotel, which is just across the road. A girl on a stretcher. Sirens blaring on the ambulance."

"Oh no!" That couldn't be Trinity. She'd learned the hard way that the deceased was taken away by the coroner. "Why do you think it was Trinity?"

"It wasn't." Dean dashed sweat from his forehead, the silver paint smearing. "A woman who worked there, though. Had an apron on. Blood on her face. I thought it was Trinity, so me and Steve ran to her. That's when one of the other hotel folks told us that Trinity was dead."

Mary Clarkson was taken by ambulance. "I was going to give her a T-shirt."

"Huh?" Dean tilted his head at her in confusion.

"Never mind. Was the woman okay?"

"She was alive, if that's what you mean. Her coworker told her he'd meet her at the hospital later with her car."

"I don't understand," Brandy said, having joined her to find out what was happening.

Charlene would have patted Dean to calm him but for his silver paint. "What happened to her?"

"She was hit on the back of the head. The guy said she was attacked in the hall. Has to be related to who killed Trinity. There's a killer on the loose in the Waterway!" Dean quivered.

And in an instant gossip took over the parade like a wave of wildfire.

Charlene excused herself before she said any more that might get her in hot water with Sam. Steve met up with Dean and they told other people who were listening in the crowd. She sent Sam a text, asking about the maid and alerting him that people knew Trinity was dead—not from her!

Sam called.

"Hello?" She kept the phone to her ear and her back to the crowd.

"The maid will be fine," Sam assured her. "She probably needs stitches. Told me that whoever hit her over the head stole an old movie poster from her while she was on duty, just about ready to go home."

"If the woman is Mary, well, she told me that Trinity had signed it that morning during her breakfast at the café. Why would someone want that?"

"I don't know. She says she doesn't either. The assailant didn't speak a word, so she's not sure if the theft was random, but that doesn't seem likely since Trinity is dead."

"Sam, this is terrible."

"I know. Death is never easy, and murder is worse." The phone was muffled and then clear again. ". . . Trinity was a beautiful star about to say hello to her fans for the first time in twenty years."

"Did you see the movies?"

"Just the original *Sirena* a long time ago."

"Do you know why she was a recluse?"

"No. Not yet." Sam sounded determined to find answers.

"There was medication on the nightstand. That might hold answers. Brandy told me that Trinity suffered from anxiety."

"You don't miss much, do you?"

The observation didn't seem very warm or friendly. "We've decided to show the movie tonight on the lawn and make it a tribute to Trinity Powers, Salem's own daughter." She waited for his disapproval.

It didn't come. "Hmm. I'll be sure to okay some extra manpower tonight for the event. Jimenez is still searching for Bobby. Not a good sign when a guy runs from the police."

"Yeah. You're right." Charlene kept the phone to her ear. "Brandy said Bobby passed the employee background check. No criminal history."

Sam snorted. "Bobby Rourke was here at the Waterway Hotel. Not only did he tell you that, but he's on the hotel security camera. I've watched the footage three times and it seems as if he was trying to slink into the lobby. There's no film of the second-floor hall, which I suggested to the manager he change. Trinity didn't like his T-shirt design and Bobby had a meltdown, taking his anger out on the actress. Temperamental artist."

Bobby was moody. He'd run. Charlene took a small peek inside the mental box where Trinity was staying for now. The shirt had been stuffed into her mouth, hard. "But why kill her? Did he go too far trying to keep her quiet? Her throat was red."

"Good observation," Sam drawled.

Considering his frostiness, she might as well tell him everything. "Trinity was lying on stationery from the Hawthorne, where she'd moved from. And I told this to Officer Jimenez, but I think maybe Grant tried to see Trinity at both the Hawthorne and the Waterway earlier today too. Trinity was trying for privacy, but everybody seemed to know where she was at." She hugged her free arm to her waist. "How did she die, Sam?"

"We won't know until the medical examiner tells us. Don't rush the process, Charlene."

She scuffed her shoe against the sidewalk. Brandy was reading her phone. Serenity had joined Tina at the table with the remaining T-shirts. They were supposed to be at the finish line at two thirty, so she had a few minutes.

"My guest, Dean Sanchos, saw the ambulance in front of the hotel. I guess an employee told him that Trinity was dead and that Mary had been hit over the head. Dean and his brother think that there might be a killer loose at the Waterway."

"They might be right. Or wrong. This could have more to do with Trinity, but an investigation is about finding answers. I have to go," Sam said. "Please go home."

Charlene rolled her eyes. "Can't do that. The show must go on for tonight, but it will have a different vibe than intended."

"I'll double the patrol for the event as soon as we get off the phone," Sam said. "Be safe, Charlene."

"I will."

Sam gave a rueful chuckle. "I've heard that so many times before."

"I mean it every time."

"I don't want you taken to the hospital by ambulance again, not on my watch."

His rumbling overprotectiveness actually made her blush. "Sam!"

"I saw your excuse for a purse today. No room for pepper spray."

"That's true. You take care too. Bye!" Her heart was warm as well as her cheeks.

Brandy joined her. "Sam?"

"Yes."

"He makes you glow."

"We're only friends."

"Yeah. Just like me and Tony. But that is not what I want to talk about. Did Sam say we couldn't do the show?"

"No—the opposite! He's going to double the

police to make sure it's safe. Bobby is still on the run."

"Ugh. Let's go find Kass and Kevin at the finish line, with big smiles. Not a whiff to them that I might be a killer."

"Stop that!"

The friends hurried without further conversation. Brandy wouldn't purposefully hurt a fly no matter her tart and sometimes overbearing personality. Her loyalty to her family and friends would make her a formidable opponent. Was there more to Brandy and Trinity's past than elementary school woes?

Not the time to ask as they reached the block with the finish line on one end. The float, with Ariel Glitter driving, blasting the original *Sirena* soundtrack, rumbled toward them.

Fans were disappointed that Trinity hadn't shown yet there was nothing to be done but let the show go on. Most people didn't know that Trinity was dead.

Kass Fortune, in a skintight mermaid skirt with a sparkling bodice, her brown, waist-length hair in braids with shells and feathers, saw them first and waved her pad of paper. Kevin, the other judge, turned toward them too.

Kevin Hughes had opted out of merman attire and chosen tie-dyed summer shorts and a blue tee. He was blond to Kass's dark, and the pair were fast friends. He managed the bar at Brews and Broomsticks and operated a paranormal tour company. Kass owned a tea shop and read fortunes through the leaves. She sometimes helped with Kevin's tours.

Kevin's girlfriend, Amy, was in the parade on a theater float with some of her friends. Kass was now dating Franco Lordes, a historical film expert she'd met a few months before. He was not as skinny these days, though because of his height, he would probably always be thin, but Kass had turned him on to Salem's food scene. Gourmet burgers with a local beer—delish.

What a family she'd created here, and Charlene couldn't imagine leaving, not even for Sam. She'd have to convince him that she was a compelling reason to stay.

"Where in the hell is Trinity?" Kass asked through her wide smile. "People are asking for their money back."

"What?" Charlene couldn't believe it. "This is for the Clean Oceans project." Charity—who would want their entry fee for the parade back?

"You know Trinity, right?" Kass asked Brandy. "Text her. Call her. Drag her here by the hair . . ."

Brandy cleared her throat. "Can't do that."

"Oh no. What's wrong?" Kevin shifted his gaze from Brandy to Charlene. "Something happened to her?"

"Why would you ask that?" Charlene said, unable to meet his discerning gaze.

"I heard a rumor about ten minutes ago that something happened to her at the hotel," Kass said in a low voice. "I asked Kev if he'd heard. So, that's why."

"She died at the Waterway," Charlene said, trying to make her tone casual. Nothing to worry about. It didn't fool either of them.

"*Dead?*" Kevin repeated.

"Sheesh." Kass bowed her head and murmured a Wiccan prayer.

Charlene had learned, barely, to hold her tongue rather than blurt out news to her friends. She kept the manner in which Trinity had died to herself.

Brandy moved her shoulder to stand in solidarity with Charlene. "It's not Charlene's fault. I sent her to look for Trinity, who was a no-show. For a reason, as it turns out. Did you choose the winners?"

"What?" Kass asked. "We can't possibly continue with the prizes or the show."

"We should skip the Neptune coronation, I agree." Brandy was cool as a winter breeze as she said, "We're going to offer a scholarship in Trinity's name and still give out the cash prizes. That should calm the crowd a little."

"The movie?" Kevin asked dubiously.

"We're going to show the film as a way to honor Trinity's life." Brandy's tone was final with no room for discussion. Charlene was impressed. "People can choose not to come, but we have all of the tourists in from out of town and they will need a place to gather. To mourn."

The number one float arrived and parked. Other floats were coming in as well, with happy mermaids and music.

Where was Alannah in all of this? Charlene wasn't forgetting that the pair had had a feud—a very public one.

Ariel Glitter jumped down, her makeup melting

after two hours in the sun. Her blond wig was droopy. "Where is Trinity?" she said in dismay. "This is my fault."

"What do you mean?" Charlene put her hand on the woman's arm.

"Last night at the party we had a few words." Ariel exuded misery, and Charlene recalled Barb saying that people had been drinking and blowing off steam. That Ariel probably wouldn't remember it. "She basically told me that I could drive the float without her. I never dreamed she meant it."

"Why didn't you say that earlier?" Like, at the registration table, when Ariel must have suspected Trinity wouldn't show.

"What did you fight about?" Kass asked in a gentle tone.

"My costume. Trinity said I was stealing her persona and I wasn't good enough for that. Too . . . big." More tears rolled down Ariel's cheeks. "Fat. She called me fat, actually."

"What did you do?" Charlene wanted to hug the woman who Trinity had been cruel to for no reason but her own.

"Nothing!"

Uh-huh, Charlene thought. That didn't sound even close to the truth.

Ariel clasped her hands together. "I'll go apologize to her right now. I'm so sorry for ruining the parade. Everyone is so mad that she's not here. It's my fault!"

That was two people claiming blame and an artist on the run.

"Ariel," Charlene said in a soft voice. More floats were parking, the participants ready with questions and wanting refreshments. The idea was for folks to buy food at the park or freshen up between two and six, when the prizes were to be given out. The movie would start at eight. Were they making the right decision?

"Yes?"

Brandy shook her head at Charlene where Ariel couldn't see her. Could Ariel have killed Trinity? It was possible for Ariel to have gone to the Waterway before registration, but she'd been on the float and couldn't have hit the maid.

She went with her intuition and said, "Ariel, Trinity passed away."

The woman gasped and stumbled back. Kass gave her a can of fizzy water. "Here!"

"Thanks. Oh my gosh." Ariel popped the tab, her hand shaking. "What happened to her?"

"We don't know exactly," Charlene said, "but the police are investigating."

"Well, we can't have the movie tonight without her. She's the star! She will always be a star." Ariel was pale as could be beneath her makeup. She guzzled the fizzy water.

"Actually, we want to honor her life, so we're going to continue with the show as planned," Charlene said.

"Oh." Ariel took another deep drink. "Are you sure that's not . . . insensitive?"

"Trinity wanted to return to Salem, her home, to make an appearance after so many years. How else can we give her the accolades she deserves?" Charlene asked. "Her dad still lives here."

"I know that. I know everything about her. I've loved her since I was ten years old and saw her in

Sirena." Ariel squished the empty can. "I wanted to be her so bad."

Charlene thought that was a little creepy.

"There's Grant now!" Ariel pointed behind Charlene. "Does he know?"

Charlene looked to the house Trinity had grown up in as Officer Bernard, a tall Haitian police officer, spoke to Grant on the doorstep. Grant nodded, then stumbled.

Officer Bernard patted Grant with compassion as the man sobbed so loudly, they could hear it across the lawn.

"Guess he just found out," Charlene said, her heart full of sorrow for the man who'd received news nobody wanted to hear—the death of a loved one.

They watched, helpless, until he went with his friend inside the house again. Would Grant be okay with the movie playing practically outside his front door?

CHAPTER 5

Alannah's float, number fifty-one, was the last to park. It was decorated as a scorpion—what had poisoned Josh in the movie. Dom brought it in and parked it crookedly. Alannah beelined straight for Serenity and Brandy.

"Is it true? What happened to Trinity?" The mermaid actress broke down in sobs when Brandy simply nodded.

Serenity hugged the young woman as Dom watched the pair, his eyes hard. Did he know something about what happened that morning?

Could he have harmed Trinity, thinking he was defending Alannah somehow? Just words. Had the feud escalated, or was there a different reason Trinity was dead?

Sam and Jack had both told her that human beings were complicated. Charlene was anxious to return to the B&B and talk to Jack, her best friend, about what had gone on today at the parade.

Her phone dinged a text from Minnie, saying that the Sanchos brothers had returned to get the paint off of them and rest. They'd told her that Trinity was dead. Was it true?

Charlene texted back that it was, and that she would explain later.

Minnie sent a praying hands emoji.

Alannah wiped her tears and reached for Dom without looking at him; he stepped to her side as if that had been rehearsed onstage. Actors. Charlene didn't trust what she was seeing from them. Ariel's reaction, by contrast, had been heartfelt and real.

"I know that there was some, well, friction," Serenity said diplomatically, "between you both about your portrayals of Sirena, but I hope you'll come to the twenty-fifth-anniversary showing of the movie."

"You're still playing it?" Alannah's brow rose.

"We are." Serenity clasped her hands together with composure. "To honor Trinity's life."

"Of course we'll be there. There is nobody who can compare to the original," Alannah said, her tone brittle. "I studied Trinity's movements frame by frame."

"It's not like she helped you," Dom said angrily. "Which is why your rendition of the story is equally as good, if not better."

"Trinity didn't help you?" Brandy asked.

"No. I had my agent call her, and I sent emails and a letter, wanting to do her part justice because it is such an iconic role." Alannah shrugged.

"That must have been hard," Charlene said. Enough to make anyone angry.

Bobby Rourke hadn't pleased Trinity, and neither had Ariel, or Alannah. So far, the only person Trinity had been kind to was the maid.

"I got the hint after three months passed with nothing from her that I would have to make my own Sirena." Alannah twirled a long curl.

"I saw your version of the movie," Charlene said. "The music makes it come to life."

"Thank you. I hired the same swim ballet coaches—well, the two who were still alive anyway." Alannah gave a snarky laugh. "They totally helped with the choreography. But the thing is, I will give credit where it is due, Trinity was naturally graceful."

Dom swiped his bare chest, not sharing an opinion.

"That can't be taught. So, I decided to shake it up a bit," Alannah patted her hips, "because this is what I can do better than most people."

Dom grinned, revealing pearly white teeth. "Oh yeah. You can move, babe."

The chemistry between them was good, but not as dynamic as the original—or had that all been Trinity?

"It's difficult to rise above, but I just focused on what I could do with the part and showcased my swimming sisters in the film—one of them is in the synchronized swimming Olympics," Alannah said. "Water ballet isn't a thing in the United States, but it could be, you know? I'd love to see a revival of water dancing."

"It's a sport?" Brandy asked.

"Yes." Dom's brow rose, as if he couldn't believe Brandy wouldn't know that. Well, Charlene hadn't either.

"I'll have to check out some videos," Charlene said.

"The Chinese have an amazing team—men and women both," Alannah said.

Charlene reached for Alannah's hand. "I have to confess that I just saw the *Sirena* movies on Friday."

"Not into living, breathing mermaids?" Alannah laughed, this time a genuine sound that made Charlene like her a little better.

What would it be like, making a movie where the previous star wouldn't give you the time of day? You'd have to keep your chin up, maybe play defense instead of offense. "I'm surprised Trinity never answered your emails," Charlene said. "I mean, just to be polite, right?"

"I heard that she lives in her compound with the doors locked and the shades drawn, scared of her own shadow," Dom said. He made a circle with his finger near his head. "Crazy."

"She told me that she suffered from terrible anxiety," Brandy said. "She rarely left the house."

"Maybe she was right to be paranoid," Serenity said.

"Fact." Dom sighed and looked longingly toward the food trucks. "I'm starved. I'm down with coming back for the show and all, but I'm also ready for a shower and to put some clothes on. Grab a drink in the Hawthorne bar. That hotel has class."

Serenity nodded. "Thank you both for being here. I loved your version of the movie too. In fact, well, this might be an imposition, but could we ask you to say a few words tonight before the show? If it's too much, I understand."

Alannah seized the chance at being in the spotlight like a true star. "Of course. We'd be delighted to step in."

Dom nodded. "All right. See you later."

"Five thirty?" Serenity asked. "To go over some lines beforehand."

Alannah raised her chin. "Sure."

Hand in hand, the pair left the place their float was parked. Alannah glanced back over her shoulder at a tall man in a Team Alannah cap that seemed to be in charge of the float. They would all need to be dismantled and most had teams.

"Hi," Charlene said, admiring the scorpion on the conch shell. "You did a nice job on this float."

"Thanks. I'm Ned Hammond, Alannah's fan club president. They weren't planning on being in the parade at all until I persuaded her that I could whip something together."

Ned was about forty, with thinning, dark hair, brown eyes, and both ears pierced. A goatee. He exuded shady vibes.

Like, he'd go the extra mile. Even if it was a little bit of a crooked mile.

Would he have had time to visit Trinity before the parade started, and maybe get across his point that he was Team Alannah all the way? His hands were big, the knuckles nicked. Probably from building the float.

"That was nice. What do you think of the feud?"

Charlene asked. Brandy, Kass, and Kevin were looking over Kass and Kevin's notes with Serenity.

"Obviously, I think Alannah Gomez has more
talent in her little finger than Trinity Powers has in
her entire body."

"She can certainly dance," Charlene agreed. "Have
you met Alannah before today?"

Ned considered this and held his chin, tugging
his goatee. "Well, on video calls, but not in person.
Doesn't change the fact that I'd do anything for
her." He squinted at Charlene. "You know. I'd
hook her up."

She got the picture loud and clear that Ned was
fine with breaking the rules.

"Why you askin' all these questions? You security or something?"

"No. I'm helping with the parade."

"Huh." Ned leaned closer and shoved his hand
in his pocket, bringing out a C-note to show her.
"Can you sway the judges at all?"

"I can't." Charlene backed up a step. "Well,
thank you, Ned, for joining us today."

"Yep." He pushed back the brim of his cap. "You
know where Alannah went to? I'd like to buy her a
beer."

"Their hotel. The Hawthorne."

"They ain't really together, Alannah told me."

"They aren't?" Dom and Alannah had seemed
tight to her.

"Nah. It's for promotion of the movie that they
act like they're a couple. Contract said for a year."

"Their movie contract?"

"Yeah. It's a Hollywood thing. Pretty common," she said."

"Well, good luck with that."

Ned laughed. "I know I don't have a chance long-term with someone like her, but sometimes a man might be in the right place at the right time. Stranger things have happened."

Charlene was not going to argue with that. Shady. She watched his expression and said, "I don't know if you heard, but Trinity Powers passed away."

Ned turned the color of chalk. "No way."

"It's true." She studied him for any sign of guilt. Any tells of distress or fear. Nothing. "Listen, when you take the float apart, be sure to use the recycling bins we've set up, all right? Proceeds of the parade go to Clean Oceans, so we should all do our part."

Quiet, Ned got to work on the float.

Charlene returned to Kass, Kevin, and Brandy. Serenity was speaking with Tina at the long table. Tina held the cashbox under her arm as they tidied to go.

"Well, what did you find out?" Brandy asked. "What a character! Looks like he might have done some jail time."

"Ned. He didn't know about Trinity being dead."

"That's strange. because Alannah and Dom had heard, and he was on the float with them."

Charlene turned back to watch Ned, who studiously ignored her as he focused on the float pieces. "He would have had to have known. You're right."

"Why would he lie?" Kass asked.

"Why would he act so shocked?" Charlene said.

"Alannah and Dom are actors," Brandy said. "Maybe we were all just played."

Charlene exhaled with frustration. "It's too early for a glass of wine, but dang, it's been a long day. It's only three."

"Says who?" Brandy tapped her watch. "I prefer the five-o'clock-somewhere line of thought."

Brandy had a point. Before Charlene could suggest it, Natalie, Linc, Jewel, and Aqua moved as one toward her.

"Charlene!" Natalie's cheeks were flushed. "We need to return to the B-and-B—Aqua hurt her ankle. We'll call a taxi."

"Poor sweetie—don't worry about that. I can take you home," Charlene said. "Give me ten minutes."

"Did you hear about Trinity?" Linc murmured in her ear.

"Yes. You?"

"Just rumors." Linc sighed, continuing to speak in a low voice. "Nobody seems to know what happened." Natalie was consoling the girls. Jewel wanted to help, but Aqua didn't want her to touch her leg.

"I'm sure that we will find out more soon." Charlene trusted Sam and the Salem PD. "Is Aqua all right? Should we go to the ER?"

"I think she's just tired. It's not swollen or anything." Linc shook his head. "I've heard how hard you've worked on the parade, so it's too bad about the festivities tonight."

"We've decided to continue with the events. Show the movie as a tribute to Trinity. Alannah is going to speak."

Linc's brow furrowed.

It seemed to be a mixed reaction between understanding and poor taste.

Spin, spin, Charlene thought. "She's a Salem native and I know it would mean the world to be honored this way. We're going to have a Trinity Powers scholarship of some kind. As members of the New Business board of Salem, we want to make sure that we do the right thing by her."

"Oh, yes." Linc nodded. "I get it."

Charlene gave Linc her keys and pointed to her vehicle. "That's my blue Pilot parked across the street. Why don't you get everyone inside and I'll just be a minute. Traffic is moving again, so it should be no problem getting home."

"Great. Thanks, Charlene." Linc herded his mermaid family toward the SUV.

"You better be back here at five thirty," Brandy said when Charlene went to explain that she had to run them home.

"Mom!" Serenity shook her head at her mother. "We know the names of the winners; we've chosen the winning floats. We've got the money accounted for and we can give Tina a check in front of the audience to make them part of the donation for Clean Oceans. Charlene, take your time."

"Don't listen to Serenity," Brandy said. "I was hoping we could talk to Grant before the event tonight so he's not sideswiped by the movie still going on. I want you to come with me."

That was not a mission Charlene wanted to accept, but she also understood why Brandy would consider it necessary.

This was a man she'd known since childhood. It was a matter of respect, and absolutely the right thing to do.

"I'll be back at five, five fifteen at the latest—where are you going to be?"

Brandy gestured toward the brick building on the corner. "The Hawthorne Hotel bar, getting a big glass of chardonnay."

At that, Serenity sighed.

"What?' Brandy said, defensive against another critique from her daughter.

"Can I come too, Mom?" Serenity batted her lashes. "I can't have you drink alone. It's not right."

"Since when do we care about what other people say?"

"Since you started dating the politician."

"You're an evil child." Brandy took Serenity's hand. "Come on, let's go."

CHAPTER 6

Charlene hurried to the Pilot, where the Southern family had piled in with the AC and radio cranked high. Linc was shotgun in the passenger seat and the girls were in the back, with Natalie between them to make sure that Aqua and Jewel had space as they were bickering over who had more room. Tired and cranky, it was time for a cooldown back at the B&B.

"I texted Minnie to let her know we are on our way," Charlene said over the music. "She reminded me that we have ice cream in the freezer." She'd never had a sibling or children but had picked up a few tricks during the last two years. Ice cream was a gift from heaven.

"Ice cream!" the girls chorused, immediately in much better moods.

"Charlene, you are a lifesaver," Linc murmured across the console. "You don't get this kind of special treatment from a hotel."

She smiled at him, loving this direction her life had taken in Salem. "Happy to help."

Charlene maneuvered around mermaids, mermen, and floats in disarray until she reached Crown Point Road, the street that led up to her bed-and-breakfast.

Jack waited for her on the porch, his stance agitated. Uh-oh. He'd probably heard about Trinity's death from the Sanchos brothers and would be worried for her.

She parked and everyone spilled out, Aqua hamming it up with her ankle until Linc carried his daughter inside. It was sweet how the little girl rested her head against her dad's shoulder—the blue paint didn't smudge, unlike the silver body paint the Sanchos brothers had used.

Minnie met them in the foyer and led the way to the living room. "Poor sweetie! Prop your foot up on the stool, here."

Jewel appeared a tiny bit put out at the attention her sister was getting, but Minnie had experience with kids and understood right away what to do.

"Jewel, dear, why don't you help me bring out the ice cream? Normally we don't allow our guests in the kitchen, but since you're so strong, I know you'll be the perfect helper."

"I will!" Jewel stuck to Minnie's side, and they returned to the kitchen.

Jack laughed. "She's good."

"She sure is!" Charlene said with a smile.

"What did you say?" Natalie asked.

Jack chuckled. "Gotcha. What happened to her?"

Charlene gave Jack her shoulder and faced Natalie. "She sure is a good helper—Jewel."

"Oh, yes." Natalie kneeled to get a closer look at Aqua's injury.

"I am too!" Aqua tugged at Charlene's hand.

"How did you hurt your ankle?" Charlene leaned over the little girl's foot, clad in a cute sandal with thin straps. The tiny toes were dirty from all the walking she'd done. Jack stood next to Charlene and goose bumps dotted her skin.

"I was running really fast, so fast, to beat the float." Aqua grimaced and her eyes welled up. "I tripped."

"Not much support," Jack observed. "It doesn't look swollen. Can you have her move her foot?"

Charlene gently touched Aqua's shin. "That sounds very fast! Can you move your foot?"

Aqua did, and even flexed her toes.

"It's not broken or sprained," Jack said. "Probably just a tweak."

Somehow, Charlene refrained from commenting on a *tweak* being a medical diagnosis.

"It's fine, hon." Natalie straightened and kept her gaze on Aqua. "After a rest and some ice cream, I bet you'll be good as new. Unless you don't want to go back to the park later?"

"I do!"

"Well, we'll see." Natalie smiled at Linc over their daughter's head.

Minnie entered the living room balancing a tray

crowded with bowls of ice cream followed by Jewel, who carried the spoons and napkins in a special holder. "We've got sprinkles too!" Jewel announced.

"Wow!" Linc said.

Jewel handed out the spoons and napkins, tilting her head at Charlene. "Minnie said you wouldn't want ice cream?"

Minnie probably wanted a moment with Charlene to find out about Trinity. "Not right now, but it sure looks good."

"I've got an iced tea ready for you, Charlene, on the kitchen counter." Minnie headed out of the living room and Charlene stayed on her heels.

"Thank you!"

"Now, tell me what happened to Trinity!" Minnie pulled her cell phone from her pocket and placed it on the counter. "The Sanchos brothers didn't know much, and I can't find it anywhere on the news."

Jack appeared in his spot at the dining room table. "It's horrible that she's gone. Natural death?"

"She was killed," Charlene whispered. "Sam hasn't released the news yet, but he will eventually. An employee at the Waterway let it slip to Dean and Steve that Trinity was dead, but of course not how."

"How?" Jack and Minnie asked in unison.

"A T-shirt stuffed in her mouth." Charlene touched her throat. "And red marks on her neck." Her body shook. She'd put it all from her mind as best she could to get through the day.

"That's a very personal crime," Jack said.

Charlene nodded at Jack as she sipped her iced tea. It did seem up close and personal. And what about the marks on Trinity's neck?

"What happened?" Minnie asked, keeping a cautious eye on the hall. Charlene shut the pocket door, enclosing the kitchen.

"Trinity didn't show up at the parade and she was supposed to be on the float. Brandy asked me to check on her . . . she suffered from awful anxiety and rarely left home. I saw medication on her nightstand, but I don't know for what."

"You found her!" Minnie exclaimed.

Charlene nodded, keeping Brandy's spell to herself. "Brandy had offered her five thousand bucks in addition to paying for the hotel and flights. Maybe she needed money so much she was willing to face her fears?"

"Poor woman!" Minnie placed a pod for herbal tea in the Keurig and hit the button. "I wonder if that's why she never made more movies?"

"That's hard to treat," Jack said. "Without medication and therapy."

Charlene focused on Minnie's question. "Maybe so. Her father, Grant Powers, was hoping to have a reconciliation while she was here in Salem since they haven't spoken since she got mad that he'd commented on her personal life to the tabloids."

"Grudges hurt those who hold them more than the recipients, often times," Minnie said wisely.

Charlene took another large swallow of refreshing iced tea. "I'm going back to the Common early to help Brandy, who knows Grant from her childhood, break the news that the show will go on tonight—to honor Trinity's life."

"Oh?" Minnie cupped her mug. Lemon zest wafted from it.

"This was Brandy and Serenity's debut project and it has a lot of eyes on it," Charlene explained. "Bad press isn't acceptable, so . . . the prizes and party aspect from the parade will be downplayed and the movie will become a tribute to celebrate Trinity Powers, a Salem native."

"Did you help with that?" Jack asked, his eyes dancing. "I recognize some Charlene magic in turning that around."

Minnie blew on the tea in the mug. "When you say it like that, I understand. Also, why Brandy wants your help to break it to her dad . . . you have a way with words, Charlene. Brandy can be . . . abrasive."

"I'll do my best, but it won't be an easy message to deliver." Charlene sipped again, the cool liquid quenching her dry throat.

"What does Sam say?" Minnie asked. "Since you found her?"

"Don't talk about the case." Charlene wrapped a small napkin around the base of the tall glass. "It's difficult because I want to help. I could ask around, talk with folks, but Sam would be upset if I did." She placed the glass on the counter, the condensation caught in the napkin. "Brandy thinks Trinity was a diva, the artist Bobby Rourke had words with her because she didn't like his T-shirt design—the maid I talked with at the Waterway had her sign an old movie poster and I guess Trinity was nice to her, but she's the only one. Oh, and Ariel Glitter, her fan club president, got into an argument with her last night to the point that Trinity told her she wasn't going to be on the float. In the past, Alannah asked for her help with the movie and Trinity completely ghosted her."

"That's awful!" Minnie said. "Hollywood must have really changed her. She didn't like the T-shirt design?"

"Brandy says she was spoiled even before then." Charlene tugged the hem of her shirt. "I think this is pretty. Artsy. It was in her mouth."

Minnie put down her mug after a fortifying drink. "Could the artist have done it?"

"Bobby had the time, and I guess the motive." He'd sat in his truck to get himself together before flirting with Tina, the Clean Oceans representative.

"Artists can be temperamental. Passionate," Minnie said.

"True." Passion. Temper. Mary Clarkson. "Somebody hit the maid over the head to steal the poster she'd had signed by Trinity. I don't know if her attacker would be a different person or the same one as who killed Trinity? Dean wondered if there was a killer on the loose in the Waterway."

"Good question," Jack said. "I would chat up the maid, Charlene."

Charlene didn't answer Jack but made a mental note to check on poor Mary Clarkson, and maybe deliver the T-shirt to her because she hadn't been able to get one herself. Proactive, to give something and then, if conversation came up, well, that happened sometimes.

"I think it's terrible that someone so beloved by our city has been killed here." Minnie straightened a dish towel on the oven rack. "I'll pack up some cookies for you to bring to Grant Powers. I just can't imagine receiving that kind of news."

Minnie loved her family above all else and they were close. Charlene was working on that closeness with her own family . . . and, with her dad's help, putting off their move to Salem by appealing to her mother's friends in Chicago.

Her neck tingled. It had been a week since their last phone call, which was odd.

"Would you like an assortment?" Minnie asked.

"That would be perfect, thank you." Charlene shook her hands to get rid of any negative energy. "Now, what can we do about happy hour? I'll need to leave right at quarter to five to meet Brandy."

Minnie scoffed. "Not a thing, Charlene, not a thing. In fact, why don't you go rest for a bit and I'll take care of this? Spinach and bacon bites, homemade coleslaw, and pulled chicken for sliders."

"You're the best, Minnie."

Charlene refilled her iced tea and took it to her suite. Once there, she raised the volume on the TV so that she could speak to Jack about the murder.

He was already in his armchair by the time she opened the door.

Handsome smile, turquoise eyes, dark hair. He was elegant and poised, intelligent and caring. Charlene didn't mind that her best friend was a ghost.

"Tell me what you saw," Jack said.

He flicked his fingers toward her, and a gust of air tickled the tip of her nose.

"Hey!" She removed her shoes. "What was that for?"

"You were too serious, Charlene. Sit, and share that heavy load with me."

She did, scooting her back against the inner left side of the love seat, drawing her knees up to her so that she could look her fill at Jack. Never a hardship. His essence was better than air-conditioning on a warm summer day.

She told him everything up to finding Trinity. "I called Trinity's name and opened the door—totally transfixed by the T-shirt in her mouth. It had been jammed in there, widening her jaw."

"What about the red at her neck? Was it all the way around, like a garrote?"

"No! Not that thin, either . . . I didn't notice the marks right away . . ." She had an awful thought and stood, putting the tea on the low table. "Stand up for a sec."

Jack did, and she circled her hands around his throat, well, almost around his throat—if she was to touch his actual ghostly makeup, it would chill her to the bone. She'd learned that lesson the hard way.

"You wonder if she could have been choked?"

Charlene nodded. "But if so, why the shirt in her mouth?"

"Anger," Jack said.

She stepped away from him and turned. "That would point the finger squarely at Bobby Rourke."

"Could it have been?" Jack returned to his chair.

"Perhaps." Charlene rubbed her arms. "He was certainly upset enough when he arrived this morning at nine thirty. The maid, Mary, said she saw Trinity at breakfast around nine, when she received her autograph. I've told this to Sam. He was surprisingly okay about the movie going on tonight at the Common."

"If he doesn't have the killer, they might show up." Jack tapped his fingers on the armrest.

She shared, "Jimenez was chasing after Bobby Rourke earlier—he kind of melted into the crowd when he saw her."

"That doesn't look good for him."

"I know. However, if I've learned anything over the last two years, it's not to jump to conclusions." She grabbed her pad and pen from the desk and then returned to the love seat.

"We've grown a lot," Jack admitted with a wry smile.

Charlene drew mermaids and conch shells. "Jimenez still doesn't like me. Do you think Aqua will be fine to go to the park tonight?"

"Yes," Jack said. "It's good that Aqua is resting, and I'd suggest better shoes to support her ankle, but other than that, she's okay. Kids are resilient."

Charlene knew that Jack had very much enjoyed being a doctor when alive and was considering starting an online practice in some way. His cyberskills were decent enough that he could probably forge all the necessary licenses.

"How's the MD idea coming?"

"Slow but steady. Right now, I'm content. Are you, Charlene? Happy? I see these couples at the B-and-B and I worry that you don't have someone." He searched her face.

"I have you," she teased.

Jack grew very serious instead of going along with the light flirtation they had between them. "You know what I mean."

Charlene tossed her pen at Jack's image, and it splintered. The pen hit the wall. Did he suspect her feelings for Sam?

Minnie knocked on her door, saving her from having to answer Jack. Two years ago, even last year, he would have been upset by her loving someone. They'd both changed in many ways.

She knew in her heart that he still would be jealous of Sam. And, selfishly, Charlene didn't want to jeopardize either relationship. Sam did not believe in ghosts, but Jack was very aware of the detective.

"Not fair," Jack said, coming back together and floating the pen to her desk.

"On my way!" Charlene hurried out of her suite feeling as if she'd dodged a bullet.

She helped Minnie carry the pitchers of lemonade and tea to the living room, where her housekeeper had already set out the food on the sideboard.

The conversation skirted around the death of Trinity. The Wheatons weren't sure they wanted to go down to the Common for the movie and were thinking pizza at Longboards might be more fun and less scary. The Southerns, in an awesome parental move Charlene hadn't expected considering their relaxed merfolk lifestyle, asked if they could join them. It would be better for the girls.

The Bonets, Sanchos, and Martins were ready to party, however. The adults were curious about what had happened to Trinity, but because Charlene didn't know, she couldn't tell them anything new.

"I'll be leaving early to help with the setup, so I'm afraid you will need to walk or catch a cab downtown," Charlene said. She hated not being full-service for them, but it wasn't too far.

"The walk was easy," the Sanchos said, and the Bonets immediately agreed.

"How is your ankle, Aqua?" Charlene asked. Her guests had all changed and showered the makeup and paint off—those who had worn it, anyway—and were now dressed in summer street clothes. She still wore her same outfit.

Aqua lifted her foot, and Charlene was glad to see sneakers on her feet. "All better." She was dressed in light blue and Jewel in purple.

"I'm so glad!"

They talked about the best floats and costumes, and the possible prize money, which let Charlene know that though it would be downplayed, people had worked hard on their creations and hoped to be acknowledged. The parade committee was walking a fine line between poor taste and satisfied customers who had paid a fee to participate. Fifty to a hundred dollars apiece wasn't cheap.

She raced back to her suite at half past four and switched out her purse for a bigger one to hold her pepper spray. Jack warned her to be careful, and she nodded as she left the suite. She didn't want to be hurt either and had no fond memories of the few times she'd been to the hospital.

"Here are cookies for Grant," Minnie said when Charlene entered the kitchen. "Drive carefully— I've got everything here under control."

"Thank you, Minnie!"

She drove to Salem Common and had to circle twice before finding a spot in a paid lot. Parking in the city was something Brandy's politician had promised to tackle if he was elected in November.

Brandy waited before Grant Powers's townhome. Charlene noted that she hadn't changed her clothes either, but sported the rainbow parade tee.

"Where's Serenity?" Charlene asked, the box of cookies in her hand.

"She's with Tina to fine-tune the details of the donation announcement. How on earth did I have such a smart kid?"

"The apple definitely fell from the Flint family tree. All three of you are beautiful and intelligent." Evelyn, Brandy's mother, was the matriarch.

Brandy side hugged Charlene, a sure sign that she'd been mellowed by the chardonnay. "What's that?" She tipped her head toward the box.

"Cookies for Grant. Minnie thought it would be nice."

"It was thoughtful, and a good reason to knock on the door," Brandy said. "My mind has been spinning over different greetings."

Charlene nodded at Brandy with encouragement. "You've got this."

Brandy blew out a breath, then climbed up the porch to give the door two firm taps with her knuckles.

The door opened right away and Grant's friend, Michael, widened it. "Oh! Hello. I'm afraid Grant isn't feeling so well right now. He's having tea in the kitchen."

Sensing they might not make it inside, Charlene stepped forward. "I have some cookies from home. We'd love to give him our condolences."

"I've known Grant since I was a child," Brandy said. "I can't imagine what he's going through."

Michael widened the door, relief in his tone. "Come in, come in. Please! I never had kids myself, and while I can keep the liquor coming, I don't know what to say to be consoling."

"Thank you," Brandy said, pulling Charlene with her into the dim foyer of the townhome. A row of hooks was on the wall to her right, a closet to the left, and a carpet runner ran the length of the narrow hall.

"This way." Michael's body was almost as wide as the hall, which opened to a square kitchen with a narrow window, the drapes drawn. Built-in shelves were crammed with books and snapshots.

Grant hunched over a large mug of tea, yes, but the tang of whiskey suggested that Michael had liberally dosed the beverage with spirits, as he'd told them. The bottle was next to it. Grant wore the same short-sleeved, button-up shirt from before, his silvery-brown hair a mess, as if he'd been yanking on it.

"Mr. Powers. Grant," Brandy said. "We don't mean to intrude."

Charlene gave Brandy the box and Brandy placed it on the table as she said, "Homemade cookies."

Grant raised his watery gaze. "How kind."

Michael swept a stack of papers from the place mat and set them on the counter next to the kitchen sink. The kitchen hadn't been redecorated in forty-plus years, with a black phone on the wall and a phone book beneath, on a butcher-block table.

"Please, sit," Michael said. "Can we get you tea? Whiskey?"

"No, but thanks," Brandy said. "We won't stay long. Grant, I'm so sorry for your loss."

Grant nodded and stared into his mug.

Brandy peered imploringly at Charlene.

Charlene shuffled forward. "Grant. Sir."

"Yes?" The man looked up at her with such pain. What had happened between father and daughter, truly?

"I—" She cleared her throat. "We just wanted to alert you, so you aren't alarmed, that the event for tonight will still go on. The movie."

Michael sucked in a breath.

Charlene braced herself for Grant's reaction and hurried on to explain before he said no. What would they do then?

"Grant, we are not making this a mermaid party as originally intended. Instead, we want to honor Trinity's life as Salem's star. There will be some sort of scholarship in her name. Also, we are discussing changing the Mermaid Parade to the Sirena Parade in a nod to Trinity's iconic role."

Charlene sat across from Grant and took his hand, staring into his eyes. "Salem loves Trinity," she said in a soft voice, seeing his agreement in his gaze. She dared to ask, "What do you think?"

Brandy's shoulders stiffened.

"Yes." Tears poured down his cheeks. "Yes. My daughter would really have loved that."

Brandy eyed the ceiling and gave a discreet exhalation of thanks to the Goddess.

CHAPTER 7

Charlene relaxed slightly in her chair, nodding at Brandy, who had visibly brightened. It was a tragedy, and yet, with the right direction, the event could be salvaged in a way that all parties might flourish in the long run.

"Should I say a few words tonight?" Grant asked. He peered across the table to Charlene, then glanced at Brandy.

Charlene scanned the kitchen and noted the pictures in frames on a shelf by some cookbooks. Happy memories from over forty years ago with Grant, Trinity as a child, and probably his wife, taken before they moved to Hollywood.

Brandy folded her hands before her on the table. "If you'd like."

Michael, attempting to be the voice of reason, tapped the whiskey bottle. "Do you think that's a good idea, Grant?" Subtext: He's been drinking.

"I'll shower and get cleaned up." Grant scrubbed his jaw. "What time should I be there?"

"The movie starts at eight. So . . ." Brandy looked at her watch. The clock on the wall read five thirty. "We can do the announcements of prizes at six; that might take until seven. My daughter has a schedule, but we can fit you in. Why don't you say what you'd like at seven thirty?"

Michael nodded to the pen on top of the stack of paper. "I can help you write something down on note cards, Grant."

"You have a way with prose, Michael. He's let me read some of the draft for Trinity's biography." Grant tossed back the rest of the mug of tea and winced, from the whiskey or the heat of the tea, Charlene didn't know. "Would you ladies like to see some pictures of my daughter? I was showing Michael a scrapbook I kept."

Grant gestured to the stack of papers on the counter that had been on the table.

"I'll get it." Michael rifled through them until he located a six-inch-thick photo album. "Here you are."

Grant opened the cover. Trinity as a baby. Trinity in the arms of a lovely woman with light brown hair and violet eyes. The three of them in candid shots and portraits. "This is her with Madeline. Madeline was the best mom and wife."

Brandy studied the pictures, a smile flitting around her mouth at the memories. "That's our kindergarten school photo. Individual and class pictures."

Charlene rose and stood behind Brandy to get a better view of about twenty kids with big eyes and teeth. Brandy was easy to pick out with her auburn hair and bright smile.

"Trinity's next to me. We used to be so close," Brandy said with sadness.

"I remember." Grant sighed and reached for the whiskey bottle, adding a dollop to his mug. "She used to love me too. It's my fault that they left."

"What do you mean?" Charlene asked.

"Madeline and I fought all the time. It was obvious Trinity had something special. And her imagination was incredible. She adored her mermaid stories."

Brandy nodded.

"How was it your fault she left?" Michael asked.

"It's not important now." Grant finished the whiskey and wiped his cheeks.

"It's good that we're just across the street," Michael said. "Brandy, what is your phone number if . . . circumstances change?"

As in, Grant passes out or changes his mind. Brandy told him, and Michael entered it into his phone.

Grant stood, and Michael was right behind him to keep the man steady. "Easy, now. Are you going to be okay to walk up the stairs?"

"Maybe I need a minute. . . ." Grant sat back down.

"You don't need to speak," Brandy said softly. "I promise to be very considerate of Trinity's memory."

"I owe it to my daughter." Grant's voice wavered. "I didn't support her dreams to be a water ballet star. I thought they would fail, and they would crawl home in defeat. To me. I would be the victor."

Charlene also sat back down, heavy with despair.

Now they would never have the chance to reconcile.

Brandy reached across the table for his hand, patting it.

"Madeline kept me in the loop so far as news went, but . . ." Grant bowed his head. "I was a stubborn fool. Now, it's far too late."

Brandy squeezed his knuckles. "I'm so sorry."

"Not anything you can do. I need to make things right. I screwed up." Grant tilted his head. "I told the press about our falling out in hopes of reaching her after her mom died, but Trinity never responded."

"Why is that?" Charlene asked.

"I don't know." Grant sighed and stared into the empty mug. "I sent her a letter Friday at the Hawthorne Hotel. The clerk there is a friend of mine and let me know when Trinity arrived."

"You sent a letter?" Brandy asked, exchanging a glance with Charlene.

"Yes. Asked her to meet me at the bandstand last night."

Instead, she'd moved hotels. Charlene had seen a partial envelope beneath Trinity's body at the Waterway. Her mouth dried.

Grant slumped in his seat. "She didn't show."

"No." Brandy blew out a breath, her gaze sharpening on the older man. "She didn't. Why is that?"

Grant shook his head. "It will haunt me for the rest of my miserable life, not knowing the answers to so many questions."

Brandy checked her watch. The kitchen clock

read five forty. "I'm afraid we must go, Grant. Please, don't feel like you need to be there. You are welcome, but know we will do the right thing by Trinity."

Charlene rose and murmured goodbyes. Her emotions were in an upheaval—sorrow for Grant but also concern. He'd sent a note and Trinity switched hotels. What if Trinity had a reason to fear her father?

Michael followed them to the front door. "He's a mess, poor man. I'll keep you posted on what he decides to do. It's nice of you to give him that space for closure."

Brandy nodded. "Of course. I'll have my phone— can you confirm either way by seven fifteen?"

"I will. Bye now." Michael gently closed the door behind them.

Charlene followed Brandy, speed walking down the sidewalk, and hitched her purse strap to her shoulder. She caught up at the corner. "Why are you going so fast?"

Brandy tugged Charlene to her with narrowed green eyes. "Did Grant . . . harm Trinity?"

Charlene gave the townhome behind them a glance and shivered. "That's preposterous. But . . . he said that it was his fault Madeline and Trinity left."

"He expected them to come back with their tails between their legs," Brandy said. "Not nice, but there was never any evidence of abuse." She peered over her shoulder, her mouth tight. "Grant tracked her down at the Hawthorne and sent her a letter. Trinity moved right after that. Maybe it had nothing to do with Alannah or her fans, as Bobby suggested."

"Did Grant offer to be with them in Hollywood, once he realized they weren't coming home?" Charlene's mind went to the worst possible scenario. "Maybe they didn't want him to join them." Her spine tingled. She whirled again to the townhome, but nobody was there. "Could they have escaped his cruelty?"

"We'll never know," Brandy said, straightening. "Nobody is alive to tell us what happened then, except for him. I never saw any evidence of that in all the years Trinity and I were school friends."

Jack was very good at researching online. Charlene would ask him to work his magic to see if Grant Powers had any secrets.

They crossed the street toward the Common. Barbecue and cotton candy scented the air from the food trucks. Kass waved at them from in front of an arepa stand. Her braids dangled and danced as she moved, no longer in a mermaid outfit but patchwork jeans and a flowy shirt.

"There you guys are!" Kass moved up the line to order. "Want anything? The jalapeño cheese is my favorite."

"No, thanks," Charlene said. She was still full from the sliders Minnie had made.

Brandy shook her head.

Kass shrugged. "Suit yourself." She faced the vendor and ordered two. Once she'd paid and gotten her food, they stepped away from the people milling around.

"Have you seen Serenity?" Brandy asked.

"She and Tina are near the table." Kass tore off a piece of arepa, made of corn and stuffed with cheese and jalapeño. "How was Grant?"

"Grant okayed the movie going on," Charlene said. "He believes that Trinity would have loved the honor." But what did he really know of his daughter?

Brandy stepped toward the gate leading into the lawn, Charlene and Kass with her. "Let's focus on creating something good from this tragedy. As the Goddess wishes, so mote it be."

"So mote it be," Kass seconded. Her special talent involved seeing ghosts and reading one's fortune from tea leaves.

This closing phrase, "so may it be," was why Charlene knew Brandy couldn't have forced Trinity to come to Salem against Trinity's will. The Flints and Kass were good witches.

Brandy bowed her head briefly. "Serenity and Tina might need to alter the schedule to allow Grant to speak. Knowing how much Serenity relies on scheduling, that should go over like a sour grape."

Kass swallowed her bite of arepa. "The timing of the floats went beautifully even without Trinity being there. I think Serenity did fab. Any news from the Salem PD about who done it?"

"Not yet." In fact, Charlene hadn't heard a peep from Sam since their phone call. "When I talked with Sam earlier and let him know the event was going on, he said he'd send extra police coverage."

They passed the long registration table with the remaining T-shirts. A young man sat next to the boxes wearing a Clean Oceans polo. Serenity and Tina were there, chatting with Kevin.

"So," Kass asked in a low voice, "since Bobby has evaded the police for mere questioning, what should we do with these T-shirts? There's not many left."

Charlene asked for one for the maid, stuffing it in her purse. She hoped that Mary Clarkson was all right, but she hadn't had two seconds to check on her.

"Let's hang on to them." Brandy eyed the evening sky. The blue had shifted to cloudy gray, as if to match the somber mood. "Serenity, have you heard from Bobby?"

"No, and neither has Tina." Serenity's long auburn hair was loose past her shoulders. Like Brandy and Charlene, she still wore the rainbow *Sirena* T-shirt. "Bobby gave her his number before all this went down and Tina tried to text him, but he's not answering."

"Still on the run." Kass pointed with her wrapped second arepa to a bunch of people with hot-pink shirts that read "Team Trinity For Life." "Gotta love human ingenuity. Some enterprising gentleman started selling those this afternoon. He's also got Team Alannah, but since the rumors are spreading that Trinity was murdered over the feud, those aren't as hot an item."

"Murdered over the feud?" Charlene could unfortunately imagine the crowd turning from peace and love to violence. She was glad Sam would have extra people at the event, which was due to start in twenty minutes. Searching the throng, she didn't see him. Would he personally attend?

"I heard that too." Tina sipped something from a clear glass—no straw, in her nod to no plastic to save the ocean. The Clean Oceans pamphlets stated plastic straws were one of the worst offenders for harming sea life.

Kevin held a bottle of beer with a mermaid label. "I've had three different people ask me why we're going on with the show."

"It's in honor of Trinity that we continue." Charlene gestured toward the row of townhomes not quite visible from where they stood. "Grant already approved."

"He did?" Kevin asked in surprise.

Brandy shifted to Serenity and Tina. "Grant asked if he could speak at the tribute for Trinity tonight. I said yes."

"Tribute to Trinity," Tina repeated. "Nice."

"Are you kidding?" Serenity waved her cell phone. "We have the whole schedule marked already, with barely a second of wiggle room."

Charlene bit the inside of her cheek. Brandy had known any changes wouldn't go over well.

"Seven thirty. Just a few minutes. Would you deny a grieving father?" Brandy countered.

Tina shook her head and placed her hand on Serenity's lower back. "Of course not."

"Fine. Give me a minute." Serenity read the schedule on her phone with a huff. "We asked Alannah and Dom to speak, which I thought was very cool of them to agree to, considering the crowd tonight. Should they be before Grant or after?"

"That's a tough call," Kass said. "Grant will probably really tug at the heartstrings!"

Kevin thoughtfully sipped his beer. "This is Alannah's chance to be in the spotlight, but because of the online feuding, she's not in a top position. Who wants to be famous for bad-mouthing a dead woman?"

"What could be so awful?" Tina asked. "I like her. Or I did until I saw her true colors."

Kass read aloud from her phone some of the things Alannah had posted about Trinity and summarized, "Snarky, which can be funny in the right environment, but a lot are downright mean. Trinity didn't seem to engage, but her fans did on her behalf. Ariel Glitter is a fierce protector. She and Ned go back and forth a lot."

Brandy's phone dinged an incoming message.

Charlene studied the people on the grass and metal bleachers—yes, there was laughter, but in clusters, not an overall feeling of joy, as there had been at the start of the parade.

"Did Trinity personally ever answer?" Charlene was curious since Alannah had said Trinity had pretty much ignored her. It seemed odd for her to engage. Maybe that was her only outlet.

"It would be impossible to know for sure. Trinity's social media pages could be run by anyone. Didn't have to be Trinity," Serenity said.

Charlene nodded. "When I worked for the marketing company, a lot of those pages were handled by assistants."

"That's why you're so good at finding quick solutions!" Serenity said to Charlene. "You were in marketing. That can be a very cutthroat business."

"The company Jared and I worked for in Chicago was at the forefront of encouraging work-life balance, so the competition, while fierce, wasn't bloodthirsty. Kind of a we-all-rise-to-the-top philosophy instead of 'every man for himself.'"

"I forget you had an entire life before arriving in Salem," Kevin said. "I think of you as one of us."

Charlene grinned at Kevin. "You are so sweet!"

"How long will you need to speak to get things started?" Tina cupped her empty glass. "Since we need to move the schedule, we might as well do it all at once."

"True," Serenity said with a wince. "Mom, I've got you scheduled for a seven-minute intro, welcoming people. Maybe we can cut it to five?"

"I need to stay out of the limelight." Brandy looked at Charlene with determination. "Charlene can start the show."

"Me?" That hadn't been the plan at all.

"Yep." Brandy swallowed hard. "I just received a text that Tony is on the bleachers with his family."

"He's got a family?" Serenity asked sharply.

"Divorced!" Brandy said. "But teenagers. Two girls who are both Team Alannah. They wanted to meet her, but now I'm not sure it's a good idea. What if Alannah had something to do with what happened to Trinity?"

"I hope that isn't the real reason you wanted the show to go on, Mom," Serenity said. "To impress your secret boyfriend's daughters."

Kass and Kevin exchanged a look.

"Not so secret if you keep talking about it, Serenity." Brandy raised her chin at her daughter.

"We won't say a word," Kass said, a little hurt in her voice.

"Me either," Kevin promised. He turned to Charlene. "Well?"

"I'm not a big talker," Charlene promised. "Five minutes or less—what should I say?"

Brandy reached for Charlene's arm. "What you said to Grant earlier will be good enough. You convinced him."

"He was already on board!" Charlene protested.

"You'll be fine!" Serenity and Tina bowed heads and sat at the table to compare notes. Within five minutes of them all working together, Charlene had something short and sweet, to the point. She'd made a bulleted list in the notebook she carried in her purse.

They decided that even if the city didn't approve a scholarship from the funds, Brandy would donate it from her personal bank account if necessary.

"A scholarship to what? Acting school? Water ballet? How to be a mermaid?" Charlene tossed out ideas to brainstorm.

"Can't we leave it open?" Brandy shrugged, showing Serenity her watch and the time.

"No." Kass and Kevin chorused Charlene's *no.*

"And are we going to name the annual parade the Sirena Parade?" Brandy asked. "Put that in for sure."

"Yes." Charlene added that to the bullet points. They had to keep the crowd happy.

"How much are you willing to spend?" Kass asked bluntly.

"Scholarships for college range from one hundred bucks for a grant to full tuition." Charlene knew that because of helping Avery the year before.

"Not full tuition!" Brandy shuddered at getting stuck with that bill every year. "Can we make it a one-time deal?"

"Sure." Charlene nodded. "I like the idea of it being for a college here in Salem."

Brandy nodded, tapping her fingers to her chin. "Yes. Okay. How about the Trinity Powers Grant for a thousand dollars to a school in Salem of their choice. Applicants must be interested in the arts. We will do one student per year, for the next," Brandy gulped, "five years."

"That's generous," Charlene said. "Shall we just say that the information will be on the City of Salem website shortly?"

"Yes." Brandy looked at Charlene, Kevin, and Kass. "Yes?"

"Great!" they all said.

"Your politician friend will approve," Charlene whispered to Brandy. "This will give the city something to offset the murder with."

"And here I was feeling so good until you said that." Brandy checked her watch with a yelp. "Serenity! It's almost six! Whose idea was this to be an annual event?"

"Mine, Mom!" Serenity said. "I may have been a little ambitious."

"How could you know that the guest of honor would die?" Tina said. "On the positive side, the parade raised five thousand dollars for the Clean Oceans project. Half of ten thousand. That's a big deal."

Which meant Salem had earned five too, less expenses. Charlene borrowed a mirror from Brandy, who had a compact in her bag. "I wasn't prepared to be in front of everyone." Her hazel eyeliner had been smudged and her lipstick was long gone. She brushed her hair but kept it in a ponytail, then added powder to her nose and shiny lip gloss.

"Ready?" Serenity asked.

"Yes." Nerves tumbled in her stomach, and Charlene sipped from a can of fizzy water. As soon as this was over, she was having a very large glass of the Flint's Vineyard pinot grigio being sold at one of the vendors outside the grass.

Charlene made her way up the steps to the stage and took in the crowd of people dressed as merfolk, or in Team Trinity or Team Alannah T-shirts. There was Seth Gamble, Avery's boyfriend, with his mom, Dani, and his younger brother. Sharon and John Turnberry. Oh, and Sam. She relaxed to see him by the bleachers. She waved at her guests, the Martins, the Sanchos, and the Bonets, then tapped the microphone.

"Salem welcomes you!" People quieted, and Charlene did her best to sound reassuring as she skated over the facts of Trinity's death without updates on the incident. She stayed away from words like *murder* and *crime*, pouring her energy into a different side of the truth.

"Trinity Powers was born in Salem and went on to be one of the greatest water ballet artists ever."

Charlene paused to nod at the burst of applause. "She personified beauty and grace."

"She's dead!" a man with a goatee and a ball cap shouted. "Killed!"

A Salem PD officer was immediately at the man's side. Was that Ned?

Mouth dry, Charlene continued, "Today, we mourn the loss of Trinity's beautiful soul—she will not be forgotten! We will honor her memory in Salem by offering a school scholarship for budding artists."

Cheers erupted from the lawn and the bleachers.

Charlene decided to scrap the poignant parts of the speech and keep it to the facts. The crowd was so emotional, it wouldn't take much to rile them up. She closed with, "As always, we are grateful for our community, which includes the Salem Police Department, the vendors, and the organizers of the parade. Now, I'd like to introduce Serenity Flint and Tina Setzer, who will share the generous donations you've made possible to keep our oceans clean."

Charlene raised her hand in farewell. Tina and Serenity passed her up the stairs and Serenity gave her a thumbs-up. She searched for Sam in the shadows on the grass, drawn to his broad shoulders like a homing beacon.

Sam nodded at her in approval but stepped back when Brandy barreled forward.

"Charlene, Michael just texted. Grant is on his way across the street right now. And he's not thinking too clearly."

"Drunk?" She put her hand to her throat, still

undecided about his motivation. Love. Hate. Two sides of the same coin.

"Plastered. Michael is trying to keep him quiet but . . . Goddess help us. I can hear him coming."

Charlene turned toward the entrance of the Common. Michael was doing his best, but Grant had a mind of his own.

"It's my fault she's dead," Grant shouted. "My fault!"

CHAPTER 8

Sam appeared at Charlene's side. "What's going on?"

"That's Grant Powers, Trinity's dad. He wants to say a few words about his daughter tonight. When we spoke earlier this afternoon, he was supportive of the film going on, and the scholarship in her name."

"He said her death is his fault. What did he mean by that?" Sam took two protective steps in front of Charlene.

Charlene tugged Sam's lightweight jacket. "He's been drinking and he's devasted about his daughter being dead—especially when he wanted so desperately to reconcile with her."

Sam smoothed his long mustache. "And now he can't. Why were they fighting?"

"I don't have specifics, but he blames himself for not supporting her and her mother, his wife Madeline, when they went to Hollywood. Trinity was only ten years old."

Sam sighed, turning away from Grant to study Charlene. "Why am I not surprised you know all this?"

"I brought him some of Minnie's cookies," Charlene said.

"I'd spill my guts too." Sam's full lower lip twitched. "The almond biscotti?"

An answering smile flickered around her mouth. "An assortment."

"The man didn't stand a chance."

Minnie had an adorable crush on Sam and he loved to tease her. It was all in good fun by both parties. Brandy had intercepted Grant, followed by Michael, near the long table before making it inside the gate.

"Anything you can share with me about what happened to her?" Charlene asked Sam as they walked toward Brandy.

Sam shook his head. "Not yet."

That was par for the course with them, so she switched topics. "How's Mary Clarkson, the maid?"

"She had stitches and was released. Her poster is missing."

Charlene appreciated that Sam was slowing his steps to match her stride or else his long legs would outpace her. "I'm glad she's okay. Did you ever catch up with Bobby?"

"Nope."

Not enlightening. Charlene grabbed his sleeve. "I'd prefer the culprit to be the artist rather than her father."

"Softhearted, Charlene," Sam murmured in her ear. Tickles from his mustache made her sigh.

"You need a thick skin to keep your emotions in check."

"If I was a detective or a police officer, you would be right." Charlene tilted her head to hold his warm, brown gaze. "But I am a bed-and-breakfast owner, which means that my emotions can be on my sleeve for all to see."

Charlene continued toward Brandy. Sam spluttered, then caught up with her. She turned as Serenity, on the dais, handed Tina a check for five thousand dollars made out to Clean Oceans to the approval of the crowd.

"That's a generous donation," Sam said, staying at her side as they meandered around blankets and camp chairs.

"It's half, as promised! We're trying our best to salvage the Mermaid Parade. I forgot to tell everyone that we are changing the parade name to Sirena!" She patted her pocket where she'd stuffed the list. "And I even had notes."

"You did great." Sam touched her arm.

"This parade was something Serenity and Brandy worked together doing and I know they wanted it to be a hit. Mermaids are fun people, Sam, and they seem to have the money to spend on their hobby. Tourist dollars are wonderful for Salem."

"It's a sad truth that most people are pretty amazing, but the small percentage who aren't, like whoever killed Trinity, create a bad taste. I'm glad that you're focusing on the positive from the parade."

"Thanks, Sam."

They finally reached Brandy, Michael, and Grant. Brandy was smoothing down Grant's jacket, his black suit older, his hair still damp from his shower. His beard was trimmed and he smelled of cologne.

Michael handed Grant his notes. "You can do this, Grant."

"Thank you, Michael. Thank you, Brandy." Grant stuffed his hand into his jacket pocket. "I'm sorry about running over here. The truth is that I'm afraid."

"Of what?" Brandy gripped his upper arm.

"That I will never get Trinity's forgiveness." Grant drew in a breath.

"What did you do that was so bad?" Sam asked.

His deep voice dropped between them, a different tone than the others, and everyone looked at Sam. The twilight sky behind him created shadows in the trees. Clouds peeked between roofs and branches. His jacket was open over jeans and boots, his badge clipped to his belt.

"Who are you?" Grant squinted to keep Sam in focus—the fault of the whiskey, not the evening shadows.

"Detective Sam Holden." Sam reached out his hand to shake Grant's. The man hesitated, but then accepted the clasp. "I'm sorry for your loss."

Grant's mouth quivered. "Thank you. Is there any word on what happened to Trinity?"

"No. I'm sorry." Sam's words were sincere.

"I will be angry tomorrow," Grant said, body alert, "but right now, I just need to focus on thanking her fans."

"Thanking them . . ." Sam let the words hang.

"For their love for her. I remember when she was a little girl how she would stand in front of the mirror and practice her dance moves before an imaginary audience." Grant sighed. "She would practice for hours, her speeches, too, as if she could imagine the future and her success. She could see it, even as a child, her fame."

"Creating reality," Michael said, a little in awe.

Sam turned to Michael, his hand out. "You are?"

"Michael Brown. I am writing Trinity's biography."

"Very talented man. Helped me with my notes." Grant pulled them from his pockets, and a breeze fluttered the papers to the grass.

Charlene got them, looking at them to make sure they hadn't been ruined. Michael had neater penmanship than Charlene, especially when she was in a hurry.

"Charlene?" She turned to Sam, who waved goodbye before he faded into the crowd.

Ariel Glitter joined her and offered a hug. She showed her loyalty to Trinity in a hot-pink Team Trinity T-shirt and a pink-and-silver-scalloped mermaid skirt. "That is so nice, about the scholarship. Just want to warn you, though, that Ned Hammond is talking crap about Trinity and saying the city of Salem must've been paid off or something." Ariel scowled. "I really don't like that guy."

"Who is Ned again?" Brandy asked, walking forward with Grant and Michael.

"Ned Hammond—he's the captain of Alannah's fan club," Charlene explained. "I have several guests who are Team Alannah and several who are Team Trinity."

Ariel pointed out all of the hot-pink Team Trinity shirts in the park. "She's gained a lot of followers since her death." She put her fingers to her throat.

Charlene noticed that Ariel was not the slender, dainty type and had very large hands. Almost masculine. They'd argued—and Ariel had been willing to apologize to Trinity . . . had she tracked her to the Waterway?

Charlene had to control herself or she'd be thinking anybody might have a reason to kill Trinity as her imagination went into overdrive.

The truth was, Ariel couldn't help the size of her hands. Charlene pointed out the police officers in navy blue. "If there's a problem, I want you to tell one of those guys, okay? You will be safe! Don't worry."

Ariel looked at Charlene like she might have a screw loose. "*I'm* fine! I wrestled semiprofessionally for a while. I just think that Ned might be a problem is all. Let's have a little respect for the dead, yeah?"

Grant's shoulders shook with emotion. "Thank you for standing up for her."

The pair embraced, Ariel's bouffant blond wig making her slightly taller than the older man. They'd met earlier that morning at the parade.

"It's time," Brandy said, tucking her arm through Grant's.

Charlene gave him the notes that he read over again. He raised his chin. "I'm ready."

"Good luck," Ariel said.

"You'll do great," Michael said, following Grant.

Charlene went after them and asked Ariel, "Where is Ned?"

"I'll show you." Ariel led the way to where he'd been, the same spot the heckler had been, but the space was empty. "He's not here anymore."

"It's all right." Charlene hiked her purse over her shoulder. "Remember what I said—don't hesitate to tell the police if he bothers you."

Ariel rolled her eyes and slammed a fist into her palm instead.

Charlene stepped back from the dais as Brandy helped Grant to the microphone. He wouldn't let go of Brandy, so she had no choice but to be on the stage. "Congratulations to all of the participants in the parade today," Brandy said, making the best of it. "Before we begin the movie that made Trinity Powers a household name, I'd like to introduce Grant Powers, her father, who still lives here in Salem."

Applause sounded and roared as people made as much noise as they could to show their support for the man on the stage.

"Thank you." Grant bowed his head as if in prayer, then lifted it to scan the crowd. Brandy scooted to the far side of the platform so that he was in the spotlight, and she was out of it.

"Trinity Powers was not always an easy person to understand, but she was dedicated to her craft from a very early age." Grant shuffled his feet and gripped the microphone, creating a screech of feedback as he read the note cards.

Kass showed up to Charlene's right and Kevin to her left.

"Not what I thought he'd say," Kass whispered. "No wonder they were fighting."

"I knew she was star material, and that Salem would not be big enough to hold her," Grant continued.

Salem natives rustled uncertainly. This wasn't the tribute they were expecting. Charlene made out Sam standing near the bleachers, intent on Grant. Did he think the grieving father could have killed his daughter?

Grant crumpled the notes and stuck them in his jacket pocket, deciding to wing it. "I used to tell her stories of the merfolk who lived beyond Salem Harbor. I gave her a magic conch shell to call them to her. Before she grew to hate me, she loved me."

Some of the crowd booed.

Michael shook his head—this must not be part of the speech he'd prepared for Grant.

Brandy, on the dais, searched for Michael and then Charlene in the crowd. Her eyes widened in silent appeal to Charlene—Michael was focused on Grant, as if to will the right words to him.

"I cut her out of my life first," Grant said. "I was trying to control her, trying to make her conform to my wishes. I was so wrong." He slumped.

Stomping on the bleachers grew louder as the people conveyed their disapproval. Brandy joined Grant and murmured something to him, helping him upright.

"I apologize to you, Salem, her fans here tonight, since I can't apologize to dear Trinity." Grant sobbed. "I loved her so much and now, now it's too late."

Brandy wrestled the microphone from Grant and handed it to Serenity, who had practically dragged Alannah and Dom behind her up the stairs.

Charlene didn't miss the twist of the starlet's mouth as she demurred, nor Serenity's hard gaze as she murmured something about a contract. Grant and Dom passed each other on the steps, the young man crowding the older one in a cocky display.

"Don't like that guy." Kevin clenched his hands loose behind his back. "Not at all."

"Or Alannah," Kass said. "I thought her movie reached the younger generation, but there is something to be said for class."

"You're so right." Charlene had lost sight of Sam, Brandy, Grant, and Michael as the audience came off the bleachers to the crowded grass.

"And now may I present Alannah Gomez and Dom Preston!" Serenity gave the microphone to the starlet.

"Hi, Salem!" The intro to her version of *Sirena* began on the speakers. Her hips moved accordingly. Team Alannah clapped and whistled.

"Our condolences go out to Mr. Powers on his loss. On Salem's loss," Alannah said. This earned a wave of approval from both teams.

"Oh, that's nice. Alannah better behave or I'll delete my copy of her film to the trash." Kass's hips moved too. "Isn't she pretty?"

"We want to apologize," Dom said, not sounding at all sincere, "for any misunderstandings between Trinity and Alannah. These things get taken out of context or blown out of proportion to the original intent."

"Notice that he's barely holding back a smile," Charlene said.

"I know, right?" Kass stopped dancing.

"You read us some of the comments earlier, Kass," Kevin said. "Pretty clear and direct messaging."

"Yeah. Darn it." Kass snapped her fingers. "Why can't people just be nice?"

Alannah took the mic from Dom. "Of course, Salem has Team Trinity for life! As it should be here in her hometown. I'd always wondered why she left." Her tone suggested that now she knew.

Serenity, on the edge of the stage, hurried toward Alannah. "And now it's time for," she started to say but didn't finish as Dom danced with Serenity to cut her off from announcing the start of the movie.

Thinking he was being cute? Team Trinity's fans didn't like it. Charlene saw Ariel shout to Serenity to make sure she was all right.

"Back off, Ariel Glitter." Alannah shimmied up to the edge of the platform. "Weren't you fired? Trinity didn't want you!"

"Hey!" several Trinity fans protested.

Team Alannah, in blue shirts, crowded the ground before the dais, rocking it.

Charlene had a terrible feeling that things were going down in flames and worried about Serenity on the stage as chanting people crowded around the flimsy structure that wasn't meant to be jostled in such a manner. "Let's go!"

Kevin, Kass, and Charlene made their way to the

front, and Serenity on the platform. It was almost impossible to move in the crush.

She heard Ariel yell and arrived near her to see the mermaid with the blond bouffant wig haul her fist back and slug Ned Hammond in the nose.

Blood gushed.

Kevin grabbed Charlene and a stunned Kass toward the bleachers to their right and out of the way of the dancers on the grass.

Alannah and Dom were dancing like fools, but Brandy had Serenity to the side, protecting her daughter as the structure wobbled. The Flints hurried down the stairs.

"Charlene! Over here!" Sam shouted as he waved to her, his head and shoulders visible above the crowd. Brandy and Serenity huddled near him. Charlene was at his side within minutes, Kass and Kevin behind her.

By the time they reached the interior side gate of the park the crowd was in complete chaos and singing along to Alannah's *Sirena* soundtrack. Salem PD had created a clear path for those who wanted to leave the grass to the sidewalk. Thank heaven that Sam had ordered extra policemen.

"What a nightmare," Brandy said with a groan. Charlene waited outside the gate with Grant and Michael, watching in horror as Alannah and Dom danced on the shaking dais.

"That is not going to hold," Sam said. He spoke orders into his radio to clear folks back.

Ned Hammond, against all logic, climbed to the stage and joined in the dancing, never mind the blood on his face from where Ariel had punched him.

"What idiots!" Kass said.

"You guys stay here." Sam hurried inside the park toward the fray. He could see as well as they could that those closest were going to be hurt when the rickety structure collapsed.

The Salem PD whistled and herded folks back away from the stage. Those who didn't want to go took their chances. Alannah and Dom moved sensually in sync until Alannah gave Dom a little push over the side—he whirled his arms off balance and landed on the grass with a curse.

Alannah just laughed down at him.

The metal brackets of the dais buckled to the left, spilling folks over like the *Titanic* going down. Ned Hammond was there to catch Alannah as they fell, rolling with her so she didn't get hurt when they hit the lawn.

Officer Bernard strode toward Brandy and Serenity, on the outside of the iron gate, halting six inches before them. "Who is in charge? We need to make a call."

"Movie night is canceled," mother and daughter said in unison.

Charlene nodded, relieved the long day was over.

CHAPTER 9

"Charlene!"

The long day was *almost* over. At the urgent cry, she turned to see Ariel limping toward her, her blond wig askew to show dark hair beneath. One of the police officers was watching the bedraggled mermaid with suspicion and Charlene raised her hand to say that it was okay. Ariel was no danger to her. She hoped.

Charlene went back inside the park. She had her hobo bag with the pepper spray but honestly couldn't reach it if the wrestler decided to charge her. Broad shoulders, big arms, and hands, bigger grin, Ariel didn't appear the least repentant about scrapping with Ned. Her Team Trinity T-shirt in hot pink had bloodstains on the front.

Once Ariel reached Charlene, she asked, "Are you okay?"

Ariel's grin widened. "Yep. Bruised up a bit and broke my fake fingernails, but it felt good to let go, don't mind saying. Ned had it coming. Serenity's a good girl just taking care of business and not part of the stupid feud."

Charlene agreed with all of that. "I saw Ned catch Alannah as they fell."

"Yeah." Ariel grumbled. "Did you see her push Dom off the stage? Man, was he mad."

"Don't blame him a bit."

"Me either." Ariel wiped her palms on the front of her long, scale-patterned skirt that had split down the side. Like something from a horror movie, maybe. Zombie mermaids?

Charlene shook her head to clear that image. "Is there something I can help you with?"

Ariel leaned toward Charlene. "I just wanted to warn you about Ned."

"Oh?" Charlene scanned the Common and found Ned talking with a police officer. Neither appeared happy. Was Ned nervous? "About what?"

"He's in love with Alannah. Obviously."

Charlene had figured that out already.

"Ned's jealous." Ariel picked the rest of a fake fingernail from her pinkie finger. "From what I learned today, I don't think Dom cares. They're an appearances-only thing, for the movie."

Ned had said as much, but she'd thought it was wishful thinking on his part. "So, you think Ned has a shot with Alannah?"

"In his dreams!" Ariel snorted. "No. Alannah's just using him. Ned would do *anything* for her. That's what I wanted to tell you." Her sly expression had Charlene's guard up. "Saw you with that hot cop."

Charlene's feet hurt from the long day, and she

shifted her weight from one leg to the other. "Sam Holden? He's a detective."

Ariel inched closer to Charlene with a curious glance. "Do you know how Trinity died?"

"I can't say," Charlene said, feeling boxed in. Where was Sam, come to think of it? The police were doing a good job of clearing the lawn and sending people home. She'd like to be one of them.

"Was it on purpose?" Ariel asked, her eyes overly bright. "Since you found Trinity, you might have noticed something."

Alarmed, Charlene straightened. "Who told you that?"

"Tina. We were having a chat about the parade next year. She also said that Bobby Rourke, the T-shirt artist, ran away from the cops. Hasn't been heard from since this morning."

Tina was a gossip. Had she been around to discover the identity of Brandy's secret boyfriend? That could be a problem. Charlene would need to warn Brandy and Serenity that Tina had loose lips. Why did Ariel want to know these things? Charlene furrowed her forehead.

Ariel didn't catch the warning to back off but asked instead, "Did they catch him? Bobby?"

Edging backward, Charlene decided to be vague. "I have no idea."

"Him running like that makes me wonder if Trinity died of foul play." Ariel cracked her knuckles. "Her poor dad up there on the stage. You think Bobby did it?"

Charlene found Ariel to be very pushy and didn't like it. "I wouldn't know."

"He was a Trinity fan. I loved the shirt design. I'm saving mine in a special place because it will be a collector's item someday. You should see my collection!" Ariel shrugged. "And now that she's gone? Not to be crass, but the value will skyrocket."

"Crass" was an understatement. Mary's signed poster had been a collector's item and stolen that day. Could it have been Ariel? Ariel was very strong. She was a top Trinity fan. Alannah had shouted from the stage that Trinity had fired Ariel. Had that been true? She edged back from the woman and looked around for Alannah.

Alannah stood with Ned and flirted with the policeman, who was more relaxed now that he was the subject of Alannah's smiles. Alannah glanced toward Ariel and Charlene. Charlene stepped to the side, out of the starlet's sight. She wanted to go home and regroup. "Is that everything, Ariel?"

"We *must* find out what happened to Trinity. Between Bobby and Ned, I'd go with Ned since he has a record. Did jail time for something. Not sure." Ariel smacked her big fist to her open palm. "He's in love with Alannah, who hated Trinity. Could mean Ned would hate Trinity too. You get me?"

Charlene followed the logic, though it wasn't concrete but subjective. "You think he might have hurt Trinity on Alannah's behalf?"

"You saw Alannah push Dom off the stage so she could be with Ned!" Ariel said this like that was enough proof for her. Charlene thought Ariel was trying too hard to direct conjecture away from herself.

"Being selfish doesn't make her a . . ."

"Killer?"

Charlene raised her brow at Ariel, ready to leave. "That's not what I said at all. You could ask the police. They might talk to you. In fact, if you know anything at all, you should make an appointment at the station with Officer Jimenez."

"Don't brush me off, Charlene." Ariel curled her fist at her side, eyes bulging with temper. She was digging around to find out what Charlene knew. Charlene went on the offensive.

"When did you see Trinity last?" Charlene held Ariel's gaze. "Your party that she bailed early on? Or did you see her this morning at the Waterway?"

"I didn't go there." Ariel's lower lip jutted out.

"Were you fired from being the president of her fan club?"

"No. Can't get fired since it's volunteer." Ariel studied the broken nails on her right hand. "I wanted to apologize, even though Trinity was totally out of line. She had no respect for me."

Charlene tilted her head. "You thought you deserved an apology from Trinity—but needed to make up because of the parade situation. That must have stuck in your throat."

"Maybe it did. I didn't do anything about it. I know my place in the shadow of the star. I'm the one to who set up the original Sirena page and website." Ariel's gestures were so emphatic that her wig slid, and she straightened it before it fell.

"You said volunteered. Did Trinity hire you for the non-paid position?"

Ariel shrugged.

Charlene pressed, "Did you set up the account with her blessing, or did you do it on your own?"

As she'd discussed with Serenity and Brandy earlier, the fan pages didn't need to be authorized by the star. So long as there was no wrongdoing, it wouldn't be an issue.

"I was ten when I first saw *Sirena*. I was enthralled by Trinity Powers. I couldn't believe they never made a sequel. She did two more movies but not water ballet films, and she lost her audience's approval. *Sirena* was, is, a classic."

And Ariel hadn't answered Charlene's question.

Dom had joined Alannah and Ned and all three were talking. The police officer had moved on. Guess flirting with the cop had kept Ned out of trouble.

He'd been disruptive, and if he'd been to jail before, it probably wasn't a place he wanted to go again. Still, Ariel was trying her darndest to keep suspicion off of herself.

"Was there something else that you and Trinity argued about?" Charlene adjusted the strap of her bag over her shoulder. "Once the police question those in her circle, they *will* find out. It might be best if you went to them."

Ariel gave a furtive look around to make sure nobody else would overhear her. "Trinity didn't like me copying her costume for the parade, that's all. I lost my temper. I'm in anger management classes to control it."

Charlene was glad the woman was getting help—before she ended up in jail, as she'd just ratted out Ned. "Ned and Alannah are coming toward us."

Ariel raised her fist, her eyes narrowed as she

:ed Ned Hammond, fifteen feet away. Ned chuck-
l and touched his swollen nose, undaunted by
eir previous skirmish.

"I think you should go," Charlene said to Ariel.
)uickly, so that there isn't more violence here
night. The park's mostly empty, but there are
ll some families around." Like the Cortes family.
1e politician's daughters were intercepting Alan-
h.

Ariel nodded. "I'll call you if I think of anything
se. And you can call me!"

Not likely. "I'm in the Salem directory, Char-
1e's Bed-and-Breakfast—go!" Charlene shooed
·r hands to get Ariel to leave before Ned reached
em. Ariel went toward the exit and Charlene was
awn to Tony. What would he think of this fiasco
night?

Tony was distinguished, with silver hair, tall, slim.
is daughters wore blue Team Alannah T-shirts
d appeared to be in their early teens.

"I apologize," Alannah said with an impish smile
Tony, then to his daughters, "for the crowd get-
1g out of control. I get carried away myself when
comes time to dance. I'm so sorry!"

"You are so pretty!" the youngest girl said.

"You are!" Alannah countered. "And I adore
ur mermaid skirts."

Ned backed up several paces so that Alannah
1s there with the girls and the politician. Dom
ok Ned's place and Ned turned to Charlene,
·ting with a smirk that she'd come closer.

His demeanor exuded readiness for battle that
dn't quite deflate when he saw that Ariel was not

with Charlene. She held her ground when he
joined her, not looking behind her to give Arie
away.

"Ned." If worse came to worst, she could throw
her hobo bag at him, and there were still severa
Salem PD officers present. "Trouble with the police?

"It's cool." Ned's nose flared in anger. "Where i
Ariel?"

"She went home. You should too." Charlene ca
sually gripped the strap of her purse in her palm
"The damage here tonight was extensive. Shoulc
the city of Salem send you a bill?"

His shoulders lowered at that. Not that Char
lene could—she didn't think. She'd have to asl
Brandy.

"Like I told that cop, Ariel started it. Sh
punched me in the nose. I should press charges!"

"Ariel was worried for Serenity, the announce
on the platform." Charlene didn't back down. "
heard you calling out comments in the front row
trying to stir up trouble."

He lifted his lip without confirming or denying

"This was supposed to be a family-friendly even
celebrating the twenty-fifth anniversary of th
movie *Sirena*. Now, there is no movie at all and
lot of damage the city will have to repair." Th
more she thought about it, the hotter Charlen
got.

"Not my problem," Ned said.

"Do you live here in Salem?"

"Yeah, so?"

"Not only should there be pride in where yo
live but you pay taxes. If those taxes go up to cove

city improvements because you destroyed the lawn in the historic Common, well . . ."

Ned scuffed a bootheel to the grass. All around them, the streetlights went on as night fell. Salem was a safe place to be most of the time.

"You don't need to lecture me," Ned said. "I ain't a kid."

She bit her lip to keep from telling him that he'd been behaving like one. "Are you in love with Alannah?"

The change in subject lowered his defenses and Ned started to answer in the affirmative, then held his tongue.

"Do you manage her social media accounts? For the fan club?"

Ned tucked his thumb in his jeans pocket. "I do, but she also has her own page that she does herself."

"And yours clearly states it's a fan club site?"

"Yep. Alannah insisted because she plans on doing a lot more movies than *Sirena*. She don't want to be a one-shot wonder, like Trinity."

Charlene held up her palm, not wanting to hear any slander.

"That's a fact, not a negative opinion." Ned studied her closely. "About Ariel . . ."

"Yes?"

"Don't trust her," he said. "She's a liar."

"How so?" Ariel had warned Charlene about Ned. Who was telling the truth?

"Lots of folks were talking about an argument she and Trinity had last night. I made sure to tell the cops about it, too, just now." Ned grinned. "Doing my civic duty."

"What about?"

Ned reminded her of a fox, canny and untrusting. "Trinity was going to sue Ariel if she didn't take down the fan club page—all the social media sites. Ariel runs three or four of them. Sells merchandise that Trinity doesn't see a penny from."

Oh. And if Trinity was hurting for income, that could be a problem. "She told me they'd argued." Charlene gave Ned the eye right back. "She also told me that you'd been to jail. Not to trust you either."

"What?" Ned blustered.

But she could read from his expression that it was true. Ariel's plan to paint Ned as the guilty party had gotten paint on her too. Charlene would suggest to Sam that he check out Ariel Glitter as well as Ned Hammond.

Trinity might have been within her rights to sue. What if Ariel had had to pay restitution or something? Would she have had the cash?

The mermaid lifestyle wasn't cheap. Some of the tails were worth five grand. Might Ariel, who had a temper, have killed Trinity by accident? Or had it been calculated? Charlene's stomach tightened with dread.

Alannah and Dom sauntered over at the same time as Brandy did, probably curious as to what the politician might have said, and his daughters, who'd wanted to meet Alannah. Ned oozed away as they arrived.

Charlene read her watch. It was only eight thirty. "Brandy! How are things going? Can I do anything to help clean up? My couch is calling to me."

"Serenity has a crew of people to take the bleachers down in the morning." Brandy glared at Alannah and Dom. "The stage was ruined, of course."

"I am so sorry about that!" Alannah said. "I talked to that gentleman over there—I didn't know he was a councilman in the city—and offered to pay for the damage—he said it wasn't necessary."

"He did?" Brandy's eye twitched.

"His daughters are fans! Who knew?" Alannah clasped Dom's forearm and leaned against him. "You know, if Trinity hadn't died, I might have won this ridiculous popularity contest."

"You would have, babe," Dom said. "Hands down."

Charlene brought her purse strap back to her shoulder, tired to the bone. "It's a moot point now."

Alannah's brown eyes lasered on Charlene, as if realizing that she wasn't impressed with her. "So, were you and Neddy catching up? I saw you with Ariel too."

"Charlene has a way with people," Brandy said. "It's a gift."

Charlene hid a smile at that. "It comes in handy running the bed-and-breakfast. Brandy, if you have things under control, I'm going to head home."

"A bed-and-breakfast?" Alannah asked, not taking the broad hint that Charlene wanted to leave. "Where?"

"Crown Point Road." Charlene had been raised to be polite, so she explained, "The historic mansion has eight rooms on a large piece of property. The widow's walk has a view of the wharf and the harbor."

"It sounds so romantic. Doesn't it, Dom?"

Dom nodded, but she could tell this was really Alannah's deal. What did the woman want? The actress had Ned and Dom under her thumb, and she'd flirted Ned—and probably herself—out of paying for the damage done tonight.

Charlene was not an Alannah fan, even if the music was good. She looked at Brandy, who nodded.

"I'd love to see it," Alannah continued.

Charlene's skin tightened in alarm. She didn't want Alannah there. The woman wasn't kind; maybe that was it. Or could her intuition be warning her that Alannah was an enemy? Could Alannah, perhaps through Ned, be responsible for Trinity's death?

"I'm full through Friday with the guests for the Mermaid Parade. Maybe next time you're in town you can make an appointment and I'll show you the place."

Alannah's brow lifted. She'd expected a different answer.

Brandy gestured toward the politician and his daughters. "Do you know Tony?"

"No. Just met him." The man was glancing back at Alannah—and Brandy. Was that a warning in his intense gaze?

"Maybe I should send him a bill," Brandy teased—but not really.

Alannah tittered. "Oh! Did I cause some trouble? That seems to be my thing lately."

"No trouble," Charlene interceded. She didn't want Alannah to give herself so much credit.

This young lady was something else. An actress, a dancer, a water ballet artist. Could she also be a killer?

CHAPTER 10

Charlene, at last, escaped the quagmire of the Common and didn't stop until she was in her SUV. As soon as she'd started the engine, her cell phone rang. Avery's smiling face showed on the screen.

She answered via Bluetooth, her heart happy despite the tragedies of the day. "How are you, sweetheart?"

"I'm fine! Just wanted to see how you are? Seth told me the *Sirena* movie was canceled, and Trinity died? What happened?"

"We aren't sure exactly." Avery was going to school to get her criminology degree, so she knew that Charlene couldn't answer unless Sam gave her the go-ahead. Bless her, she didn't press.

"Should I be worried about you?"

"Oh, no, hon! I'm fine." Charlene stopped for a red light. "The mermaid costumes were out of this world. I hope we do the parade again next year. It raised five grand for Clean Oceans."

"That's amazing, and a worthy cause."

"I couldn't agree more. How is school?" The light turned green, and Charlene stepped on the gas, careful of the pedestrians. Tourists weren't always cautious when in vacation mode.

"It's only been a week. I'm loving it, Charlene. Thank you for all your help getting into college."

"You did the hard work—I was just there for moral support. And ice cream."

"Lots of ice cream! So, I'll come home on Friday for the weekend, but text me updates about Trinity, 'kay?"

"Okay." Charlene would share what she could. "Love you!"

"Love you!"

She ended the call and within five minutes was home and parked before the house. The lights were on and, best of all, Jack and Silva waited on the porch for her. She exited the SUV.

"Welcome home," Jack said.

Before she could reply, the front door opened. Charlene blew out a breath. That was close. Jack grinned as she climbed the steps.

Natalie Southern widened the door. "You're home! Are you all right? Ned Hammond has been posting 'Alannah Wins Salem' all over the place, with videos of her dancing on the stage as it collapsed."

Jack disappeared and reappeared by the staircase. He hadn't known that. "What happened?"

Inside the foyer, Charlene said, "The movie was canceled."

"Canceled? Why? Did Alannah do something wrong?" Natalie's excitement dimmed a little as it dawned on her that her hero might have clay feet. "I can't believe it."

"I'm not sure of the details." Charlene looked around for her daughters, wondering how much to reveal.

"The girls are upstairs taking a bath to get all the makeup off. Linc is supervising so I could greet you." Natalie sighed guiltily. "I've been listening for your car."

Charlene chuckled. Natalie's curiosity might be as great as Charlene's. "Where are the Wheatons?"

"They went bowling after pizza. We took the girls to the shops. They're nice people for sure, but boys are just a very different energy." Natalie brushed back her hair. "Elementary." She laughed at herself. "Nobody else is back yet."

"Well," Charlene said, closing the door, "I don't know anything more about Trinity's death, but we tried to salvage the hard work people had put into their floats and costumes to grant the prizes. We were keeping things very low-key."

Alannah, Dom, and Ned had ruined that.

Purposefully.

Natalie was Team Alannah.

Charlene raised her guard and kept her tone casual. "I think the fans of both mermaids were simmering and angry about Trinity."

"And it came to a boil. I was hoping the videos were wrong. I'm sorry, Charlene. Sometimes people just get carried away during public gatherings. I guess we haven't changed that much since all those years ago when the witches were hanged."

Jack sighed. "As a species, that doesn't bode well."

"You might have a point," Charlene conceded. "On a happier note, the parade raised five thousand for Clean Oceans."

"That's great! Well, you take care. You must be exhausted after such a long day." Natalie squeezed Charlene's wrist. "I'm going to make sure the girls don't spill too much water."

"Thank you!"

Natalie hurried up the stairs to the suite to join her family.

Charlene went to the living room and flipped on a soft lamp on an end table. Just being home revived her spirits. She opened the gorgeous bar Parker Murdock, a local craftsman, had custommade for her and studied the wine choices for what appealed most.

"You look tired," Jack said kindly. He appeared by the mantel, and the mirror above it didn't reflect his image.

"I'm done for the night." Charlene poured herself a very large glass of cabernet sauvignon from Brandy's winery and sipped, then sipped again.

The oak and cherry notes coated her palate. "This is just what the doctor ordered."

Jack chuckled. "As usual, I enjoy it vicariously through you. Have a seat, Charlene. Or should we go to the suite?"

Charlene nodded and topped off the glass. On second thought, she brought the bottle with her and returned to the privacy of her cozy space, careful to lock the door behind her.

"Ah." She sighed as she sank into the plump cushions of the love seat. Her legs trembled with fatigue after twelve hours of walking around the parade and then the movie night that hadn't happened. Ups and downs like a roller coaster.

They sat in companionable silence for several moments as Charlene just let the day replay in her mind. So much had happened. She looked around for her cell phone.

Jack snapped his fingers, and it appeared on the cushion next to her.

"Thank you," she said. "I don't know if I'd have had the energy to get up right now."

"You're drained, Charlene. Even though I'm riddled with curiosity, I can wait until the morning if you'd rather not talk about it."

"You are a wonderful friend—but I would never do that to you." She laughed. Melting into the cushion, she sipped her wine and exhaled. "I don't know where to start."

The television was on low as background noise to cover their conversation, showing a travel documentary about Peru. It was lovely.

She hadn't thought of travel since Jared died. He'd been her everything. Her lesson from that had been to make friends so she wasn't so isolated. It had been just the two of them. How they'd loved each other!

His loss had devastated her and now, after three and a half years, she was in a place where the grief had dulled. It was a part of her, but not as all-encompassing as it was.

There was room in her life to date Sam . . . slowly. Behind the scenes for them both at this point in their lives. To have a ghost as her best friend. Her life now was full. It was not by any means easy, but it was hers.

"Why the smile?" Jack asked.

"I'm happy," she said. "Avery called. She heard about Trinity and the canceled movie showing. She'll be here on Friday."

Jack grinned. He loved her, the daughter he'd never had. Sometimes she wished that she could introduce Jack to Avery. Avery would be open-minded; she was sure of it. Charlene didn't know why she was able to see Jack when nobody else could—except Silva.

"How did she hear about it so soon . . . Seth?" Jack said the young man's name like it was toxic.

Avery and Seth Gamble had started dating a few months back. "He's a good kid. His mom, Dani, was there too."

The Gamble home was haunted, and Dani could see the little girl ghost as if it were an echo in their kitchen. The spirit wasn't similar to Jack at all, and Charlene hadn't glimpsed her when there. Charlene would never invite Dani inside the B-&-B, just in case. Just like Kass, who also saw ghosts, and never came inside either. Sam could come in all he wanted as he didn't believe in ghosts, end of story.

"I suppose," Jack said. He was very protective of them and had saved their lives more than once. Charlene knew it, but Avery didn't—that she had a specter protector.

Charlene sipped her wine, her eyes half-closed.

"I'm glad you're happy, Charlene." He fluttered her hair. "But there is something different about you lately."

Silva meowed from the kitchen on the opposite side of the closed door, saving Charlene from having to answer her too-astute ghost.

Jack unlocked the door and opened it slightly to let the cat in, then closed it and locked it once more without Charlene having to move a muscle.

"I owe you," she said. The cat leaped onto the love seat next to her with a rumbling purr.

"You can pay up by dishing on what happened tonight," Jack said.

"That is fair." Charlene patted Silva's soft fur and went through the events of the day and evening, giving him all the details that she hadn't shared with Natalie. Not only was Jack Team Trinity, he was also an awesome sounding board.

"Grant Powers was a mess! It was good that Brandy was there to help him, but she might have blown her cover with her politician boyfriend."

Jack chuckled. He was well aware of Brandy and her taste in men, the two of them having grown up in Salem together. "What did *you* think of Grant?"

Her mind was fuzzy from being so tired. "He seems like a decent guy, but he's carrying a load of guilt. Trinity and Madeline moved to LA when Trinity was ten years old. He expected them to fail and crawl back home. They didn't. Can you use your super cyber-skills to see if there was anything that happened between them around forty years ago?"

"You got it. Anything specific, or just general snooping?" Jack waggled his brows.

Charlene laughed. "Trinity disowned Grant over something. He claims not to know what it is. My mom was awful, but I still stayed in touch." Her mother's constant criticism hadn't allowed for a cozy childhood.

"Your mother has changed," Jack said. "She's softer. And you had your dad."

Dad had made up for hurt feelings as best he could by taking Charlene on all-day outings that often ended with ice cream. "Maybe I'm biased because I had such a great father, so I'm very curious as to what happened between Grant and Trinity. They won't have the chance Mom and I did to reconcile." Since her move from Chicago, Charlene and her mother had developed a less adversarial relationship.

Jack nodded in understanding. "I'll look."

"Thanks." Charlene patted Silva, stroking her soft ears, then her back.

"Anything else?" Jack teased.

"As a matter of fact, yes. I'd like it if you could uncover more about Trinity Powers. Why did she have such severe anxiety? She was at the top of her game. What changed? There must have been a reason for her to never really leave her LA home." Charlene sipped her wine thoughtfully. "Would her dad get an inheritance?"

"Oh, smart question." Jack approved. "Discovering who benefits from her death might lead to the killer."

"Exactly. I saw pictures of the three of them in Grant's house when we delivered Minnie's cookies. Madeline is his wife. In the photos at least, they appeared to be a happy family. Then Grant didn't support the move to Hollywood. Is that enough of a reason to never speak to him again?"

"Good questions."

"I have so many when it comes to Trinity—she

was secretive and private, rude. Yet nice to a young maid who asked for a collectible poster to be signed while she had breakfast. Could that behavior be the result of her anxiety?"

"Maybe she was just hungry," Jack joked. "Seriously, it might be as simple as that she wasn't taking her medication. I wish I knew what that prescription bottle said because then I'd have more answers. Any chance Sam will tell you?"

"You're a riot, Jack." Charlene scowled, upset with herself. "If anything, I should have taken pictures of the room and the letter beneath her for us to go over later, but I wasn't thinking clearly. It's hard to act like the dead body you discovered isn't a real person." Her eyes welled up and a tear dropped onto Silva's fur.

"I'm sorry," Jack said, gently soothing her face with cool air.

Charlene rested her head on the cushion at her back. She had to focus on what she could do to help. "Can you find out if Trinity had money or not? Ariel Glitter ran several fan pages and sold *Sirena* merchandise. Ned told me about their argument, and Alannah said Ariel was fired. Ariel admitted to the disagreement but didn't answer my question on whether Trinity had chosen Ariel, even as a volunteer. What if she was doing it all behind Trinity's back?"

Jack shifted on the armchair. "So, Ariel is a person of interest, as is Bobby, and Grant."

"I guess so." Charlene sipped her wine and raised her brow at Jack. How could he keep all of this straight?

"What?" Jack showed both palms with a cute

hrug.

"You should be taking notes!"

"I've got it all here," he said, tapping his temple.

"Then *I* should be taking notes." Charlene laughed at herself.

"Want your pad of paper?"

She yawned loudly. "No. I want to go to bed, and we can do this in the morning when I have a fresh mind."

"That's probably the best idea. Any last thoughts?"

Finishing her tasty red, Charlene placed the empty wineglass on the low table. "Yes. Ned Hammond might have been to jail, and he's in love with Alannah. Alannah and Dom are for the movie only. Why didn't Trinity do a second movie, Jack? I mean, a sequel to *Sirena*, a blockbuster, would have been money in the bank. I think that's important to find out."

She got up and blew Jack a kiss, then took Silva and collapsed into bed—so beat that she didn't dream at all.

CHAPTER 11

On weekday mornings, Charlene and Minnie provided a light breakfast of cold cereal, muffins, toast, fruit, yogurt, and, of course, coffee, tea, and juices, as they did this Monday too.

The Sanchos brothers were checking out today, having taken an extended weekend to meet Trinity Powers and the other mermaids. Though their King Triton costume hadn't placed in the contest, they were returning home with a juicy story of a killer at large. The Bonets were moving up the coast to Portland for a few more days of vacation, but the Martins, Wheatons, and Southerns were here through Friday morning.

Salem offered so much history that the Wheatons and Southerns were interested in teaching their kids. Over their coffee and muffins, the Martins bickered about where to spend the day. Plymouth or Boston?

Charlene sensed an undercurrent between the

couple and got the feeling the argument wasn't really about where to spend the day.

Sam arrived at nine as she was finishing her coffee. Minnie called for Charlene, and she excused herself to see what the detective wanted. He wore a lightweight jacket over slacks, his badge on his belt. Sam at work. Good—she hoped that he would have answers about Trinity and what had happened to her.

"Morning, Sam!" Charlene heard the pleased tone in her voice and cautioned herself to keep her cool. It was difficult not to stare at his lips and that glorious mustache that did indeed tickle in the best ways when they kissed.

He saw her gaze on his mouth and winked, then backed up with amusement. "Charlene."

"Coffee, Sam?" Minnie asked, not seeing the wink as she had half her attention on the dining room and what might need to be replenished.

"Yes, ma'am. Can we talk in the kitchen, Charlene?"

"Sure." She walked down the hall, feeling Sam's gaze on her back. Her straight, dark brown hair was down today. Was he watching her?

"I need to question one of your guests: Andrew Martin," Sam said.

Charlene stopped at the small, rectangular kitchen table and faced Sam. Her stomach clenched and banished any romantic thoughts. She was like a mama bear as she said, "Why?"

"While I was scrolling the security film at the Waterway Hotel, I discovered footage of a man acting suspiciously as he entered the hotel Sunday around noon. The guest had booked a room under the name Andrew Martin. I called his home number and the person house-sitting for them told me Andrew and his wife were staying here. At your bed-and-breakfast. Small world, huh?"

Too small, it seemed. In all of the chaos yesterday, she hadn't had the time to ask Andrew about it—not that it was her business. He could do whatever he liked. Well, except murder somebody. She gave a single nod.

Sam removed a tablet and pen from his pocket. "Was he there?"

"I don't know." Charlene swallowed, her throat dry. "I thought I saw him at noon but didn't ask, and I forgot in the tragedy of finding Trinity. I thought maybe he wanted an autograph or something."

He wrote that down. "It didn't cross your mind to mention it?"

"Sam, he's a guest! And I wasn't sure it was him." Her heart pounded with alarm.

Sam looked toward the Keurig with hope in his eyes. "Dark roast?"

"Fine." Charlene was a little upset, but Minnie had offered, so, well, she was a good hostess and could be polite. She centered a mug under the spout, put in a pod, and hit the button.

The rich scent of coffee filled the narrow space. Jack appeared by the fridge.

"Morning, Sam," Jack said with a raised brow. "Any answers?"

Charlene handed Sam the mug, careful to keep her fingers to herself.

"Heaven." Sam cradled the mug to his chest and

observed Charlene. Sensing her chilly demeanor, he blew on the java without any flirting.

"Sam!" Charlene barely restrained herself from stomping a foot in frustration. "I told you what I know."

The man could draw out a moment like no other. "Trinity Powers's death is being treated as a homicide. Which you probably surmised."

"Right. Trinity had no reason to stuff a T-shirt in her own mouth." Charlene was impatient. "Or put marks around her own throat."

"Right." Sam drank his coffee, wincing at the heat. "She didn't die of suffocation, but she was asphyxiated. Choked to death."

"Choked, like you thought, Charlene," Jack said.

Charlene gave a slow nod, recalling the scene just yesterday. "Why would she have the shirt in her mouth?"

"I don't know," Sam said. "Yet. We will find answers. I'll talk with Andrew. And once we get our hands on Bobby Rourke, that will fill in some blanks."

She was glad that Sam wasn't focusing solely on her guest. "No clue where Bobby is?"

"No, but he'll surface eventually. I've got officers watching his place, his bank, and the studio space he rents to paint in. The landlord agreed to put a bolt on the door until we catch Bobby."

"Sam's putting some effort in," Jack noted with a chuckle. "Could be that Brandy's politician is laying on the heat. Isn't he up for reelection?"

Charlene didn't turn toward Jack but wondered if he was right. They'd have to do some digging on Tony Cortes too. They hadn't had a chance to go over what, if anything, he'd learned about Grant and Trinity last night while Charlene had slept.

"That's narrowing things down," Charlene said. "Does he have local parents? A steady girlfriend? He flirted with Tina quite a bit at the registration table."

"No parents here. A lot of female friends, but nothing serious. He was a waiter for a while, so that widens the net too. Handsome, friendly." Sam sipped his coffee. "At large. Anything else you can tell me, since you neglected to mention Andrew?"

Charlene placed her hand on her racing heart. "I didn't know it might be important!" She thought of all she'd learned yesterday. "I talked with Ariel Glitter and Ned Hammond. They're both fan club presidents and don't like each other. To the point of suggesting they could each have a reason to want Trinity dead."

"Ariel is the big blonde who punched the guy with the goatee? That's Ned?" At her nod, Sam jotted down both names. His phone dinged repeatedly, but he ignored it. "I'll be sure to pass this information over to Officer Jimenez." He put the pad and pen back in his pocket, sipped his coffee, and put the mostly full mug in the sink. "I have to go. Do you mind if I talk with Andrew Martin now?"

Charlene knew Sam was just being polite and hoped that Andrew had a good explanation for being at the hotel, like getting an autograph from Trinity. "Discreetly, of course."

"Of course." Sam sighed, as if smooth was his middle name. It might be, Charlene admitted to herself.

Jack disappeared as Charlene followed Sam. They entered the dining room and Sam asked to speak with Andrew out on the porch. Barb was having none of it.

"Why him?" Barb asked.

"I have some questions regarding the events of yesterday," Sam said calmly.

"He can answer them here, can't he?" Barb insisted. Her eyes flashed with anger and hurt. "He was with me all day."

Andrew shrugged, but his eye twitched. "I can answer them now."

Sam smoothed his mustache and pursed his lips. "Why don't we step outside? If not here, Mr. Martin, we can go to the station. Your choice."

Andrew, pale, stood and went out with the detective. Barb threw her napkin over her plate, her face scarlet.

"What's wrong?" Lottie Wheaton asked.

"Not a damn thing." Barb left the dining room in tears.

Charlene wanted to help her but had no clue where to begin. The Martins seemed to be having marital troubles. She checked the carafes for coffee and water, but everything was full. Minnie was in the kitchen doing dishes and had already taken care of refills.

Grabbing an apple, Charlene polished it on her shirt, glancing toward the open dining room door when Andrew ducked his head in. He saw Barb gone, cursed, and left the room, then ran up the stairs. Sam didn't come back in.

No explanations. Typical.

Charlene didn't know what to do, so she pasted

a big smile on her face and bit into the apple, taking a seat at the head of the table, conversing about activities for the day. It was hard to ignore what had just happened in the dining room of her bed-and-breakfast.

"Does this have to do with Trinity?" Dean asked. "It was on the news that she was killed. Murdered."

"The cops think Andrew had something to do with it?" Steve sounded dubious.

"Right now, they are simply gathering information," Charlene assured them. "Sometimes one little fact can lead to tracking down a criminal. If you've heard anything suspicious or that might help, you should let the department know before you go. Coffee?"

Dean and Steve exchanged looks, then shrugged and went back to their breakfast. "Nothing new," Dean said.

"Bobby Rourke is a person of interest." Linc slathered cream cheese on a toasted bagel. "The artist who designed the shirts. The cops can't find him."

To act like her B&B was in a bubble wasn't working, Charlene thought as she chewed and swallowed another bite of apple.

"And what about Alannah?" Dean broke off a section of banana nut muffin.

"What about her?" Natalie asked. She sounded defensive of her favorite mermaid actress.

"You weren't there last night, but she totally encouraged that stage coming down." Steve sipped his orange juice. "I think she did it to stop Trinity's movie from showing."

It was obvious the brothers had discussed this

and come up with their conclusions. Charlene hadn't considered that there would have been a purpose behind the destruction. Were they right?

"She did?" Terry asked. The Wheatons had chosen not to go downtown for the show because of Trinity's death and the possible danger of a killer on the loose in Salem.

"I think so!" Dean said.

Her guests turned to Charlene, who shrugged and explained, "The police were there to calm the rowdy crowd at the Common. I heard Alannah apologize for letting things get out of control." Charlene privately agreed with the Sanchos.

"See?" Linc told Aqua and Jewel. "An apology goes a long way." Charlene didn't think it would be easy to explain bad behavior to good kids. Alannah was their idol.

"Alannah should be held responsible," Steve said. "I unfollowed her. I am totally Team Trinity now. I hadn't picked a side before."

"She's dead!" Dillon's eyes were big in his face, his features awkward until he grew into them. "What will happen to her fans now?"

"Good question, kiddo." Charlene wiped her fingers on a napkin and wrapped the core of her apple inside. If Alannah was smart and played her cards right, she could gain those fans for herself and possibly do a sequel right away.

Maybe it was up to the producers, though, and not the actors? Charlene didn't know much about how movies were made.

Lottie steered the subject back to the Peabody Essex Museum, where they were going for the day.

"How much time should we allot for that, Charlene?" Terry asked.

"You'll easily fill a day. There are many exhibits. If you're interested in boats, they have the history of the first merchant vessels built in the US, along with a replica of the *Friendship* that's on the wharf across from the Custom House."

"We are going on an excursion tomorrow for that," Lottie said. "I just wasn't sure if we should try to fit something else in today."

"We did the Peabody last time we were here," Rose said. "I wished we had two days scheduled for it. But then again, we love Salem. It's our fourth visit. Charlene, we will be back. Your bed-and-breakfast is the best."

Dirk nodded and covered Rose's hand with his. "It is."

Charlene smiled, very glad to hear those words. "You know . . . anything over five days, I give a ten percent discount for repeat guests."

"I'll check our calendar!" Dirk said.

"You won't be back for the second annual Mermaid Parade?" Lottie asked. "We will be—if it's still going on next year."

"We had fun, partying with mermaids, but it's not our thing," Rose said.

Natalie brought her hand to her mouth in pretend shock. "What? You don't want to spend thousands on costumes and travel to various festivals just to hang out with other merfolk?"

"We have other things to spend our extra money on—like saving for a house," Dirk said. The young couple had only been married a few years.

"That is perfectly logical," Linc said in agreement. "It takes a bit of whimsy to dive into the mermaid culture. I love it, and my family does too, but it's not for everyone. No hard feelings."

Charlene liked Linc's attitude. Too bad not everybody was as easygoing.

By noon, the Sanchos and the Bonets were checked out and Charlene was upstairs helping Minnie clean the rooms. More singles were coming on Saturday, in addition to having Avery home on Friday. All four suites would have new guests Friday afternoon. She hummed under her breath as she vacuumed, playing with Silva, who liked to chase the machine.

By one, they were ready for lunch. Minnie had made turkey and Swiss sandwiches with hot mustard on whole wheat bread, iced teas, and lemon cookies for a sweet bite afterward.

Charlene hadn't seen Jack since that morning, when Sam was there. She hoped he was all right. There were times he disappeared without reason, and she feared that one day he might just never return.

"So," Minnie said as she got up to put the dirty dishes in the dishwasher.

"Yes?" Charlene scraped crumbs into the trash, tossing Silva a piece of cheese.

"Did one of our guests have something to do with Trinity's murder?"

Charlene whirled, her hands on her hips as she thought of Andrew and Barb. "I hope not! That would be awful for business."

"Unless you spun it right," Jack said.

Charlene gulped. His voice was behind her, his body not to be seen. She was just happy he was back.

"Why did Sam want to talk with Andrew?" Minnie asked.

"I don't know . . . well, maybe I do." Charlene sighed and studied her fingernails—she'd painted them with pink glitter in honor of the parade.

"What?" Minnie pressed the Start button on the machine. It was quiet, so they could still talk over the hum. "Spill!"

"Yesterday morning, I thought I saw someone who looked like Andrew Martin around the Waterway."

"Was Barb with him?" Minnie asked.

"No! And Barb clearly said that Andrew was with her the whole day. They are Team Trinity. Maybe he went in to meet Trinity, you know? Get a picture or an autograph. But then, why wouldn't he just say that? And Sam said he'd rented a room under his own name."

"Could he have killed her?" Minnie gulped and touched her throat.

"I don't see it." Charlene washed her hands and then dried them on a paper towel. "If you're a fan, you wouldn't hurt the person you've idolized."

"Seen *Misery*?" Jack slowly manifested by the counter.

Minnie shivered and glanced behind her. "From what I've gathered about our guests, they are very supportive of their favorite mermaid. I saw on the news where rabid soccer fans were killed when they stormed the field after a call they didn't like. There's another side to this whole fan thing."

"A dark side," Charlene agreed.

"What do you think of Andrew?" Minnie asked. "Could he be hiding something?"

"He has to be, considering that he was at the Waterway. Without Barb. He'd rented a room!" She hated to follow that line of thought.

"Oh no." Minnie brushed her hands together, having arrived at the same conclusion of an affair. That would be better than murder. "I hope we're wrong and Andrew clears up the matter with the police."

Charlene nodded. "Amen to that."

Jack said, "Charlene, you should come to the suite."

She turned to him and tilted her head. Could it wait?

"I overheard Sam asking Andrew on the porch if he'd been to the Waterway the morning Trinity was killed. Andrew said no."

Oh! Charlene wasn't sure how she felt about learning this news by Jack eavesdropping. On the other hand, it wasn't as if Sam had stuck around to talk with her. Andrew hadn't either.

She cleared her throat. "Minnie, thanks for lunch. I'm going to pop into my suite and do some paperwork for an hour or so."

"Take your time. Happy hour summer harvest cold soup is on the menu. I'll bake some corn biscuits to go with them."

"You're the best!"

Charlene went into the room and turned up the volume on the TV.

Jack waited by her desk. He'd opened her laptop for her and scooted out her chair too. What a gentleman. She still was on the fence about his eavesdropping.

"Don't be mad," Jack said, easily reading her. "Sit down."

Oh. "I need to sit?" Her nose scrunched.

"It's a good idea."

She did. "Okay."

Jack paced between her and the TV.

"What?"

"Well."

Charlene rolled her eyes. "Hurry! You're as bad as Sam!"

Jack came to an abrupt halt. "Fine. In addition to Sam having Andrew on video cam going into the Waterway Hotel before Trinity was killed, there is footage of a man who could be Andrew—you can't see his face—leaving with a woman, heads together, an hour later."

CHAPTER 12

"And I guess the woman he's with is not his wife, Barb?" Charlene empathized with how Barb had left the dining room so abruptly.

Jack shook his head. "Andrew refused to admit it was him on the camera, but from how they've been bickering, I think Barb suspects something is going on."

"Andrew says he's innocent?" Charlene, agitated, sat forward. "Barb lied for him this morning in the dining room. What did Sam do?"

"Said for them not to leave Salem, and that the next time would be questioning down at the station."

"And Andrew didn't cave?" Charlene had been the recipient of Sam's glares and she knew how powerful they could be.

"No. But I saw Andrew's expression and believe he's lying. Sam does too. I don't know how he keeps from just arresting the liars to put them in jail. He didn't tell Andrew that he knew he had rented a room, just kept it to himself." Jack stopped pacing. "I think Sam has a lot more patience than I've ever given him credit for."

Charlene laughed. Sam had been patient with her, certainly. "The lie you saw—was it guilt over killing Trinity or is he covering up an affair?"

"One way to find out if he won't talk—ask his lover. Who is she?"

She frowned. Who did she know who might help? "Mary Clarkson is the maid at the Waterway. I have a T-shirt for her as a thank-you that she never came to collect because she was bonked over the head."

"Do you think she'd talk to you?"

"I don't know. Maybe if I frame the scenario just right—like, try to prove my guest is innocent . . . it might work. She seems like a nice woman."

"Unless he isn't," Jack said. "Innocent."

"Stop switching sides!" Charlene accused, only half-joking.

Jack spread out his arm, his hand brushing through the TV. "If he's guilty, we need to be on our guard at the B-and-B. I can keep watch here while you go out and converse with others." He smiled at her softly. "We're good at solving these puzzles."

"We are!" If she could give him a hug, she would, but she knew better.

"So," he said, turning on her laptop, "while you were sleeping, I did some research on Grant Powers, and Trinity. You might find this to be interesting reading."

Charlene scooted to the edge of her chair.

Grant as a much younger man, Trinity, a toddler, with her mom, Madeline, at Salem Harbor. Trinity held a conch shell to her ear, and the caption read, *Calling Mermaids*. The grainy image was forty-seven years old, and an article followed.

Grant Powers worked at the Peabody Essex Museum in the restoration department. It seemed he'd discovered a mermaid legend from one of the ships coming from Fiji to Salem that if you called to a mermaid through a conch shell and she heard you, she would grant you a wish.

"This is adorable," Charlene said, turning to Jack, who stood to her right. "Trinity's expression is pure magic, and it's obvious Grant loves her. Madeline isn't looking at the camera, but she's very pretty. How could Trinity cut this man from her life?"

Jack maneuvered the browser. "The next article, in the *Salem News*, about Trinity is when the *Sirena* movie was released twenty-five years ago. Grant called her selfish, pleading with her to answer his phone calls."

Charlene scanned the article and sighed at the image of a distraught Grant, twenty-five years older than in the first photo, asking his daughter to talk to him.

That was something her mom might have done if Charlene hadn't been in touch. If a week went by without a call, her mother was impossible. Speaking of, it had been about that long since their last family phone chat.

"The other things I found are Madeline Powers's obituary. It was in the *Salem News*, even though she died in Hollywood, and then notices of Trinity's two other films—neither were successful."

Grant must have informed the local paper. He'd had a scrapbook of everything Trinity had ever done. At what point did that go from paternal pride to stalking?

She placed a hand on her stomach and looked at Jack with concern. "Jack, could Grant have killed his daughter?"

"I don't know why—if he's being honest with you about why his family left Salem and him behind. The money thread was a bust, as in, Trinity Powers was in debt up to the chimney on her house along the California coast."

Honesty. She didn't know the man at all. "Grant has lived in the same place since Brandy can remember. He retired from the Peabody Essex Museum, so he would have some sort of pension. It might be safe to assume that whoever killed Trinity, it wasn't for the money."

Jack shifted the mouse so the next browser showed Google Earth. Trinity had lived in a gated compound on a property so overgrown she couldn't enjoy the view of the ocean in the distance. "It's a beautiful home, but with back taxes owed, it would still be in the negative if Grant did inherit it. Perhaps she had life insurance?"

Charlene tapped her finger to the desk, appalled on Trinity's behalf by the trap she'd been in. Was it due to her anxiety? Until coming to Salem. Had Brandy's spell been that powerful? Or had Trinity been desperate for the five grand Brandy had paid for her to be in Salem?

"This makes me very sad, Jack. She was a talented star whose fame was assured. What happened?"

Jack accessed yet another open browser. He'd been busy! "These were her next two movies. Trinity was doing interviews then, so not quite to the hiding-at-home stage. This suggests to me that she suffered from a severe trauma. What triggered it? Medication would ease the anxiety. SSRIs, like paroxetine. It helps most when combined with therapy. I'd love it if you could convince Sam to tell you what was in the hotel room."

"Fat chance." Charlene jotted a note on the pad of paper next to her computer. "I can ask Brandy if Trinity mentioned medication. What did you call that . . . SS?"

Jack used his modulated doctor's voice. "Selective serotonin reuptake inhibitors are a class of medication typical in treating depression, among other psychological conditions. As I said, they perform best with therapy."

"SSRI is a lot easier on the tongue." Charlene liked having her handsome doctor in the house. "I haven't told Brandy anything about what I saw in the room because Sam asked me not to, but she might be able to help."

"You'll find a way to get her to open up without breaking your word to Sam."

"You have too much faith in me sometimes!" Charlene protested. "What else did you find?"

"While researching Trinity, Ariel Glitter's name came up as her fan club president on social media." Jack stroked his chin just a tad smugly. "Ariel Glitter's real name is Sandy Knickerbocker."

"Sandy Knickerbocker?" Charlene recalled Ariel's insistence that Ned had secrets. Well, he wasn't the only one!

"Born in Iowa and raised on a farm," Jack continued. "The farm failed, and she moved to Boston for college, where she was picked up as a semipro female wrestler."

"Seems silly to ask if she had a history of violence?" Charlene drummed her pen to the pad of paper.

Jack chuckled. "You have a point. Ariel Glitter was her wrestling name as well as her mermaid name. She was *retired* after knocking out an opponent unfairly. She avoided jail by agreeing to anger management classes." He grinned from the computer to Charlene. "I revere the internet."

Charlene returned his smile and then went back to the screen. "But no arrests." Ariel had controlled her impulses since then. "I did tell you that she punched Ned in the nose?"

"Yes," Jack said. "So, she's had eight years of *mostly* good behavior. The Trinity Fan Page was something she started in Iowa before college, so that would be at least fifteen years ago, possibly twenty. It's hard to compare now, but Ariel Glitter very much resembled Trinity as *Sirena*." He pulled up a picture of Sandy/Ariel in college. Very pretty, with long, dark hair.

"But not the eyes." Charlene moved the cursor over Ariel's eyes, which were brown and not Trinity's violet. "Trinity was very cruel to Ariel about her size on Saturday night. Why would Trinity fire Ariel after so many years of her running the fan clubs, unpaid labor?"

"I don't know. It wasn't mentioned anywhere online. I'm not sure that Trinity ever directly used social media, which means that Ariel controlled most of the content. But look at this." Jack opened a Word doc entitled Ned Hammond. "Ned Hammond did five years for assault. He started his fan club presidency while behind bars. He's only been out of jail two years."

Charlene shivered at the picture of Ned's mug shot. He was missing teeth on the right side that had been replaced. "This is pretty brutal. Ned was very threatening at the park last night and didn't care who saw him. He's got nice teeth now."

Probably had false ones put in. Maybe even on the government's dime. She didn't want to go down that rabbit hole, but it was bothersome that Ned could start a fan club from jail with access to the computer. Jail was supposed to be a punishment, not a time to daydream about your new love.

Then again, it spun things toward Ned about Alannah, and what he'd do, maybe, for her against Trinity.

Charlene was startled by Minnie's knock—time to prep for happy hour.

She stood and stretched. "Good work, partner. I'll be back when they all head out for dinner. Could you do some research on Dom Preston? He's been on the fringes of everything. The costar, not the star."

"You got it!" Jack resumed his seat before the computer.

However, that didn't happen. The Wheatons surprised her with an invitation to a dinner cruise—

the ticket was already paid for, and Charlene couldn't say no. Salem's harbor was lovely, and a part of her wished she had a conch shell to call a mermaid.

The next morning, Charlene showered fast, having slept through her alarm. It was Tuesday, and she had to upload pictures of the mermaids from the weekend to her Tuesday blog as well as the website. She'd built quite a following.

Charlene chatted with her guests in the dining room over pastries and coffee. Andrew and Barb hadn't yet joined them. Half of her mind was on the bookkeeping and pictures and the blog on the Mermaid Parade—minus the death of Trinity—when Linc said, "Do you mind?"

Charlene blinked—busted for not paying full attention. "I'm sorry—you were saying?"

Linc laughed. "No worries! Is it okay if we have a late checkout on Friday?"

"Not a problem," she said automatically. Because the Bonets had already left, her early Friday check-in was already ready for her next guests.

"Careful, there." Jack chuckled. "Murder on your mind?"

"I was thinking about the Mermaid Parade." Charlene faced Linc, but also answered Jack. "I'm going to put some pictures on the website. Is it okay if you're in them?"

"I want to be in them!" Aqua and Jewel said.

"I don't care," Dillon seconded. Charlene figured that was ten-year-old code for he'd like that a lot.

Last night at dinner she'd gotten to know the family better, and had enjoyed their company very much. Dillon had been able to drive the boat, even.

"I've got some great ones of the parade that I can send you," Terry said.

"Perfect. I'll have you sign a permission form before you go, for the minors." Charlene drank her coffee. "I know the Wheatons are headed to tour the *Friendship* today. What about you, Southern family?"

"We're going to the wharf to finally see the House of the Seven Gables and all the shops. The reason we would like a late checkout on Friday is that the girls get to be part of the pilgrim reenactment on the pier."

"Awesome!" Charlene said. The twins bounced in their seats with excitement.

"No witches," Aqua told Charlene. "Pilgrims."

Jewel's eyes widened. "Witches are so scary. Like, really scary."

Charlene used to think so before moving to Salem from Chicago and discovering that witches were everyday people like everyone else—for the most part.

"Have you guys been to Fortune's Tea Shoppe?" Natalie shook her head.

"Well, my friend Kass Fortune owns it, and she creates custom tea blends. She's a good witch and will read your fortune from your tea leaves."

The girls squealed but seemed more excited than scared.

"A good witch? See, my sweets, they aren't scary.

Those were just stories." Natalie nodded at Charlene with thanks.

"They've been getting the bad witch vibes from some of the shops," Linc said. "Maybe seven or eight would have been a better age to bring them to Salem."

"It's hard to know for sure . . . if you want, I'll call Kass and let her know you're coming." Charlene had learned that having an open mind was key, and the Southerns seemed to embrace that philosophy already. "She can set up a special tea party for them."

"Tea party!" Aqua and Jewel chanted.

By nine a.m. both families had departed for their day of fun. Charlene was in the foyer arranging a time for a tea party with Kass via text for Aqua and Jewel. Andrew and Barb came down at quarter past nine. Minnie and Charlene had kept the coffee and pastries out on the sideboard in the dining room.

"Morning!" Charlene said. "Breakfast is still available until ten."

Andrew lifted a hand and turned to Barb as they both reached the bottom step. Barb's hair was down around her face and her eyes were rimmed in red.

"There's a leak in the bathroom," Barb said.

Oh no. Charlene wanted to give the woman a hug, but all compassion—and all thoughts of getting the pictures together for the blog—went out the window as the other part of running the B&B moved to the front of the line.

Home repairs.

Thank heaven Will Johnson, Minnie's husband,

was actually on the property already to mow the grass. He did light maintenance for Charlene besides managing the outside of the mansion.

"I'll go up and have a look." Charlene sounded reassuring to her own ears as she smiled—no big deal. "We have a handyman who can hopefully get things right by the time you return for happy hour."

"Fine." Barb nodded, her mouth tight. "I'm walking down to the harbor. We'll see about happy hour."

She left without waiting for Andrew.

Charlene pocketed her phone and nodded at Andrew. There was no escaping the awkwardness Barb's departure left. "Would you like to show me the leak now?"

Andrew took off after Barb, ignoring Charlene.

"Darn it." Charlene reluctantly climbed the stairs and entered the Martins' room. The couple had clothes strewn around the furniture and floor. Barb's floral-print suitcase was on the foot of the unmade bed, open and empty, as if she'd been packed to leave, but then Andrew had unpacked for her—not wanting her to go.

The closet was open and the mermaid costumes on the floor rather than hung up with pride. Andrew's black suitcase was on the luggage rack, closed.

She peeked into the bathroom. Towels were piled around the base of the pedestal sink to sop up water. The bowl had overflowed. Time to track down Will and his toolbox.

If Minnie was magic in the kitchen—and she was—Will was just as magical everywhere else.

That afternoon at three thirty, just before the guests were due to return, Will called for her to come upstairs.

She'd been juggling several things but hurried to meet him and couldn't believe her eyes. The bathroom floor was dry, the sink draining with ease. Will shuffled his feet, offering a gold band to Charlene.

"Pipe was clogged with a wedding ring," Will said.

Charlene sighed. "The Martins are having some marriage problems." As in, Andrew was cheating. Was he also a killer? She shook her head. "Thanks, Will. I'll send you a bonus for the plumbing work."

"You pay me plenty, Charlene. Happy to help."

Will gathered his toolbox. She closed the door behind them and made sure it was locked, putting the ring in her pocket. Poor Barb.

Will left out the front door, blowing a kiss to Minnie, who smiled and winked at her husband of many, many years. She got fresh towels for the Martins and raced them upstairs. After a quick tidying up of the bathroom only, Charlene returned to the kitchen to help Minnie, but the housekeeper already had things set up in the living room.

Today was the kind of day when Charlene felt a kinship with Silva, chasing her own tail.

Steam rose from the cheddar biscuits fresh from the oven. Bowls and spoons were on the sideboard, and a ceramic tureen of cold summer harvest soup was ready to serve. Minnie was making sure everyone had something to eat and drink.

To her surprise, the Martins were already on the

love seat, each with a glass of wine in hand. Maybe they would work things out!

"Thanks, Minnie," she said.

"My pleasure. Soup?"

"In a minute." What Charlene really wanted was a glass of chilled white wine and to catch her breath. She stepped toward the bar but then almost tripped over the throw rug when she heard Alannah's laughter, along with Dom's.

Charlene turned toward the mantel, where Jack usually stood, and there was the couple, center stage. Alannah wore a power-red minidress. Dom was in black jeans and a black silk T-shirt. What was this about?

Aqua and Jewel were beside themselves that the actress was there, and they chattered nonstop with their favorite mermaid ever. Linc and Natalie took a lot of pictures as Jewel did her *Sirena* dance. Alannah applauded politely. Dom looked bored.

Charlene knew they knew she was standing there, watching, but Alannah controlled the scene. She fumed but hid it, waiting.

After a calculated moment, Alannah raised her head and her hand. "Charlene!"

"Hi, Alannah." Charlene kept her neutral expression in place. "Dom! Where's your man, Neddy?"

Alannah winced slightly, probably recalling that she'd referred to Ned as Neddy on Sunday evening after they'd destroyed property on the Common. "Who knows?"

"Who cares?" Dom asked with a smirk that was supposed to be charming but fell short.

"Charlene—I hope you don't mind that I invited Alannah to visit the B-and-B?" Without waiting for an answer, Natalie preened like the teacher's pet. "She might be doing a movie at a bed-and-breakfast. Isn't that exciting?"

"It would be very exciting," Charlene agreed. *Not here.*

Jack manifested himself between Dom and Alannah. The couple widened and shivered.

She bit her lip to keep from laughing.

"This is interesting," Jack said, studying the pair. "Alannah is not as beautiful as Trinity, but Dom is more handsome than Mickey. Maybe the studio is hoping for another blockbuster."

"A mermaid movie filmed here? I don't think this is the right place. Maybe something closer to the bay?" Charlene suggested.

"Will there be a sequel to *Sirena*?" Natalie asked, swept away by the idea.

"Perhaps," Alannah said mysteriously. "Studios make plans and actors are the last to know."

Lottie patted Dillon, who was besotted with Alannah. "That would be exciting!"

"There wasn't a sequel to the original," Barb said. Her tone wasn't as enthusiastic about the project.

"It would be a completely fresh script!" Alannah exuded confidence that everything would go her way. "Everyone in town has great things to say about your bed-and-breakfast, Charlene. I just had to see it for myself."

She didn't allow a full smile as she believed Alannah's confidence was an act. Why was she here, especially after Charlene had told her it wasn't a good time? "That's sweet."

Alannah moved away from the fireplace toward Charlene, as if to have a private word. Charlene stayed put. The actress twirled a lock of dark hair around her finger. "I was curious if you knew any more about poor Trinity's death?"

"No."

"You were talking with a very handsome detective," Alannah said with a pout.

Natalie seemed to suddenly realize that maybe bringing Alannah had been a mistake and looked from Charlene to Alannah. Dom watched from several paces back.

Barb stood, bringing Andrew with her, her arm possessively around his waist. "*Poor* Trinity? You were losing points in the popularity contest for being mean. Don't try to change your tune now."

Alannah whirled on Barb. "You have no idea what you're talking about."

Linc gathered his daughters to his side. "Let's remember kids are present."

Charlene wouldn't tolerate any violence in her home and nodded at Jack, by the mantel. Barb and Andrew didn't back down but stood united as Team Trinity.

Alannah stepped toward them with a sneer. "I was winning."

"The contest is over," Charlene said. "Alannah, please go. I wish you the best of luck in finding a bed-and-breakfast, but I'm afraid this one isn't for you."

Charlene, Terry, Lottie, Andrew, and Barb maneuvered the couple out of the living room through the foyer. Lottie opened the front door.

"You can't do this," Dom said, his nose curled.

"This is my place of business and my home," Charlene said. "Yes, I can."

Alannah flipped her long hair, her nails painted red to match her lipstick. "You should be careful of who you're talking to, Ms. Nosy. Butter wouldn't melt in your mouth, but you're talking to the wrong people."

"Is that a threat?" Charlene quivered with indignation.

"Let's go," Dom said, tugging her by the elbow across the threshold to the porch. "The studio told you to play nice."

"I don't need to win a popularity contest over a dead woman," Alannah spluttered. "And before she was dead, she was a has-been."

"That is not nice at all," Lottie said.

Terry shook his head and said with sarcasm, "Classy."

Charlene didn't stop as they crossed to the porch, and she walked them down to the grass. A BMW was parked behind her SUV. Jack waited by the passenger door of the sports car.

"What are you doing?" Alannah jerked her elbow free from Dom.

"I didn't want you here without an appointment," Charlene said. "Not at all, actually. As soon as I get back inside, I'll be calling Detective Holden to let him know you stopped by with a threat."

"Concern!" Alannah protested. "Neddy didn't do anything. Ariel Glitter has plenty of reasons to want Trinity dead. If you're going to butt your nose in, you should sniff in the right direction."

Dom got behind the wheel of the Beemer. "Let's go, Lan."

Alannah rushed to open the door and went through Jack. She gasped in shock and then slid in. Jack helped close the door.

Was that the only reason Alannah and Dom dropped in at the B&B, to protest Ned's innocence and point the finger at Ariel?

Dom peeled out in reverse, squealing the tires when he stomped on the brakes at the end of the drive, and then sped out of sight.

The guests on the porch, along with Jack, all burst into applause.

CHAPTER 13

Charlene gestured for everyone to go back in, feeling victorious. Even Natalie and Linc were relieved to see their favorite mermaid go. They'd kept the twins inside with Dillon.

She held Barb by the arm on the porch and pulled the wedding band from her pocket, offering it to her.

"Oh!" Barb's face blushed a fiery red as she accepted the band. "Thank you—it slipped off and I thought I'd lost it."

Not a very good lie, but Charlene didn't challenge it, simply asking, "Is everything okay?"

"Sure!" Barb put the ring back on with shaking fingers. "Andrew told me what the detective said he saw on the security film, but he's mistaken. My husband would never stray. He's a flirt, that's all. He's promised to be better."

Charlene nodded. She hoped for Barb's sake that was the truth. "You said he was with you all morning?"

Barb glanced away from Charlene, then shrugged. "We should go in. Thanks for finding my ring."

The women went inside, and the rest of happy hour was spent dissecting Alannah's bad manners and how Dom wasn't any better. The kids were bummed about their idol not being a nice person. Would it stop them from seeing a possible *Sirena* sequel?

The room was split fifty-fifty. No wonder Alannah had orders from the studio to be nice, if what Dom had said was true.

"At six years old, I'm not sure what the twins will take from all of this," Natalie said. "This is the craziest mermaid event we've ever been to . . . we thought it would be the best."

Charlene wanted to apologize, but there was no way she could have controlled any of the situation. "Where is your next festival?"

Natalie pulled her phone from her shorts pocket and pulled up a calendar. "Rhode Island, then Chicago. New Jersey. This year we're going to a mermaid conference in Key West for Christmas."

"That sounds really fun!"

"It's our first time in the Keys and we'll have a vendor booth for four whole days. I hope we do well at the event; it might be our new way to spend the holidays. Then again, we're used to snow at Christmas."

"I would love for you to send me pictures." Charlene patted Natalie's arm. "Do you think you'd be interested in returning next year for the parade?"

Natalie shrugged. "I'm undecided about it. I mean, we understand that first-runs have a few bumps, but Trinity's dead, and that's a big deal. Maybe if they find the killer?"

Linc had been half-listening, half-watching his daughters play checkers. Instead of following the rules, they were building red and black towers. Dillon was playing a game on his phone.

"I agree with Natalie," Linc said. "Who did it? Catching them is important. Their motive will guide how I feel about coming back for the parade. Random merfolk murder? Deliberate plot to oust Trinity?"

Charlene sighed. Linc had a point.

"You're not mad, are you, Charlene?" Natalie peered at her with concern.

"No!" Charlene hoped that not everybody felt that way or the new event might not make it to a second year. The pressure was on to find the killer.

"We will definitely come back to the B-and-B for Halloween when the girls are older," Linc said. "And take advantage of the ten percent discount."

"You are always welcome!" Charlene assured them.

"I'm sorry about inviting Alannah . . . she kind of finagled her way into a visit when we bumped into them by the wharf." Natalie frowned. "I didn't realize you had already talked with her about it."

"It's okay. People like that will go out of their way to get what they want." She'd seen that about Alannah over and over. Could that trait have led to Trinity's demise? She was very defensive of Ned/Neddy.

"I hate that she threatened you like that," Linc murmured. "But you handled it very well."

Charlene remembered that she was going to

text Sam about Alannah's visit and pulled her phone from her pocket. "It turned out fine."

Natalie laughed. "You herded her out like a fly in the house. Just think of the publicity the B-and-B could get if Alannah filmed here."

"With help!" Charlene gestured to the Wheatons and the Martins. "Besides, I prefer word-of-mouth—the clientele is better that way."

Jack waved to her from the threshold of the living room. "When you can." What had he discovered now? She was eager to move forward.

"You have a great place," Lottie said. "Walking distance to almost everything." She checked her watch. "We're going to grab burgers for dinner tonight. Come on, gang."

"Thanks again for yesterday," Charlene said, standing. "The dinner cruise was such a treat and I highly recommend it."

"We can't wait." Barb got to her feet, pulling Andrew up. He was holding her hand with the ring back on. "The cruise. I was able to get me and Andrew tickets for tonight."

"We're going to the arcade." Linc had his arms around the twins. "They've got a food counter that will suffice. Hot dogs and pizza. Junk food. Heaven."

All of her chicks had plans. At half past five, they'd all departed. Charlene picked up Silva to go to her suite. "Night, Minnie!"

"See you in the morning!" Minnie called.

"Hey, Jack." Charlene placed Silva on the love seat and the Persian curled up right away, as if she hadn't been sleeping all day already. It was exhausting to be a cat.

"What did you give Barb on the porch?" Jack asked. He was relaxed in his favorite armchair by the window.

"Barb's wedding band. She said she lost it, but that's what Will pulled out of the pipe that caused the water to overflow."

"Ring in the pipes? And now they're going on a romantic dinner cruise?" Jack sounded dubious.

"Barb says that Sam is mistaken about what he saw. She still is defending Andrew. She must not know that he'd rented a room."

Marriage was a journey. There were peaks and valleys. If they truly loved each other and Andrew wasn't cheating, then she hoped it worked out for them.

If he was "stepping out," as they used to say, then, well, Barb might be better off by herself or with another.

Some women were afraid to be alone and would settle for bad behavior rather than sleep by themselves.

As a widow, it had been a hard adjustment not to reach for Jared in the night, but she'd managed, and now shared with Silva. Sam . . . she shut off all thoughts of the handsome detective in her bed and focused on the TV. It could never be her bed.

"Did you want to tell me something, Jack?" It was nice to just sit and be still for a minute after the earlier Alannah drama.

"No—I was simply curious about what happened on the porch with Barb." Jack propped his elbow on the armrest. "Have you texted Sam yet?"

Charlene shook her head and pulled her phone from her pocket. "What should I say? Alannah didn't give me a direct threat, just snuck her way into the B-and-B."

"Insinuated that you shouldn't be asking questions," Jack countered seriously. "Considering that her rival is dead, I don't think you should brush it off."

"All right." She quickly typed a message explaining how Alannah had tried to point the finger at Ariel and away from Ned, then sent it to Sam. Her stomach rumbled. It was five thirty and she hadn't eaten much. Just a bowl of cold soup and a biscuit, appetizer-size.

Her hobo bag had tipped sideways, and she saw the rainbow-colored cloth rolled inside—the T-shirt for Mary. "I should drop that off and see how she's feeling. I can't imagine good after being attacked. Also, she might have seen Andrew and who he was with."

Her phone dinged and she looked down.

"Sam?" Jack asked.

"No—Kass. I've been invited to the tea shop with Brandy and Serenity to go over the details of the parade. They probably just want to know more about the case, but I don't have news." Charlene was tempted to stay home with a peanut butter sandwich, curled on the love seat with Silva and Jack to binge Netflix.

"Or," Jack said, "they might know something. You can mention Trinity's possible medication to Brandy and bring the T-shirt with you to drop off at the Waterway."

Charlene sighed. "I don't want to cause Mary trouble by leaving the shirt at her job. I should find her phone number."

Jack rose and opened the laptop, searching for Mary Clarkson in the Salem directory. "There are two listings for M. Clarkson, not Mary."

Charlene reluctantly rose and went to the page. There would be no rest for the weary tonight. The addresses for M. Clarkson were on opposite ends of town. She copied the information and sent it to her phone. "I'll call on the way. Thanks, Jack."

"Always welcome," he said.

She went to her room for a gift bag to put the T-shirt inside of to make it more presentable than simply rolled up in her purse. "I hope she's feeling better. This will be a nice pick-me-up. Wish me luck, Jack!"

"Luck!"

With a spring in her step, Charlene left and plugged her phone into her Bluetooth, with the new information on M. Clarkson.

She dialed the first number with the closest address to downtown. A man answered. "Yo."

"Hi!" she said. "Is Mary Clarkson there?"

"Nobody here by that name."

"Oh—well, sorry to bother you!"

Charlene backed out of the driveway and called the second number. "Hello," she said. "Is Mary there?"

"No Mary here." This woman sounded as old as Methuselah with a pack-a-day smoking habit.

"Hmm. I'm trying to reach Mary Clarkson."

"Can't help you." The older woman hung up.

Well, shoot.

Charlene drove to Fortune's Tea Shoppe and lucked out with street parking a block away. She left the T-shirt in the SUV and walked down the sidewalk until she reached the storefront.

A dozen or more beautiful teapots filled the shop window. She went inside and was transported by the scents of dried flowers and herbs that Kass created her lovely teas with. Her specialty when it came to psychic ability, in addition to seeing ghosts, was reading the tea leaves left in a cup after a customer drank.

In the center of the shop was an indoor water fountain in the shape of a robust goddess that gurgled merrily.

Charlene greeted Kass, who stood behind the waist-high long counter, and Serenity, who was seated on a stool with a delicate porcelain mug on a saucer before her.

"Hi!" Charlene said, taking a stool next to Serenity. "How's it going?"

"Hello . . . it's all right. Could be better." Serenity sipped her tea. "I'm trying to focus on the profits made for Clean Oceans and not the fact that Trinity was murdered and her killer is still at large."

"Good idea." Charlene placed her purse on a teapot-shaped purse hook that allowed it to dangle next to her rather than being on the floor. It was considered bad luck to do that, as if you didn't care about your money.

"Tea?" Kass asked.

"Sure. I'll take something herbal." Charlene didn't see Brandy anywhere.

"Citrus? Floral? Spice?"

"I love the orange spice you put together—yes, that one, please!"

Though Kass had often offered to read Charlene's tea leaves, she chose to live her life as it came. Knowing would just make her worry.

"Where's your mom, Serenity?" Charlene asked. How could she bring up Trinity's possible medication in this setting? She'd play it by ear.

"On her way." Serenity stirred honey into her cup.

Kass placed a small ceramic teapot before her to steep, with a timer in the shape of a lemon. "Thanks. The Southerns' little girls would love a tea party with you."

"It should be fun. Natalie and I spoke on the phone—if they can't fit it in this time, then they will the next visit to Salem." Kass had her long hair in a thick braid to her waist and wore a summery half apron over a sleeveless dress.

"There is so much to do in Salem. I've been here two years and haven't managed to see it all yet." Charlene noticed Serenity glancing from Kass to Charlene. "What is it?" Nerves made her stomach clench. "Does this impromptu meeting have to do with Alannah and Dom? They dropped by my B-and-B today, trying to point the finger at Ariel Glitter instead of Ned."

"No!" Kass stuck her hand in her apron pocket. "That's some nerve. Did you report her?"

"I texted Sam, but he hasn't answered. So . . . why the tea?"

Serenity sighed. "Detective Holden might be

busy. Officer Jimenez arrested Bobby this morning trying to break into his art studio."

He'd been on the run for three days. Charlene jumped when her steeping timer went off, jostling the cup on the counter. "Arrested?" It would have been nice for Sam to tell her, but he didn't have to. At least it wasn't Andrew in jail.

"Bobby says he's innocent." Serenity sounded like she believed him.

Sam and Jack had both pointed out that criminals didn't tend to be honest folks by nature. If Bobby was a killer, why would he care if he told a lie?

"So, Mom called a lawyer and is bailing Bobby out." Serenity's silver and gold rings clinked against the porcelain cup as she drank her tea.

Charlene's eyes widened in disbelief. "What?"

"Her reasoning is that Bobby passed a criminal check to be hired by the city." Serenity's demeanor was calm. Serene as her name. "Neither of us gets a bad feeling from him. Kass doesn't either."

Nervous, Charlene folded the paper napkin beneath her cup. "What happens, then?"

"Mom is bringing him here so we can hash it out."

Getting answers from the source was much more important than tracking down Mary at the Waterway. Charlene put her phone on silent. Before she could ask more questions, Bobby and Brandy entered.

Brandy had her lipstick freshly applied and walked with her head high. Her auburn hair was straight to her shoulders, while Serenity's was in a messy bun. Bobby slouched and smelled like he could use a shower and a shave, the scruff on his jaw almost black. His curls were tangled.

"I want to go home," Bobby said sullenly rather than greet the ladies.

"I'll take you there as soon as you answer some questions." Brandy was no-nonsense.

"Hi," Kass said, then offered to make them tea.

Brandy had black tea and Bobby chose a green tea sweetened with honey. Brandy went around the counter next to Kass and Bobby plunked to the only vacant stool on the opposite side of Serenity. Kass's full-time employee, Areema, watched in the front of the shop for walk-in traffic.

"I'm starving, man," Bobby said. "Got anything to eat?"

"Biscotti all right?" Kass showed him a selection of individually wrapped hard cookies perfect for dunking.

"Thanks." Bobby unwrapped the first cookie and bit into it. "Can we hurry this up?"

Kass offered one to Charlene. Almond. Delicious.

"You owe me," Brandy said. "Be good and this won't take long. Why did you run Sunday morning?"

"Like I told the cop." Bobby shrugged insolently. "Had a little weed on me. No big deal. I just didn't want to get busted with it. I panicked."

Charlene recalled the vape falling from his pocket and how he'd needed to relax in his truck. "Pot is legal. You could have tossed what you had and turned yourself in."

"Running made you look guilty," Serenity said.

"True!" Kass said. The steeping timer next to the pot clicked as the seconds passed.

Brandy crossed her arms, her brow up as she stared at Bobby. She was in no mood.

"Ugh." Bobby's shoulders hunched over the tea. "So maybe it was more than pot. I didn't know what to do."

"Why don't you be honest?" Brandy said. "You may have heard rumors about my family. The Flints."

Bobby scraped back his wild curls from his forehead. "Yeah. You're witches." He looked at Kass, then Charlene. "Are you, like, a coven or something?"

Charlene glanced at Brandy for a clue as to what she was supposed to play in this drama. They all believed Bobby to be innocent. Salem PD wouldn't arrest someone without probable cause.

"Not a coven," Brandy said. "*Worse.* We are on the parade committee and now I've got to figure out what happened to Trinity Powers. Did you kill her?"

Bobby turned as pale as the white ceramic teapot before him. The steeping timer went off and Kass poured him a fragrant cup. It steamed and the scent was earthy and fresh, with a hint of lemongrass.

"No! No." Bobby unwrapped the second biscotti and took a bite.

Serenity watched him calmly, soothingly. Kass reached for the timer and put it aside, offering a third biscotti.

"You saw her that morning," Brandy said. "Trinity. You told us that already, which is why you were a person of interest. What reason did they have to arrest you for murder?"

He blew on his tea and then sipped.

Stalling?

"I spent a lot of money at the Salem PD just now, so you might as well give me my money's worth," Brandy said. "I believe that you are innocent."

Charlene wished she had Brandy's confidence in the young artist.

At that, Bobby relaxed. "I am! I am." He dipped the biscotti and then ate the cookie in two bites. "It's because of what went down at Ariel Glitter's party."

"What exactly happened?" Serenity asked.

Bobby looked up from his tea to Serenity. "Saturday night I was at Ariel's. There were twenty of us, give or take, all excited to meet Trinity. We'd been drinking, waiting for the star to arrive. She did, around ten that night. Walked in like a gorgeous queen, with her back straight and us all falling to her feet."

"She came alone?" Charlene asked.

"Yeah." Bobby broke off a piece of cookie. "Trinity spoke with Ariel, and that got ugly. She fired her from social media right there. Can you imagine? Then, that violet gaze found me, and she let me know that she didn't like the design of the T-shirt—that broke me, man. I'd worked with fluid lines and her grace in the water with each stroke of the brush. I'd spent hours studying the movement of waves against the shore to get it right."

Charlene studied the artist for truth. He met Brandy's gaze, then Kass's. He smelled a little like the beach, and she imagined he'd hidden out there.

She still didn't understand why he hadn't turned himself in if he was innocent but drew out the conversation. "That must've been tough," Charlene said with empathy, "to create something and then the person you admire doesn't understand your vision."

"Damn straight," Bobby said. "In ten minutes, Trinity was out the door with all of us stunned. I felt bad for Ariel, but I didn't stay. I went to the studio and worked all night on another design that I hoped Trinity would like better."

"But she didn't?" Charlene conveyed compassion in her tone.

"No. When I got to the hotel, Trinity Powers laughed in my face and told me not to bother being an artist. I had zero talent." Bobby looked at Brandy. "Trinity said it was just like you to back a no-talent hack."

Brandy straightened. "She did?"

"Yep. Guess you have a history?" He sounded sympathetic at not being Trinity's number one.

"I didn't realize she'd be bitter over something that happened to us as children. We were ten, for Goddess's sake." Brandy raised her finger. "Don't stray from the topic."

"I think Ariel killed Trinity. I told that to the cops. That Officer Jimenez will give me nightmares." Bobby scowled and rubbed the scruff along his jaw.

"Why were you arrested?" Charlene asked bluntly. The shirt had been shoved in Trinity's mouth. Could Bobby have been so upset that he'd reacted angrily? Or was he right, and Ariel was the guilty one? "Didn't you leave the new T-shirt there?"

Bobby shifted toward Charlene. "Yes."

"Your DNA will be all over it, of course," Charlene said with sudden realization. "That's hard evidence."

"That's what freaking happened." Bobby's cheeks flushed. "DNA, and they've got me on the security cam going in and out. I wasn't trying to hide it! The thing is, it was nine that morning when I was there. I followed Trinity from breakfast to her room, right, because the little creep at the front desk wasn't giving up the information—not even for cash."

Charlene nodded for him to continue.

"I was quiet as a ghost as I stayed on her heels. She was lost in thought, and I can be stealthy. I *may* have opened her door before it had a chance to close right away." Perspiration dotted his skin.

"Bobby! Why?" Brandy asked. "That's crossing a line."

"I had a feeling that she wouldn't let me in." Bobby wiped sweat from his forehead. "Because we, uh, had it out the night before."

No wonder the police had arrested Bobby. It was a surprise they'd allowed Brandy to post bail for him. Except for the fact that he was on camera at nine that morning. Before or after Mary had gotten her poster signed? What time had Trinity been killed?

"Tell us again what happened at Ariel's . . . Trinity went for you, out of the blue?" Charlene asked.

Bobby exuded misery as he admitted, "Not exactly. Trinity was already steamed about something to do with Ariel. Like, she skewered the woman. I was an idiot and just jumped in, gushing about the T-shirt, telling her she'd love it, all fanboy, and she let me have it with both barrels. I'm not sure how she'd gotten it."

"As an artist, you will need a thicker skin," Brandy said. "I thought I had a patron for you, but now I'm not sure. I sent Trinity a gift basket with one in it at the Hawthorne Hotel. Drink your tea."

Bobby did as Brandy directed and gulped more tea.

"You went to Trinity's hotel, followed her to her room, and pushed inside uninvited," Charlene said. "And you expected Trinity to react favorably? You're lucky she didn't call the police." If she had, would Trinity still be alive?

"She threatened to, and I begged her to just look at the shirt, you know? To see how I'd made her very artistic—such a different pattern than the first one. She barely glanced at it. Told me to take the damn tee and go—I was making her nerves worse. She was popping some kind of pills."

"Prescription?" Charlene asked.

"I don't know. I apologized over and over again for bothering her." Bobby finished the tea. "She slammed the door and locked the bolt home."

The bolt wasn't fastened when Charlene was there at noon. Trinity had let someone else in after Bobby left. Trinity had had a busy morning. She'd been dressed for the parade, as if prepared to go and do her part. The orange bottle had been on the nightstand.

Kass picked up Bobby's cup. "May I?"

"What?" Bobby sounded confused.

"Read your leaves."

"I guess." Bobby curled his upper lip. "Is that actually a thing?"

Kass turned the cup this way and that. After several moments, she returned the cup to the saucer.

"Well?" Bobby's knee jiggled.

"I don't think you killed Trinity . . . but you are far from innocent," Kass declared.

CHAPTER 14

Charlene looked at Kass, then watched Bobby closely for his reaction to Kass's words. He was far from innocent.

"What does that mean?" Brandy asked, her tone abrasive.

Serenity, in a calmer tone, asked, "Did you break the law?"

Bobby melted miserably in his chair. "Art supplies are not cheap. I may have borrowed things occasionally to pay for them."

Kass swirled the leaves and liquid and read again, nodding. "You have a choice, Bobby. You are at a crossroads. You can accept the opportunity presented right now, and compromise your artistic vision slightly for great financial success . . . or choose to stand by your ideas as they are. You will fail. Stealing to feed your art habit isn't okay. It doesn't bring the right energy to succeed."

Charlene was impressed by Kass's messaging.

Bobby pulled back, scared. "I want a shower.

Can you take me home?" He turned to Brandy. "You said you would take me home."

"Sure," Brandy said, not in any obvious hurry.

"I told you I didn't kill her. I bet it was Ariel!" Bobby's voice was shrill. "Never mind. I can catch my own ride home."

"I'll get you a car." Serenity asked for his address and ordered it from the comfort of the tea counter.

"Don't forget the barbecue tomorrow at the winery. If you decide to move forward with your career, that is. If you don't want to, then let's not waste each other's time." Brandy didn't look like she cared one way or the other.

Bobby, flustered, stood.

Serenity smiled, calm as a still lake. "I already took care of the driver's tip."

"Don't leave town!" Brandy called as Bobby left.

The door closed, and Kass's employee dutifully busied herself with stocking tea towels and arranging mugs, leaving her boss to do whatever she was up to.

"I can't believe that you read that in his tea leaves," Charlene said.

"Kass is the best tea leaf reader I've ever met," Serenity said.

Kass gave a humble shrug. "Ah. Anytime you're ready, Charlene, let me know."

"That's okay."

Kass laughed. Serenity's lips twitched as she sipped from her cup.

"That rat better not skip town," Brandy said. She dug around in her purse and pulled a flask free, unscrewing the silver top.

"Mom!"

"What? It's just a touch of vodka for fortification." Brandy stirred in the vodka and added honey. "Delicious." She offered the flask. "Anybody else?"

Kass added a dollop, but Charlene declined— only because she was imagining a nice glass of wine—or two—later with Jack.

"You're going ahead with the barbecue?" Charlene was a little surprised. For some reason, she'd assumed that it would be canceled.

"Yes! This is a thank-you for everyone's hard work and efforts around the parade. Please invite your guests, Charlene. I think it will be good to have the players all in one place. We need to get Bobby out of the hot seat, which means finding out who killed Trinity. Ariel Glitter will be top of the revised list."

"We'll see," Charlene said. "Sam has questions about Andrew Martin being at the Waterway. He and his wife both deny that he was there, but he's been caught red-handed on security film."

"Not good." Brandy sipped from her cup. "Bring him! Ned Hammond lives in Salem, so he has no reason not to RSVP with a yes. I'm not sure when Alannah and Dom leave—I arranged for Trinity to be at the Hawthorne from Thursday to Thursday. I'll leave a message for them at the front desk. I would have invited them already if I'd known they were coming."

"Do you have to?" Kass asked.

"Yes. To have everyone in one place who might have done the deed," Brandy said. "Charlene?"

"All right. I'll be there, but I can't promise my guests will be—all I can do is extend the invitation." Charlene glanced at her phone. No messages from Sam. She shifted on the seat. Was the Salem PD even now arresting Ariel? Or was Andrew back under scrutiny?

"Are you still going to create the *Sirena* wine, Mom?"

"I don't know. The label Bobby designed is sexy, with the swish of a mermaid tail and his artistic rendering of Trinity. A dry rosé that I believe will be a bestseller. I was thinking of it being a surprise for Trinity. I didn't realize that Alannah was going to be here until she contacted me on Friday—paid for her own room."

"Why didn't she tell you?" Kass asked. "We could have included her from the beginning and maybe diffused the feud."

Brandy shrugged. "Actresses are just as temperamental as artists, I'm finding out. Maybe she hoped to contact Trinity? Clear the air?"

"You can have the new wine without it being for either mermaid, Mom. That takes the pressure off. Maybe just use the tail."

"But is that the wisest marketing choice for the parade ongoing?" Brandy asked Charlene. "I had a loose plan for a label reveal."

Charlene twirled her cup on the saucer. "How certain are we that the parade will continue?"

"I talked with Tony earlier today and he's supportive. Alannah's apology and how sweet she was to his daughters went a long way. I've run the numbers for the cost of the parade: six thousand, not including the loss of the stage and the five-thousand-dollar donation. We're in the red."

"Twelve months is plenty to spread the word

and get the hiccups out." Charlene hoped there would never be another death related to it. "Maybe have more floats? Traffic was very congested on Oak Street. I don't believe the Southerns will return next year unless the killer is caught and they are very involved in the mermaid festival life."

Brandy sighed and traced her finger along the porcelain handle of her cup. "I was afraid of that."

"But you've offered a scholarship," Serenity said. "I think we need to be committed to this for at least five years."

Brandy added more vodka to her tea. "It has to make money or I won't support the project for year number three. I don't want to pour cash down the drain when we're supposed to be making Salem profitable."

"Small businesses take three to four years to reach a profit," Charlene said. "And the locals saw increased revenue, from hotels to restaurants." Charlene knew that Brandy wasn't including the money she'd paid to Trinity out of pocket either. Her B&B was doing well at the two-year mark, but she'd been lucky not to have any major expenses.

"Tony expects a return," Brandy said. "As a city councilman, he needs positive press for when he runs for office again."

"Maybe hold off on the *Sirena* wine label debut until we find out more instead of revealing it tomorrow night," Charlene said. "What will Grant think of his daughter on the label?"

Brandy sipped her vodka tea. "It never crossed my mind to invite Grant to the barbecue. I imagine he would be supportive of the label, as he was the movie, because it honors Trinity. Charlene, will you go with me tomorrow to see if he wants to come? We can get his permission if we need it then. Also, he's one of the players, isn't he?"

Charlene hated to agree. Today she'd managed to get the blog done, but just barely, thanks to the plumbing issues. "I should be okay to leave my place around eleven."

"I support Serenity's idea to keep the label as a general mermaid without linking it to one particular star," Kass said. "That way it doesn't matter what happens in the future."

"I do too," Charlene said.

"Would that be a big change for the design?" Kass asked.

"Bobby owes me big," Brandy said. "I don't care if he has to change it ten times."

Brandy had a point there. It seemed rude to ask how much his bail had been.

Charlene finished and placed her napkin over her empty cup. "I should get going. Hey, do any of you know how the maid is doing who was hit on the back of the head? I've got a T-shirt to give her, but the two phone numbers I've tried for her are a bust."

"What's her name?" Serenity asked.

"Mary Clarkson."

Serenity worked her magic on the phone, which she used with much more dexterity than Charlene. A minute or so later, she pulled up a picture of the maid on social media. "Her?"

"Yes!"

Serenity forwarded the information to Charlene's phone. "Now you can just message her. Lots of . . . younger people . . . don't have their cell phones listed in the directory."

"Thank you." Charlene felt pretty old about then. "That was clever."

"You're welcome," Serenity said. "Not a problem."

Charlene gave them hugs all around with a promise to see Brandy the next day at eleven in front of Grant's place to invite him to the barbecue. His permission wouldn't be needed if they went with a generic tail. Brandy wanted to gather all the players at the parade, and Grant had taken part.

She left and walked to her car. Because she was so close to the station, she sent Sam a second text that she was downtown.

To her surprise, Sam hearted her message. Taking advantage of a golden opportunity, she fired off another.

Any chance you can grab some dinner?
Yes. New quiet tavern on Smith Street?
Great.

Sam texted her the address.

Charlene combed her hair and sucked a mint, then gave her face a dab of powder and lip gloss and pinched her cheeks for color.

Her stomach fluttered at the idea of seeing Sam. She parked in the lot and saw that his SUV was already there, along with two other cars. The tavern was on the outskirts of an older section of Salem and didn't seem crowded, which was good for them and their low-profile dates.

She opened the wooden door of the tavern. Sam waited for her with a slow smile and a perusal of her from head to toe. He was in work clothes of tan slacks and an oxford shirt rolled up at the sleeves. No tie. He'd combed his thick hair and mustache and added a subtle sandalwood cologne.

Sam made sure she was alone and then kissed her cheek. The host, a man in his fifties, escorted them to a back table, dim, and placed two menus on the wooden table.

After he left, Charlene said, "When you said new, I expected modern."

"New, as in new to me," Sam clarified. "Perfect for our trysts."

They each sat down, Charlene drinking in the sight of Sam. "I like that word. It sounds romantic and slightly dangerous."

Sam sat in the chair that faced the door. Her back was to it.

"What have you had here?"

"Fish and chips just the once," Sam said. "It was good. I kept thinking of meeting you here the whole time."

"Ah!" How sweet.

The waiter arrived after a few minutes. Charlene decided on the special, a shepherd's pie, and told Sam.

"Two of your specials," Sam said, ordering for them. "Iced tea for me since I have to get back to the station. Charlene?"

"I'll have that as well. Unsweetened, with lemon."

The waiter took their menus and left, returning quickly with their drinks.

Charlene smiled across at Sam. Would he bring up the case? Should she? Bobby had been arrested and Sam hadn't said a word. She nibbled her lower lip.

"Was this a ploy to get information from me?" Sam shook his head, as if he could read her mind.

"No! I was downtown and hungry." Charlene tapped her phone, which she'd placed on the table. "Did you read my text about Alannah dropping by the B-and-B, pointing the finger at Ariel, away from Ned?"

He sighed. "I did. I conveyed that to Officer Jimenez."

The woman hated Charlene, so it would probably go nowhere.

"Okay. But since you and I are here, and I just saw Bobby, and I know that Brandy posted his bail, well, maybe we could talk about the case just a tiny bit." Charlene squeezed her thumb and pointer finger together. "He was arrested. Does that mean that Andrew is in the clear?"

Sam drank his iced tea, surveying her over the rim, as if not sure what to do with her. Was he disappointed?

"I'm sorry, Sam. I'm just curious."

He gave a slow nod. Did that mean he accepted her apology? Would he answer her questions?

"Where did you see Bobby?" Sam centered the glass on a coaster.

"At Kass's tea shop. Brandy stopped by with him."

"Why?"

"To get his tea leaves read."

Sam spluttered. "Come again?"

"It's true." Charlene raised her palm. "Even if you don't believe it. Brandy wanted to make sure that he hadn't killed Trinity, as he said."

"And?" Sam chuckled.

Charlene grew defensive and regretted bringing

up the case. "He's innocent. Bobby didn't kill Trinity, but he thinks Ariel might have. He's done a few shady things, but not that. He has to make a choice now that will affect his future success."

Sam's humor disappeared in an instant. "I can't believe you believe that."

Charlene shrugged. "Sam, I know that there is more to this world than meets the eye. Until you realize that . . ."

"What?"

"We will have to agree to disagree."

She was saved by the waiter bringing their food, placing steaming dishes in front of them, then backing away.

Because she had Jack as a roommate, she knew that there were ghosts. Witches. Psychics. Mediums.

She hadn't always believed that. What would it take for Sam to open his mind?

"The paranormal is not real," Sam said, wanting to get the last word.

The waiter stopped in midstep and came back to the table. "I'm not so sure about that. I've felt things in the cellar here that make my skin chill."

"See?" Charlene looked at Sam.

"No offense," Sam said. "But it's a cellar. It's meant to be cold."

The waiter shrugged and shared a smile with Charlene. Some folks just weren't open to other possibilities.

She wasn't going to waste a surprise dinner date with Sam arguing the point. She took a bite of creamy potatoes crusted with cheese.

"Sam! This is really good."

"Yeah." He dabbed his mustache with a paper napkin. "I would order this again."

"This could be our place," Charlene said.

"I like that." Sam studied her closely.

She smiled at him, admiring everything about him—except his stubbornness in ignoring the paranormal. Oh, well. "Sam . . . how is the maid, Mary Clarkson, faring, do you know?"

"Why?" The poor man's shoulders were braced against more questions he couldn't answer.

"I have a T-shirt for her."

Sam's brow rose in surprise.

"From the parade. She's Team Trinity and these will be collector's items. Like the stolen poster. Especially now that . . . Trinity is gone. Did she get the poster back?"

"I'm not sure. Jimenez is handling the details of the case. If she does well, she'll be up for a promotion."

"That's nice." And maybe grouch Jimenez could go to Portland instead of Sam. "I'll find Mary later."

"Why not just drop off the shirt at her work?"

"I might do that." Charlene balanced a pea on her fork, not sharing that she feared it could get Mary into trouble. "Brandy's having a barbecue at the winery tomorrow, for the parade organizers and participants. Alannah might be there with Dom. It's so sad that Trinity won't be." She put the bite in her mouth.

"Do you think that's a good idea?" Sam mounded his potatoes. "The killer hasn't been caught."

"Does that mean that you don't believe it was

Bobby? He told us about the timing on the security camera."

Sam gritted his teeth. "No comment."

Charlene continued, "It was planned before anything happened. I'm going with Brandy tomorrow to Grant's house—Trinity's dad—to invite him too."

"Why?" Sam lowered his fork, his tone suspicious.

"Brandy has known him since she was a kid. Also, there was a wine label that was going to have Trinity's artistic image on it, but now that's kind of up in the air."

"Bobby Rourke is the artist?"

"Yes."

"Will Bobby be there?" Sam shifted on his seat. "Just because he was cleared by some tea leaves doesn't fly. He has no alibi for the exact time of Trinity's death. His prints were all over that hotel room."

Charlene didn't answer. It was all she could do not to ask when that was. It would just alienate him.

"I don't think the barbecue is a good idea, Charlene."

"Would you like to come?" The words escaped her mouth in a rush. "You could be my plus-one."

"I am very tempted to do just that. To keep you from trouble." Sam's gaze narrowed, as if to ferret out any secrets she might be hiding. "Who else will be there?"

"My guests have been invited, but I don't know if they'll come."

"Andrew is not in the clear either." Sam punctu-ated the sentence with his fork. "He knows not to leave town."

She skimmed over that remark and thought in-stead of the Southerns. "I hate for them to have a bad impression of Salem when they leave."

"Murder is bad for business." Sam's phone dinged a text and he let out a sigh after reading the message.

"What?"

"I have to go. I'll get back to you about the bar-becue tomorrow, all right?"

Charlene nodded. She hadn't been serious but would roll with it. "Bye, Sam."

He paid cash for their meals. They'd both mostly been done anyway. Being in a clandestine relation-ship with a detective meant that there might be more rushed meals in her future.

Charlene would rather have stolen time with Sam than none at all. They kissed goodbye in the lobby of the tavern, and each went to their own cars.

She drove home, to Jack. On the way, she saw a missed call from Chicago but didn't answer it. Her mind was too full of Trinity Powers to navigate a conversation with her mother. She parked and went inside. Silva waited for her on the staircase and meowed a greeting.

"Hey, kitty, kitty. I know you're not hungry." Silva twisted her way between Charlene's feet as she walked to the kitchen. Dry kibble was in the bowl, but Charlene got out a treat for the cat anyway. For her own treat, she went to her wine cellar and poured a large glass of high-end pinot noir that Jack had recommended and brought it upstairs to her suite.

"Hi!" Jack raised the volume of the TV from his spot on the armchair. "What was so important at the tea shop?"

"Brandy bailed Bobby out of jail," Charlene said after a big sip. Silva jumped to the back of the love seat. "He was arrested for Trinity's murder."

"Whoa." Jack relaxed against the cushions.

Charlene laughed. It had been a surprise all right. "She had Kass read Bobby's tea leaves. They all point to the fact that he didn't murder Trinity."

"Interesting." Jack rubbed his jaw. "I always thought tea reading was a little bit of a hoax."

Unlike Sam, Jack didn't dismiss the idea that it was possible out of hand. Because Jack was a ghost, he knew that there were things in this world that couldn't be explained.

"Serenity says that Kass is the best," Charlene said. "Brandy seemed satisfied, and since she was the one to fork out the cash for Bobby, that's what matters."

"Good point." Jack chuckled. "I hope Bobby doesn't make Brandy regret her patronage."

Charlene brought him up to speed on the rest of what she'd learned, keeping her dinner with Sam to herself. She hated to have secrets, but this was a necessary omission to protect Jack's feelings.

"Serenity found Mary Clarkson for me." Charlene sat before the computer and sent Mary a message via Facebook to call so that she could drop off the T-shirt, then took her wine to the love seat and curled up in one corner.

"That's good. My big discovery is that Dom Preston is up-and-coming as an actor and doesn't have so much as a parking ticket."

As she and Jack talked, there was a part of her that wished she could be 100 percent honest with both Sam and Jack.

It wasn't going to happen without someone getting hurt.

CHAPTER 15

Wednesday morning, Charlene and Brandy, with an apple crumb cake from Minnie, arrived at Grant's house at eleven on the dot. They'd driven in separate cars.

She'd invited the guests to the barbecue at breakfast and given them the address. The winery was fantastic to tour and sample wines, no matter the reason for the get-together. Kass would be there, but Kevin had sent his regrets because he was working a shift at the bar he managed.

Mary had answered Charlene's message, saying she was off work at one that afternoon, if Charlene wanted to meet her out front of the Waterway—in the parking lot, so as not to get in trouble with Mary's boss.

Cake for Grant and the shirt for Mary. It was a little like Christmas, bringing gifts to people.

"I feel strange bothering the poor man again." Brandy lifted her own gift bag for him. "It seems important, though, so here I am."

"Here *we* are," Charlene corrected. "You're not alone."

"Thanks. I owe you."

They'd been even, but now, after being Brandy's minion for the parade, things were in Charlene's favor again.

"Fine with me." It was good to have a favor owed by a talented witch.

Brandy knocked on the door. Grant Powers answered, looking like he'd aged ten years since Sunday.

"Oh! Brandy. Charlene." Grant stepped back. "Why don't you ladies come on in? I have some time before I meet Michael for lunch."

"Is he a local?" Charlene asked.

"No. LA. Michael goes back home on Sunday. I'll miss him, truth to tell. He's very patient with an old man's rambling memories."

Brandy squeezed his shoulder. "That's probably just what he needs if he's doing Trinity's biography."

"That's what he says too," Grant admitted. "I thought it was just to make me feel better."

They followed Grant down the hall to the kitchen.

Charlene placed the apple crumb cake in the center of the table. The photo albums were still out, but the manuscript was gone. The whiskey had also been put away.

"I'm so sorry about Sunday night," Grant said. "I was overwrought. I thought I could handle myself, but I was out of control."

Brandy hugged him. "It's okay. You'd just lost your daughter."

"I will go to my grave wondering why she wouldn't forgive me." Grant exhaled and ruffled his messy hair. "I need to shove those feelings down and pretend that we got to say goodbye. It's how I managed all the years since she snubbed me."

"Pretending?" Charlene asked.

"Yes. I have a very good imagination." Grant tapped the side of his head.

"Trinity got her flair for storytelling from you," Brandy said. "We used to spend a lot of time in her bedroom, playing make-believe. She always wanted to be a mermaid."

Grant blushed, pleased. "Would you like to see her room? I've kept it exactly how it was."

Charlene rubbed her arms. That seemed a bit bizarre.

"Sure," Brandy said.

They went up narrow stairs and reached a landing. "My room is on this end, that's my office," they passed a bathroom and a closed door, "and her bedroom is at the far end."

She and Brandy followed Grant. Like the kitchen, this remained dated, with gold carpet and ivory paint.

Grant opened the door to reveal a little girl's dream bedroom. There were gauzy curtains, a castle, a chest—open, filled with stuffed animals. A closet full of dresses.

"This is just how I remember it," Brandy said in awe. She crossed the room to a series of shelves.

Grant smiled, seemingly happy that they could share this memory. "Madeline and Trinity moved when she was ten. You used to play together often."

"I loved being invited over." Brandy lifted an ivory conch shell. "No way!"

"What is it?" Charlene recalled the photo of Grant, Madeline, and Trinity at the wharf. Was this the same shell?

"A magic conch shell," Brandy offered it to Grant, "to call in the mermaids."

Grant rubbed his hands together. "You remember."

"It was thrilling," Brandy said. "Tell Charlene the story!"

He tilted his head but then nodded. "All right. I worked at the Peabody Essex Museum and discovered a conch shell with a mermaid legend from Fiji. If you were to call the mermaids using this exact shell, they would grant your wishes."

Charlene inched toward him. Grant had a storyteller's cadence, and she was drawn in.

"Trinity was the queen mermaid. She used the conch constantly and her wishes were always the same—to be a mermaid and not a little girl." Grant stroked the smooth shell. "She'd swim in the bath for hours, angry that she still had legs and not a tail."

"She insisted we treat her like a mermaid." Brandy's expression held a hint of sadness. "Even at school. She got into trouble."

"The teachers were always squelching her imagination."

Charlene smiled at Grant's indignation.

Brandy patted Grant's shoulder. "I bet they had to eat their words when Trinity became famous."

"Getting Trinity involved at the indoor pool

gave her the space she needed to grow." Grant sighed and returned the conch shell to the shelf. "What will happen to her things now?"

"What do you mean?" Charlene asked.

"I won't live forever." Grant wore a sheepish expression. "Would you like to see her special room? I've saved everything."

"More than the scrapbooks?" Charlene couldn't imagine *more* than this bedroom and photo albums.

"I wanted her to know that I cared for her and her career," Grant explained. "Every year for her birthday, I'd send flowers and a conch shell. I knew we would be reunited someday. I was wrong."

That was so sad. Sweet—but sad.

"Show us," Brandy said, her voice thick with emotion. They followed Grant from the bedroom to the hall, turning left.

"Feel free to wander." Grant gestured with pride to his collection—the second room was practically a shrine to Trinity Powers. Framed movie posters were on the wall, VHS tapes, then DVDs of her movie. *Sirena* had been translated into several languages.

"I didn't realize that. How wonderful," Brandy said. She admired the DVD cover in Japanese, then put it back.

Charlene observed the movie posters of *Sirena* on a conch shell, her lover slightly behind. It was a romance, but it was really about Sirena. She hated to even consider the idea that her dad would have harmed her somehow. Grant loved her so much. Too much?

"When was the last time you saw her?" Charlene asked, full of sympathy for them.

"I went to LA before the movie came out." Grant put his hands behind his back. "I'd been several times to visit when she was a little girl. After the divorce, Madeline wasn't as willing to let me stay at their house."

"Oh." Brandy picked up little Sirena figurines. "That must have been very hard."

"It was." Grant cleared his throat, his cheeks ruddy.

"I'm sure you had a custody agreement?" Brandy asked.

"It was just between us. I thought I could trust her. My wife. My Madeline." Grant bowed his head. "She betrayed me."

"By moving?" Charlene squeezed his shoulder.

"Not just that." Grant raised his head, and his brown eyes blazed. "Madeline had an affair with one of the men on the set of Trinity's earlier water ballet parts, before *Sirena* launched Trinity into stardom. I found out. We got divorced." He shrugged.

"That's awful! Surely you could have gotten partial custody?" Charlene said.

"In those days, the mother always got the kids, so my lawyer said not to even try. Waste of money. Which she had plenty of because of Trinity's work."

"That's terrible!" Brandy said. "Madeline was a stage mom behind the scenes?"

"Yes," Grant said. He sounded bitter.

Charlene watched him carefully. "What happened between you and Trinity? Did she take her mom's side in the divorce?"

Grant evaded her gaze and shuffled to the biggest poster of Trinity in the center of a long wall.

"What is it, Grant?" Brandy asked.

"I'm ashamed. But I told Michael for the book, so it will get out anyway."

"Oh . . ." Charlene wasn't sure she wanted to know. Right now, she admired this man.

"We argued, and I accused my wife of spending Trinity's money without working for herself. It got pretty ugly, and Trinity overheard it."

"I'm sorry," Charlene said.

"It's worse." Grant ground his teeth together.

"How?" Charlene braced herself for what he might say.

"I requested an audit of their income."

"Oh, no." Brandy sucked in a breath.

"I was right about Madeline spending more and not being honest with Trinity." Grant spoke with righteousness ringing in his words.

"Then why would she take it out on you?" Charlene asked.

"I had gone behind their backs and Trinity didn't trust me, and now she didn't trust her mom either. She said she lost us both that day."

Charlene had a better understanding of what happened now.

Brandy hugged him tight. "You probably don't feel like it, but listen, if you want, we're having a barbecue tonight at the winery. Bring Michael too."

"You are very kind, Brandy. Very kind. I am

going to stay home this time. I'm the one who is left now to see that my daughter is taken care of. Too little, too late."

The trio left the shrine and went downstairs. Charlene and Brandy let themselves out as Grant returned to the kitchen. Alone.

"That poor man," Charlene said.

"I think Trinity was a diva to her dying day." Brandy's mouth pursed with anger. "She was a brat in preschool and dance classes, even kindergarten. It was her way or a temper tantrum. She was so jealous that I had actual magical powers. In the third grade, we were walking home from school, and she told me she wished she could trap me in a conch shell. She'd never let me out. I would never be as good as her. Can you believe it?"

"That's terrible!" Charlene stopped to face her friend on the sidewalk. Brandy was a beautiful woman, but her shoulders bowed as if those memories had plummeted her back to childhood.

"We weren't close after that, and it wasn't long before they went to LA." Brandy smoothed a strand of auburn hair from her cheek, caught in a summer breeze. "I wonder if Trinity knew her mom planned on moving them and it was her way of controlling not being hurt."

"I think you're searching for justification when Trinity was just a mean girl you were probably better off without in your life." Charlene and Brandy stepped in sync toward the corner. "Were you aware she was taking medication?"

"Yes. She'd shared that Xanax and a new therapist had given her hope for a normal life. It's why she was able to travel. She teased me with possible news that she'd tell only when she arrived, but . . . that never happened."

Such a tragedy.

"Charlene . . . can you do me one more favor?"

Charlene tensed.

"Will you please drive Alannah to the barbecue tonight?"

"No way! I thought Dom had a rental car?"

"He went back to LA this morning. Please? Remember how I gave your folks the best day at the winery, no questions."

She did. Darn it. "Why can't she call a cab?"

"I want you to work your own magic, Charlene, and find out why Alannah is here in Salem. It was last minute and unplanned. I don't trust her."

"It's not magic. It's conversation." Charlene sighed.

"It's your magical power. Want to get lunch at Cod and Capers?" Brandy checked the time on her phone. "It's almost one. My treat."

"I can't. I have an appointment with Mary, the maid at the Waterway. If you're still going, would you say hello to Sharon for me?" Sharon Turnberry managed an amazing seafood restaurant with a harbor view.

"Of course!" Brandy's smile fled. "But if you can't, then I won't. I was going to do a little stargazing, that's all."

The sun was out without a single cloud in the sky. "Huh?"

"Tony is having lunch there with some political associates." Brandy's cheeks pinkened. "I thought

I'd use you as cover so I could accidentally bump into him or something."

"Brandy Flint—I am shocked. I've never seen you this caught up in a guy." When they'd first met, Brandy had been seeing Theo Rowlings off and on, but she was always the one calling the shots. This was different.

"I'm pathetic, I know." Brandy hiked her chin. "Just as well that I don't go. You're right."

"I didn't say that."

"I can imagine you saying it, and if you had, you'd be right. So. Back to the winery for me. A jealous witch is not a well-behaved witch. Maybe I'll drive by Bobby's apartment to make sure he still wants to be an artist."

"Good plan. You don't want your investment to run off."

Brandy nodded and dropped her phone into the side pocket of her black leather purse. "Thanks, Charlene. I told Alannah you'd be there at five thirty sharp. I know you like to be at your B-and-B for your happy hour at four. Appetizers for the barbecue will be served at six."

"So thoughtful of you!" Charlene started toward her SUV, her keys in her palm.

"Thanks again," Brandy trilled behind her, going in the opposite direction to her sports car.

She and Brandy were opposites in many ways, but at their cores they were each successful businesswomen who cared about their community. When she'd moved, she couldn't have imagined that her inner circle would include a ghost *and* a witch.

The weather was so perfect that Charlene retrieved the gift bag from her SUV and walked across the Common toward the Waterway rather than drive the seven blocks to the hotel.

The lawn had been cleaned up and there was no sign of the bleachers, movie screen, or stage—just beautiful trees and the historic bandstand. She passed the Hawthorne Hotel with a shiver. The building had secrets that she'd only slightly uncovered. The Salem Marine Society had a top floor that she'd never seen but wanted to one day.

The air held a hint of brine and salt from being on the sparkling Salem Harbor. Though a mile and a half away from the bay, Charlene had the loveliest view of the water from her widow's walk and wouldn't change places for anything.

She arrived at the parking lot at one and sat on a bench to wait for Mary, the gift bag next to her.

Mary exited at five after, scanning the paved area until she found Charlene. The woman hurried toward her, still dressed in her maid's uniform.

"Hi! How are you feeling?"

Mary touched the back of her head. "Fine, fine. I'll have the stitches out in a few days when I go for a checkup."

Charlene patted the bench seat. "Do you have a sec?"

"Sure." Mary perched on the edge as if ready to take flight.

Charlene gave her the bag with the T-shirt and hoped Mary would relax. "I guessed at the size. Let me know if it's wrong and I'll try to get it changed."

Mary pulled out the rainbow-colored, tie-dyed shirt and read the label. "Medium is great. Thank you. You didn't have to."

"I wanted to. You were so nice! I just thought I'd check on you and make sure you're okay."

"Oh? About the murder?" Mary balanced the gift bag on her lap.

"Well, yes—but also your head."

"I've never known anybody who was killed before, so that's weird."

Charlene couldn't say the same. "It's a shock to the system—and then to be attacked too? It's okay to feel rattled."

Mary nodded. "I keep wondering if I'd done something different, if I could have helped Trinity or saved her. If I had paid attention, would I have heard her calling for help? I listen to audiobooks to pass the time."

"You can't think like that, hon." Charlene brushed the young woman's hand. "It's a tragedy and not in any way your fault."

After a moment of silence, Charlene opened her phone to scroll through her pictures and the photos of Andrew and Barb in their mermaid costumes.

Mary tilted her head in question.

"I was wondering if you recalled seeing this man that morning at the hotel—I know it's hard to tell with the costume and the makeup."

"Actually, I admired his costume and told him so when I saw him with a blond friend in the lobby." Mary handed the phone back. "Not her."

Charlene blushed. "Do you remember what

time? I saw him around the Waterway when I came to pick up Trinity. I'd wondered if he was there to get an autograph or something."

"Why do you ask?" Mary sucked in a breath. "Does this have to do with what happened to Trinity?"

"Maybe."

"I saw him and the woman leave together from the blonde's room about twenty minutes before I was hit on the head. First floor."

So, the couple had been otherwise occupied and Trinity was already dead. Sam probably knew that, which was why Andrew hadn't been arrested. "Is that where you were attacked?"

"Yep. Near the rear exit. I just wish that whoever hit me hadn't taken my poster, you know?" Mary's fingers clenched, as if still holding on to the poster. "I heard it tear, so it won't be worth as much now to a collector. I still want it back."

"Tell me about it?"

"The poster? Well, it was one of the first ones before the studio realized that *Sirena* wasn't a traditional rom-com but a drama. It was Josh and Sirena sharing the conch shell equally."

"I haven't seen one like that." The posters in Grant's house had Sirena in the forefront.

"Well, I'm a big Trinity Powers fan," the maid confessed. "My mom knew her when she lived in Salem. Mom even went out to LA once, and Trinity was nice to her. They were kind of friends, you know? Mom died a few years ago. Anyway, I think that's why Trinity was so sweet to sign the poster."

That explained the difference between Trinity's

actions with the others and then Mary. "I'm sorry it was taken."

"Stolen," Mary corrected firmly. "The *Sirena* fans are just rabid. It's ridiculous." She lowered her voice and glanced at the entrance of the hotel. "My boss asked me what I'd seen and told me to help the police, but not talk or gossip to the news. No making the Waterway a spectacle."

"I understand."

"Thanks."

"From what I've seen, the Waterway instills good practices that the employees all abide by. That's pretty amazing in this day and age."

"It's why Trinity moved," Mary said sadly. "She said the folks at the Hawthorne didn't allow her any privacy."

"That's too bad."

"Right? Maybe if she hadn't moved here, she wouldn't be dead." Mary swiped a tear from her cheek.

What could Charlene say to that? No platitudes would fix the sad situation. Charlene gave Mary a side hug.

"I'm sorry for your troubles, Mary. Please, let me know how you are doing, okay?"

"Thanks for caring, Charlene. Do you know if there will be a service of any kind? I'd like to go. I will always be a Trinity fan."

CHAPTER 16

Charlene hurried back to her SUV, wishing she could get another peek at the movie posters in Grant's room.

Well, why not ask?

She gave Grant's front door a knock, but there was no answer. That's right—he and Michael were going to lunch.

Charlene returned to the bed-and-breakfast. Minnie was just putting away the duster. The washer and dryer were both going—bedding from the folks who had checked out yesterday.

"Howdy, Charlene," Minnie said, walking around the silver Persian cat, who liked to keep them on their toes by darting in their way and did so now with a random stretch in the middle of the kitchen floor.

Charlene knew this was Silva's code for "treats, please," and went to the jar on the counter, taking out one.

"What happened to her diet?" Jack said from his

place by the refrigerator. His dark hair was perfectly styled, his turquoise shirt the exact shade of his eyes.

Charlene shrugged. A diet was fine in theory, but what was the matter with a fluffy cat? "Hi, Minnie. How's it going?"

"Terrific. The upstairs is done, and the dryer has another twenty minutes. Want a sandwich or a salad? I made both."

"What kind of sandwich?"

"Ham and cheddar."

Charlene considered the ten pounds she thought of losing and the salad but sighed and said, "The sandwich, please. Is it already together?"

Minnie opened the refrigerator. "I know my girl!" She brought out two sandwiches covered in clear wrap. "Have a seat."

Charlene laughed. "Thank you."

"Did you find the maid and give her the shirt?" Minnie put out a plate for her too, then poured them each a glass of iced tea.

"I did! You spoil me. I love it—thank you."

"We spoil each other—you didn't have to give Will extra money for the plumbing. But you did, and thanks."

They lifted their drinks to each other in good health.

Charlene exchanged her glass for her sandwich. Minnie's ham and cheddar went beyond bread and meat—she added ground mustard, sour pickle, and shredded carrot.

Jack perched himself on the counter by the sink to watch them and listen as they caught up on the household news.

"Mary seems like a nice young lady and was grateful for the tee. Her head is better, but she would trade that for the poster that was stolen from her. Oh, and I found out why Trinity was nice to her. Mary's mom and Trinity were friends in Salem, one of the few she hadn't shed from her life."

"Was the poster valuable?" Minnie dabbed mustard from her lip.

"I don't know—but she said it ripped when the person stole it from her, so its value as a collectible wouldn't be as much. She still wanted it, of course, as she is a fan." Charlene shivered at the word. which was taking on a sinister feel.

"I'd like to see it too," Jack said. Behind Minnie's back, he floated a cat toy for Silva's amusement.

"Did Grant like the apple crumb cake?" Minnie asked.

"He seemed appreciative, but he didn't share." Charlene smiled at her housekeeper/chef, who was all about feedback on her food. "He took us to Trinity's room, where Brandy and Trinity used to play as girls. It's exactly the same. Grant *never* changed anything after Trinity and her mom left."

"That's creepy," Minnie said. "Don't you think?"

"A little. You should have seen the room next to it, which is a literal shrine. I was curious about getting another look at the posters, but Grant wasn't home when I knocked." Charlene took a bite of her sandwich.

"What did you want to see?" Minnie asked.

"Mary explained that it was a different-style poster than the one that starred just Trinity—the studio realized that marketing the film as a romance was the wrong tact for audiences because it was a drama."

"Fans and their money make the calls," Jack said.

Charlene was realizing that herself.

"I wonder why they didn't do a sequel back in the day," Minnie said.

"Me too. It seems like they aren't going to miss out on that cash cow with Alannah's remake." She finished the last bite. "Delicious, Minnie."

Minnie's cheeks pinkened with pleasure. "I'm so glad you like it. I asked the guests about the orange zest cookies, and I'll be adding them to our repertoire."

"Fine by me. Can I help you with anything for happy hour?"

"No, ma'am. I've got the menu together."

"Okay. I'm going to my suite to do some paperwork." And talk to Jack. "I have that barbecue at Brandy's tonight."

"The Wheatons have declined. The Martins are a yes but will meet you at the winery."

Charlene nodded. She would keep Andrew Martin and proof of his infidelity to herself for now. It sadly cleared him. "The Southerns?"

"Undecided. I can stay later," Minnie offered, "if you need to leave early."

"That would be great. Brandy's got me picking up Alannah from the Hawthorne at five thirty to drive her to the winery, full service. Dom already went home."

"Why can't she take an Uber?" Minnie demanded.

"Brandy wants me to figure out why Alannah is in town." Charlene got up to rinse her plate.

"There's something the actress is hiding, and Brandy thinks I can discover what. She's going to be sorely disappointed. How can I chat with someone I don't like?"

Charlene ducked out of happy hour at four thirty, leaving Minnie in charge. She changed her clothes several times, undecided as to what to wear to a barbecue at a high-end winery where local politicians and folks with money would be mingling—with a possible murderer.

"Barbecues are casual," she complained to Jack on the third try. She modeled the sundress and twirled by the love seat.

"You look beautiful," Jack said. "What's wrong with that?"

"No pockets." She patted her hips. "Where am I going to put my phone? Or my pepper spray?"

Jack laughed. "Tough choices. How about the dark blue linen capris that were your second option for pants, but with that peasant blouse you bought last week? Dressy, but stylish and comfortable. With pockets."

"You're brilliant."

"What was that?" Jack held his hand to his ear.

She was still chuckling as she added a spritz of light summer perfume, grabbed her hobo bag with the pepper spray, and her phone, ready to go.

"Perfect!" Jack announced when she entered the living room of her suite. "I wish I could go with you, Charlene. What fun we'd have. Take lots of pictures to show me when you get back. I think you're right that Brandy calling it a barbecue is de-

:eptive. Wouldn't be surprised if there will be wait-
taff in black tie."

"Jack." She pouted her lower lip. "I'm sorry you
:an't join me." And just what would she do then, if
ack was there and also Sam?

The truth was, Jack was her best friend—a
;host—and Sam was all man. She wanted them
)oth in her life.

She blew Jack a kiss before leaving and stopped
n the living room to check with Minnie. The
;uests were all gone and her housekeeper was
:leaning up.

"Good luck with Alannah, Charlene—be care-
ul!"

Driving to the Hawthorne, Charlene wondered
f she should park, but Alannah was already wait-
ng outside of the hotel. White shorts, wedge
leels, a long-sleeved tee, her long, brown hair
oose, and white sunglasses on her nose. The ac-
ress signed a few autographs, smiling sincerely at
ler fans, then got into the passenger side of the
'ilot.

"Hi! Thanks for picking me up. I wasn't sure if
3randy was pranking me," Alannah said with a
mirk toward Charlene. "But she doesn't seem the
ype. I've never met someone with less of a sense of
lumor."

"It's no joke." Charlene found Brandy very
umusing when she wanted to be.

"Dom's in LA filming a movie." Alannah buck-
ed her seat belt. "Since *Sirena*'s success, we've
)oth had plenty of offers."

"That's good, right?" Charlene pulled into traf-
ic.

"Yeah." Alannah leaned against the passenger door. "Pretending to date someone is a drag. Movie execs demand it, though. Trinity and her costar were the same."

"I'd heard that." Charlene clicked the locks just to make sure they were fastened. "Are you and Ned . . ."

"No." Alannah removed the white sunglasses to blink extremely long lashes at Charlene. "He's a necessary evil. Runs the fan clubs. But Neddy likes to party and is a better dancer than Dom."

She'd seen the pair "dance" and couldn't agree. Ned and Alannah had been barely legal on the stage. "Will you go back soon to film with Dom?"

"God no. We're doing separate projects too. Gotta strike while the public loves you. Look at what happened to Trinity. The producer must follow through with the sequel. Then Dom and I will film together."

"I'm curious about why there wasn't one back then?"

Alannah seemed pleased to know something Charlene didn't. "Oh, that's simple. There was a sequel in the making, but there were several accidents where she was hurt on the set. Trinity pulled out of them. It tanked her career. She might as well have died during production and become a national icon than a nobody."

Charlene couldn't believe what she was hearing and how coldly it was stated. Cold-blooded. All about the career. Could Alannah have killed Trinity?

Jealousy was an ugly emotion.

"Trinity was mesmerizing," Charlene said. "I

never saw her other two movies, just the original *Sirena*."

Alannah dug into her purse for a lip gloss. "Trinity Powers *in the water* was poetry in motion—her stuff on land—simply lacked that magic."

Charlene would ask some questions tonight at the barbecue . . . find out if Alannah had been around all morning of the parade, or if maybe she'd dipped out for a visit to the Waterway Hotel.

"So, how long are you in Salem for?"

"Don't worry, Charlene . . . I go home to LA on Saturday. I have zero reason to be back in Salem. Unless there is a sequel, but even then, no. I don't see it. Certainly not for the parade. I can't believe you fools are continuing with it."

Charlene gritted her teeth. This conversation was all Alannah. The young lady had strong opinions and her own agenda.

"I mean, the star died. Trinity was murdered." Alannah gestured with her sunglasses to the sky. "I'd take it as a sign from above, you know?"

She glanced at the dash. Ten more long minutes until they reached the winery. And she didn't care how much Brandy begged, she was not driving Alannah home. "Music?"

Alannah laughed. "I prefer chitchat."

Great. "What would you like to talk about?"

The actress applied a thick layer of shine to her mouth and then smacked her lips. "Like, seriously, why are you continuing with the parade?"

Charlene tapped the steering wheel. "The city of Salem is very diverse, and we're always looking for ways to reach out to the community—the parade allows us to do that."

"Bull-loney." Alannah snapped her fingers. "It's about the money. Things always come down to the almighty buck."

"Not everything. Trinity was born here in Salem." Charlene looked across at Alannah. "She has a lot of fans who want to honor her memory."

Alannah aimed her sunglasses like a pointer toward Charlene. "Whatever. It couldn't have been cheap to pay for the parade. I got the feeling that Brandy footed the bill for Trinity. Like, Salem had to bribe its star to return home. That would make a *shocking* news story. Maybe I'll give an exclusive interview before I go to the airport Saturday."

What a rotten human being!

"Why are *you* here? You weren't invited," Charlene said; to hell with being nice. "In Salem, at the Hawthorne Hotel. Were you stalking Trinity?"

"What?" The humor fled from Alannah's demeanor.

"You heard me." Charlene glanced at Alannah as she drove. "Trinity moved from the Hawthorne after you arrived. Why is that? Seems like she was trying to get away from *you*."

"If so, it's because she knew I was the winner in the *Sirena* mermaid popularity contest. Trinity avoided me like a coward rather than face me and lose."

"There was no contest—just a bunch of fans taking sides on movies twenty-five years apart." Charlene was so agitated by Alannah that she opened the glove box for some gum or a mint. Nothing.

"How little you know of Hollywood, Charlene."

Charlene shook her head. "Why don't you enlighten me?"

"Why should I? You've got it all figured out."

"You wanted Trinity out of the way," Charlene countered.

"Wrong answer. My agent told me to come, and that is why Dom and I arrived at the last minute. Ned was able to build interest in the online fighting and let it 'leak' that I would make a surprise appearance. You have me to thank for the success of your parade."

Charlene scoffed. "Why would your agent want that? Your movie came out three months ago."

"She told me that the producers are considering a sequel, so I had to be visible."

Charlene wondered if Alannah was telling the truth. Because she was an actress, it would be hard to know for sure.

"Visible in a good way. You had to be nice, Dom said, but you weren't. It would help if Trinity looked bad too?" Charlene surmised. "Could you both look good?"

"Trinity wouldn't return a freaking email. I was going to suggest to her that we apologize and make up in public. Win-win." Alannah settled her elbow on the armrest of the passenger seat. "What are you hinting at?"

"Well, that could be a motive. Making Trinity look bad for a movie role. You're incredibly jealous and you wanted the part."

Alannah clicked her nails against her phone case. "Trinity is dead. The stupid feud no longer matters."

Charlene read the dash time. Three minutes. This torture was almost over and then Alannah could be Brandy's problem. And considering how

Alannah felt about Salem, she'd reiterate that neither actress get the honor of the mermaid on the bottle. Bobby could design a new one.

"Is this much farther?" Alannah complained.

"Nope."

"I want to get something straight, Charlene. I did not kill Trinity."

Charlene coasted the SUV around the bend. A beautiful billboard announced that the Flint Winery was the next right.

"Did you hear me?"

"I did. Did you want her dead, though? Enough so that Ned acted on your behalf?"

"Ned!" Alannah blew out a breath.

"Or another person, perhaps? Dom?"

"Nobody acted on my behalf to kill anyone. You're sick, Charlene."

"You want a chance at a sequel, don't you?"

"It would be money in the bank. Unlike Trinity, I chose a man I had chemistry with on the screen. My mermaid sisters are all talented water ballet artists."

"You had to have others prop you up, it seems to me." Charlene put her blinkers on and turned right, then followed the winding drive around the grapevines to the house and beyond, to the winery. "Trinity was a star and could command the screen on her own. I've seen both movies, and yours has the best appeal for a younger audience. If those costars were *your* artistic choices, then you did well."

Alannah spluttered.

"Here we are. Enjoy the barbecue—and make sure to sample all the wines that Brandy creates here. They're all delicious, but my favorite is the pinot grigio."

Charlene parked and turned the engine off.

Alannah grabbed her wrist across the console.

Charlene arched her brow. The actress had two seconds to release her or there was no telling what Charlene might do.

"Are you dismissing me? I am a Hollywood star. They will choose me for the sequel. Me. Not Trinity—a fifty-year-old shut-in."

"Trinity is dead now, which proves my point." Charlene yanked her wrist free. "*You* had a reason to want her that way."

CHAPTER 17

Charlene flinched as Alannah slammed the car door so hard, the solid SUV shook on its tires. The actress hadn't said any more about her innocence.

Closing the driver's side door much more gently, Charlene pocketed the keys and hiked her purse over her shoulder.

Ariel Glitter hurried toward Charlene as Alannah gathered herself, pasted on a smile, and greeted Brandy, with Serenity, as if all was right in the world.

Brandy couldn't miss the tension but scooted Alannah arm in arm toward the outdoor gazebo with fairy lights, tables, and lots of wine. The scent of cedar escaped from a black barrel smoker.

"Hi, Charlene." Ariel, her naturally brown hair braided on either side of her face, dressed in snug, cutoff denim shorts and a *Sirena* T-shirt, held a bottle of beer. "Do you remember me?"

Even without the white mermaid wig, Ariel was

not a woman Charlene was likely to forget. "Of course! How are you?"

"Fine. Well, not really." Charlene stepped backward as Ariel crowded her. "I feel terrible. I can't get Trinity out of my mind." She tapped her head with more force than was warranted. "I talked with my anger therapist, and I just feel so danged guilty. It's not easy to be a wrestler. It's not a steady gig."

Charlene looked longingly toward the gazebo but could tell that Ariel needed to vent. And confess? Bobby thought she was guilty. She was here to find Trinity's murderer.

". . . so I kept the money," Ariel said. "Who should I give it to now? Her dad?"

Charlene blinked and pulled her attention from the large smoker and savory meat smells. "I'm sorry . . . could you say that again?" Something about money.

"The night of the party at my house, Trinity called me out for selling *Sirena* merchandise. She never saw a penny. It was embarrassing to be fired so publicly and I feel just awful—I had no idea she was broke. I want to give the money to her, but she's gone. Can I give it to her dad, do you think?"

"Oh! Oh, Ariel, that's very thoughtful." And didn't sound very murderous. "Let me talk with a friend of mine at the police station. They might know legally what to do, but if you didn't break any laws, maybe you should keep it."

She couldn't imagine that it would be a lot, and Ariel had just said she needed money.

"Do you think so?"

"How much are we talking?" Charlene tilted her head to smile at Ariel.

"It's ten thousand dollars."

Charlene coughed with surprise. "What?"

"Yes." Ariel patted the shirt she was wearing. "I made T-shirts and sold collectibles. My website is top-notch."

"That's great. Let me talk to my friend before you give all that away." Charlene was impressed by the woman's ingenuity. "You had the drive to create the site and sell the products, which I don't think is illegal."

"Even for the images? Maybe a copyright law or something?" Ariel truly did look repentant. A lot sorrier than Alannah.

Charlene tapped her lower lip. "I'll check."

"Bless you, Charlene!" Ariel's shoulders lifted a little.

"Feel better?"

"I do." Ariel drained her beer like she was at a rock concert and not a high-end barbecue. All she had to do was burp. "Now I'm ready for some burgers!"

Ariel jogged ahead and Charlene followed at a slower pace, curious as to who was there—Kass, Andrew, and Barb Martin—no Sam. He'd texted to say he was busy, but she hadn't really expected him to join her.

She entered the tent where Alannah was holding court with Tony and his daughters. The politician wore an upscale polo shirt with understated plaid shorts. His teenagers shone in sparkly, sleeveless dresses.

Charlene went to the wine counter and asked for a pinot grigio from a very handsome bartender.

"Here you go," Mr. Hottie said. "The wagyu steaks will be cooked in an hour or so, but appetizers are on the far table. I recommend the balsamic grapes with brie on a crostino."

Instead of tomatoes. Clever play on food at the winery. Wait. Charlene grinned at him. "Did you say steak?"

"Yes, ma'am. There will be grilled pink shrimp as well. Unless you're a vegetarian? There will be a corn and queso option."

"I am not, thank heaven. That all sounds amazing." Charlene raised her glass as the young man winked at her. Brandy wouldn't dream of having burgers and hot dogs. She couldn't wait to tell Jack. Wagyu!

Charlene said hello to Evelyn Flint, Brandy's mother, and Serenity, who were mingling around the appetizer table. Evelyn was in an ivory linen sheath with tiny cornflowers, her silver hair in a loose bun. Serenity wore a designer midi with flowing sleeves in light blue.

Charlene put down her wine to take candid photos of the event for Jack and her website.

The Martins were at a table for four, Andrew laughing with a blonde while Barb appeared *very* annoyed.

"Let me get one of you!" Kass said, snagging Charlene's phone. Kass had gone the sundress route, but hers had terrific pockets.

Charlene raised the glass and smiled.

"Ah—you look just like Jessica Biel with your hair down like that," Kass said, showing Charlene the photo.

"I wish." Charlene would also tell Jack that his help with her clothes had been spot-on.

"You do. So," Kass murmured, "you see the guy next to Tony?"

Tall, slender, and distinguished. Dark hair—probably about forty-five. "Yes."

"Well, he asked about you and wants your phone number. He thinks you're gorgeous."

Charlene picked up her wine for a big sip. "What?" She didn't know what to think about that. Maybe she was putting out some kind of pheromone.

"You've been in Salem for two years now." Kass nudged Charlene, her gaze filled with empathy. "I understand your heartache, but maybe it's time to go on a date."

She'd been on four, five counting dinner at the tavern the other day. There would have been more, but Sam had been out of town.

"I'm fine." Charlene shook her head, not wanting Kass or anyone setting her up. "You go out with him."

"Franco and I are monogamous right now." Kass showed Charlene a picture of them on a date. He'd gotten a job at Salem Cinema because the theater he'd been working at had closed. Permanently. A nice fountain was in the place it used to be.

"I'm glad for you," Charlene said. "You deserve to be happy!"

"And so do you." Kass wasn't giving up. "His name is Len Philips and he's on the conservation commission. Divorced five years ago. No kids."

"Kass!"

"What? I asked casually." Kass laughed.

"I am happy. Don't nag—you'll start to sound like my mother."

"Yikes!" Kass retreated a step and bumped into Grant, who was there with Michael, the biographer.

"Oof," Michael said.

"Sorry!" Kass brushed at Grant's shirt and the spill of red wine.

"It's just a drop—not your fault." Grant grimaced. "When Charlene and Brandy said barbecue, I thought it would be casual. I feel underdressed in shorts and flip-flops. I'm tempted to go home."

"You look nice," Charlene said.

Michael had also dressed casually, but with a vest. Was it a poor attempt to camouflage his weight, or did he really need all of those pockets? Several pens poked up, as did a pad of paper, so maybe it was for function. Charlene smiled to see a beer in another pocket. Clever.

"Would you like to get back to the table, Grant?" Michael balanced two dishes and Grant had been holding his wine. "I'll bring our appetizers."

"Yes, thank you." Grant nodded at Charlene. "Want to visit for a few minutes?"

"Sure! Let me get a plate." Charlene put an assortment of tasty bites on a small dish and joined Grant and Michael at the table. Kass followed, exuding concern.

"Are you sure your shirt is all right, Grant?" Kass asked. "I can get a napkin and seltzer water. Sangria might stain."

"It's fine, I swear," Grant said. "Don't worry."

"All right. Well, I promised Brandy I'd mingle. Bye for now!" Kass left.

"You are an amazing cook," Michael said. "We had the apple crumb cake for dessert after lunch today."

"You did? That's great." Charlene swallowed a bite of the crostino. "I must confess that it's my housekeeper, Minnie, who is the chef. She's fabulous."

"I'd be in trouble for sure if I had a housekeeper who cooked like that." Michael patted his chest. "I've always struggled with my weight. Hard to believe I used to be on the swim team."

Charlene smiled at him. "I have some extra curves that I attribute directly to Minnie's croissants."

Michael smiled back, and she noticed that he was very handsome. His eyes held humor; his hair was thick, though starting to get some gray within the brown. She'd guess him to be about fifty.

"Tell me about yourself," Charlene said. "Were you assigned this biography by a publisher?"

"No." Michael drank his beer. "I'm a freelance writer under contract. My mother passed away, leaving me a small inheritance, so I'm able to choose what I do with my time."

"Condolences on her loss." Charlene held his gaze.

"It's been five years now," Michael said. "I miss her still."

"He cared for her while she was ill." Grant nodded with approval at Michael. "It's not something that would be easy to do. I am going to die alone."

Well, that popped a hole in the party mood.

"Oh!" Charlene picked up her wine. "Grant . . ."

"I wanted Trinity's forgiveness before I died. A child should not die before a parent. It's not right or natural."

She reached for his fingers and squeezed gently. He'd wondered earlier what would happen to his Trinity collection after he was gone. "I'm sorry."

Michael sipped his beer. "I'm sure this project will keep us friends for a long time, so maybe not so lonely for you?"

Grant nodded and finished a bite of crostino. "This is the dangdest barbecue food I ever heard of. Tasty, but not potato salad, you know?"

She hid a smile.

Brandy joined them for a few minutes of small talk, then she said, "Charlene, can I borrow you?"

"Sure!" Charlene nodded at the men. "I'm glad you're here. It was nice to visit."

"Michael offered to drive me," Grant said. "Otherwise I would have stayed home. I promise not to drown my sorrows tonight."

Charlene started to step away, but then returned. "I forgot to tell you that I'd dropped by today to look at the *Sirena* posters again, but I think you and Michael were at lunch."

"We were—come by tomorrow, whenever you want. Being retired means I spend most of my time down at the bay."

"Calling for mermaids?" Brandy teased.

"Wishing for Trinity." Grant wiped a tear from his cheek.

Charlene sent him an empathetic smile as a waiter scooped her empty dishes away. "Well, bye again." Wineglass in hand, she followed Brandy. "Where are we off to?"

They left the confines of the gazebo and walked near the winery gift shop, which was closed. Brandy frowned. "Alannah has Tony wrapped around her finger."

"She's not a nice person. You should have heard her talk about Salem and how she doesn't see any reason to return."

"We can make that happen." Brandy peered inside the gazebo, her slender arms crossed. "How much longer must I endure this torture?"

Charlene sipped her wine to cover a grin at Brandy's theatrics. "Alannah leaves on Saturday."

Brandy's nose lifted. "Thank the Goddess."

"Her agent told her to come to Salem—it has something to do with a possible sequel to *Sirena.* The agent said for Alannah to be visible, as much in the public eye as Trinity, but to be nice."

"Oh?"

"Alannah was very derogative about why we were continuing the parade and concluded that it came down to money. She mentioned doing an exclusive, actually. How you had to bribe Trinity, the town's beloved star, to come to Salem."

"No!" Brandy clenched her jaw and glared toward the gazebo.

"Yes. But I pointed out that if she was told by her agent to be visible in a way to win a popularity contest between her and Trinity, and now Trinity has been killed, well . . . it gives her a motive for murder."

"That's good!" Brandy nodded at Charlene. "I knew you'd get something out of her."

"Alannah said she didn't do it. I asked her about Ned, or somebody else on her behalf, but she claims to be innocent."

"Interesting." Brandy tapped her lower lip. "You did great, Charlene. Now, if we can just keep Bobby out of trouble, I will feel a lot better."

She scanned the gazebo and saw Bobby and Tina sitting close at a table. "He chose success, then?"

"I hope so. I have two possible patrons for him if he can keep it together. Bobby had a minor meltdown about the change to the label for the wine, but Tina calmed him down."

"That's sweet." Charlene leaned into Brandy, not wanting to be overheard.

"What?" Brandy's eyes glittered. "You have more?"

"I talked to the maid, Mary, who was thankful for the shirt. She's healing but wishes that she still had her poster. It was stolen. Guess why Trinity was nice to her?"

"Why?"

"Her mom was a childhood friend like you were, only Trinity liked this woman, and they remained friends. Mary is still a fan."

"What was her name?"

"Clarkson."

"It doesn't ring a bell," Brandy said. "Does she still live in Salem?"

"No. She passed away a few years ago."

"Sad. Life is a gift."

"It is. The poster being a collector's item is why I wanted to see Grant's again. Something to do with *Sirena* being advertised as a romance at first, but then it was remarketed as a drama."

"Well, if there is a poster of it, Grant should have it." Brandy rolled her eyes. "What are you thinking? To get one for Mary to replace the one that was stolen?"

Charlene hadn't thought of that, but it might be nice. "No. It wouldn't be the same anyway, because of the signature."

Brandy blew out a breath. "Come and sit with me. It's time to eat."

Charlene watched, amazed, as the waitstaff changed the white cloths to black in synchrony, as if orchestrated, by the time they were inside again.

Brandy announced dinner. "Steak and lobster, as a thank-you for all of your work and support of the first-annual *Sirena* parade. Our servers will bring it to you!"

Applause sounded.

Charlene sat next to Brandy and wished Sam could be there. The Southerns hadn't showed either, but they might have had fun with Alannah, who was charming and on her best behavior. Kass was on her other side.

"I was talking with Grant," Kass said. "What an interesting life he's led, being a curator at the museum. That would be cool, to document treasures from hundreds of years ago."

"Are you thinking to add another skill set to your already long list of talents?" Charlene teased her friend. Kass was a psychic, a tea shop owner, a tour guide, and an actress.

"No," Kass said, smiling. "But I might try that whole blowing-into-a-conch-shell-for-a-mermaid thing. It's documented in Fiji. The first mermaids existed in Greece."

"What would you wish for?" Brandy chimed into the conversation, her attention split between Tony's table, where he sat with his daughters and Alannah, and her own.

The politician could flirt with an actress in public all he liked, but because Brandy was a witch, their relationship had to be a secret from the voting public.

"I would wish for . . . world peace?" Kass grinned.

"It's a classic wish." Brandy glanced at the table with Tony, then whispered, "When I was little, we would play mermaid and witch all the time. Trinity was so focused on wanting to be a mermaid that nothing else would do. She was a terror. I know that Grant feels bad about them not getting along and her cutting him out of her life, but she wasn't an easy child."

"She was a kid, though!" Kass unfolded her cloth napkin to place over her lap.

"She was still awful," Brandy said. "Grant would take us to the wharf and we'd blow the conch shell, wishing with all of our might for a mermaid. I think a part of me was disappointed to find out they weren't real."

"What?" Kass said with an arched brow. "Mermaids are totally legit."

"I've never seen one outside of a costume," Brandy said.

"Can you believe such lack of faith, Charlene?" Kass shook her head.

Charlene stayed out of the debate. If there were witches and ghosts, why not mermaids? "I am keeping an open mind."

Kass smacked her palm to the table. "Exactly. You should ask Michael to show you the lore he has on mermaids."

"For the biography?"

"I guess so." Kass shrugged. "He's been interested in the mermaid legend since he was a kid. He and Grant have hit it off."

"That's nice to see, for Grant's sake."

Unless Grant had killed his daughter . . .

Somebody had. Possibly somebody at this barbecue. It took some of the enjoyment from the meal. Part of the reason for Charlene being here tonight was to gather intel to find a killer.

CHAPTER 18

Charlene hadn't been so full in a very long time, but the steak, shrimp, and lobster tail would be worth the food coma.

If only she could be home on her love seat with Jack and Silva instead of here under a gazebo of fairy lights with a hundred people, all in various stages of enjoyment due to the meal, the companionship, and the wine.

Charlene slowly sipped a second glass. "You've outdone yourself, Brandy. What an amazing night."

"Just a simple barbecue," Kass teased Brandy.

Brandy smiled, pleased. "There is a lot wrong in the world, but it's hard to focus on that when there is beauty too." She lifted her glass of deep red merlot. "Grapes are in my blood."

The Flints had been in the wine business for centuries, so Charlene wouldn't be surprised if, when cut, they literally bled a sauvignon.

Her phone dinged a message, and she pulled the device from the side pocket of her purse—discreetly, of course—and saw that it was from Sam, apologizing for interrupting her at the party, but could they talk in the morning?

She sent a thumbs-up emoji and returned to the people around the table.

Kass raised a brow but didn't say anything. Brandy was too busy watching as Tony and his politician friend laughed with Alannah, who had kept up her good behavior all night.

Charlene reached for her phone again and did a panoramic video of the after-party, where folks conversed at high volume.

"For my blog," she said. And Jack. Jack would approve of the luxury here tonight. The waiters topped off drinks and cleared plates seamlessly.

"You might need to serve coffee before sending some of these people home," Kass said.

Brandy nodded. "I'm watching. Anybody who needs a rideshare will get one. Speeding tickets or car crashes would not be good for my business."

Charlene heard a ruckus at the table where Andrew and Barb were sitting. Barb's chair had toppled over and Andrew stood, fists clenched.

"Oh." Charlene placed her glass on the table and grabbed her bag. "I might take them home. You've got Alannah?"

"Tony's got Alannah," Brandy corrected. "But thank you for driving her here. Let's compare notes in the morning."

Kass nodded. "I didn't see anything out of the ordinary, and I was watching Bobby and Tina. Grant. Ariel. Ned never showed. I wonder if Alannah told him not to?"

"Good question." Charlene nodded at her friends. "Bye—great party."

She passed several people she knew and smiled, reaching the Martins. Andrew had righted the chair.

"Hello, you two."

Her guests gave her a shamefaced look. The blonde giggled from her seat. This close, Charlene guessed the young lady was in her thirties, around the same age as Barb and Andrew. A piece of cake sat before her, and a glass of sangria. Could this be the blonde Mary had seen at the hotel with Andrew?

"The chair tipped, that's all," Andrew said. "It's not broken or anything."

"Are you okay?" Charlene asked. "The chair is not a big deal."

"Fine," Barb said.

"Fine," Andrew echoed.

"I'm heading back to the B-and-B. Can I give you guys a ride with me?"

"Yes!" Barb said, sounding like Charlene had offered a lifeline.

Andrew looked at the blonde, who found anything but Andrew interesting.

"I don't know that we've met!" Charlene said to the blonde. She was pretty, sure. But not prettier than Barb. She just didn't understand straying in a marriage. "I'm Charlene Morris."

"Hi! I'm Cassie," she said.

They shook hands, the young woman's sticky from her sangria glass.

"She's on Team Alannah." Barb spoke as if this

was the greatest offense. She had to suspect that this woman was a threat to her marriage. "We are Team Trinity."

Andrew patted his pockets, as if to check for his wallet or phone or something. "I'm ready to go."

"Brilliant choice," Barb said.

Cassie giggled again and stood up. "I saw you at the parade," she said to Charlene. "Those T-shirts are so cool. I got mine autographed by the artist. He's here. Right over there with my friend Tina."

Cassie turned and stumbled. Andrew slipped his arm around her. "Gotcha!"

Cassie blushed and Andrew released her. Barb was on the verge of tears.

"Cassie," Charlene said, "do you have a ride home?"

"Yep! Tina is the designay, deshig, DD," Cassie settled on.

"You promise?" Charlene arched a brow. She didn't want to sound judgmental, but she also didn't want this woman on the roads. She might hurt herself or someone else. Her husband had been killed by a drunk driver, so the issue was near to Charlene's heart.

"Yes, Charlene." Cassie raised her hand like a Girl Scout. "I do."

Kass saw what was happening and joined them. "Hey. Cassie, right? I loved your costume for the parade." She drew the young lady to the back table that had coffee, tea, and cakes. "The rainbow tail was perfect."

Charlene smiled her thanks at Kass, then stepped toward the parking lot to do a last scan of the place before leaving, just to be sure that everyone was all right.

Grant and Michael both waved when they saw her.

"Come over anytime," Grant called from their table.

Charlene nodded and raised her palm, then led her silent but angry guests to the Pilot. The parking area was crowded as they were some of the first to leave, but that was okay with Charlene.

She'd learned what she could and couldn't wait to discuss it with Jack.

She clicked the fob to unlock the doors. To her surprise, they each got in the back seat. She was thinking one of them would call shotgun to avoid the other.

Maybe there was hope for them, but Charlene wasn't happy at how Andrew seemed to disrespect his wife.

She kept the music on low. "That was some barbecue, huh?"

"Yeah. Never had steak and lobster on the grill before," Andrew said.

Barb, behind the passenger seat, stared out the window, opting for silence. Couldn't blame her at all.

"What did you think of the wine?" Charlene asked. "Oh, you were drinking the sangria."

"It was delicious. Maybe had one or two more than I should have."

"You got that right," Barb said, finding her voice.

Andrew sat back with a huff. "You remember when you used to be fun?"

Ouch. Charlene raised the radio a smidge and followed the winding road to the main street leading to Salem.

They stopped at a light and the music paused. Charlene heard them whispering back and forth, and Barb said, "I lied for you to the police. Lied!"

Andrew said, "Shut it!"

Barb sniffed. "Is that who you were with? I'm not stupid!"

"Just keep your mouth shut about it. You are my wife."

"You are my husband," Barb countered. "You are supposed to be faithful. It's a big part of the whole marriage vows thing."

The radio returned to music. Charlene was glad of that because she didn't want to eavesdrop any more than she already had.

They arrived back at the B-and-B with each of them stubbornly pouting. Barb and Andrew slammed their doors and hurried inside, not waiting for the other.

Charlene bowed her head. Was there anything she could do for the couple? She said a little prayer, then entered the house where Silva greeted her in the foyer. Children's laughter sounded from the living room, so she went in that direction.

The Southerns were playing a game of Jenga on the floor before the fireplace. Jack appeared and studied her, then gestured toward the family.

"They are a wonderful unit," Jack said. "Unlike the Martins upstairs. Are you okay?"

She nodded.

"Hi!" Natalie seemed at ease crossed-legged on the area rug. "How was the barbecue?"

"Steak and lobster, my friends," Charlene replied with a laugh. "And shrimp! You missed a feast."

"A barbecue is supposed to be hamburgers and hot dogs," Aqua said.

"And lots of watermelon," Jewel said.

"That is the traditional way, you're right." Charlene allowed her purse to slide off her shoulder to her palm. "What did you guys do?"

"We had pizza," Linc said. "Antonio's Pizzeria. Great prices for their pies."

"Pizza pie," Jewel laughed.

"Apple pie is better," Aqua said.

"I like it all." Natalie patted her stomach.

"Me too!" Charlene agreed. "Can I get you anything before I retire for the night?"

"No—you've been such a wonderful hostess." Linc glanced at Natalie.

"Though we hate to leave, we've decided to go home tomorrow." Natalie settled on her palms as she peered at Charlene behind pink bangs.

"But check out is Friday!"

"We know," Natalie said. "It's just that with everything that's happened, we're antsy to get the girls back in their routine."

"Understandable," Jack said. "They sure are terrific parents."

Charlene sighed. "I understand. Let me refund your stay for one day."

"Absolutely not!" Linc shook his head vehemently. "We've had the best time at your B-and-B. So welcoming, and very much someplace we'd like to return."

"Let me give you a gift certificate then, okay?"

Charlene genuinely cared for the family. "You're welcome back anytime. You'd have a credit."

"You don't have to do that." Natalie's eyes twinkled. "But we accept."

"We might come for a romantic weekend," Linc said. "Eh, Nat?"

"With us?" Aqua asked. "We like Charlene's too."

Natalie sighed and exchanged a glance with her husband. "We'll see."

"That means no." Jewel pouted.

"They're catching on to parent code quick!" Linc laughed and tickled the girls, who knocked down the Jenga tower.

"On that note," Charlene said, "I'll see you in the morning over breakfast. What time will you head out?"

"Leisurely, so around noon," Natalie said. "Thank you for understanding!"

"My pleasure. Night!" She shouldered her purse and picked up Silva.

Jack walked with her toward her suite. "Why can't all our guests be like the Southerns?" he asked. "Beat you there!" He disappeared.

Charlene stopped in the kitchen, deciding to make a cup of tea. Green, with honey and lemon. She met Jack in her suite. Not as fancy as Kass's, but still satisfying on a full tummy.

Jack closed the door for her and raised the volume of the TV. She dropped her bag on the coffee table and perched on the edge of the love seat.

"Did you have fun?"

"I did. Wagyu steak and lobster tail—Brandy throws a spectacular party." She got out her phone to show Jack the pictures and video later. For now, she savored a sip of tea.

"Not a single hot dog?" Jack laughed robustly.

"Nope!"

"How was Alannah?"

"A real brat," Charlene said. "She can't wait to get out of Salem on Saturday."

"Good riddance." Jack soundlessly brushed his hands together.

She gestured with her teacup to her phone on the coffee table. "I shot a video, too, so you could get the full experience. The winery is magical at night."

"Thanks." Jack ignored the phone, more interested in hearing her account of the barbecue than pictures. "What did you learn on the car ride? I hope it was worth it."

"I think so. Alannah's in Salem because her agent told her to be visible while Trinity was making her first public appearance in twenty years." Charlene sipped and briefly closed her eyes with enjoyment. Tea was perfect after such a rich meal. "She mentioned that the producers are interested in a sequel to *Sirena*, and she wants to star in it. Gives her a motive for killing Trinity."

"Besides jealousy." Jack settled into the comfy armchair.

"Exactly. She'd be the only mermaid option for Hollywood—there aren't a lot of water ballet stars who are beautiful and can act too."

Jack drummed his fingers soundlessly on his knee. "Tell me what else you discovered?"

"Well, Ariel Glitter has ten grand that she's

made from her website marketing Trinity as *Sirena*. She feels guilty because Trinity called her out on it at her party. She's wondering if she should give it to Grant or something. What if she was breaking fan club rules?"

"I don't know anything about fan sites," Jack said, "but I'll check the fine print of the law. Celebrities and public figures might be protected."

"Thanks, Jack."

She took another sip and curled her legs up to her side, snuggling into the cushion. Silva meowed at the kitchen door. "I'll get it," Jack said. "Don't get up."

"All right. I won't." A ghost was very handy sometimes.

"Do you think Ariel might have killed Trinity?"

"I thought it a possibility until she wanted to give the money back," Charlene said. "She seemed truly sorry. I think Bobby just wants the heat off of himself."

Jack nodded. "Who else was at the party?"

"Brandy and her under-the-radar politician boyfriend. Cracks me up. She knows that they can't ever be a thing in public, but she doesn't care. She was very hot under the collar about Alannah sucking up to him. Honestly, Tony was a little too flirty for my taste. I don't know what she sees in him."

Jack sprawled his legs out before him. Silva curled up next to Charlene on the couch. "She likes her men to be powerful."

"You're right. His daughters are the perfect age to be fans of Alannah, who seemed to be on her best behavior once we were there."

She cradled her warm mug and petted Silva,

who stretched her paw toward Jack as she leaned her head to Charlene's leg.

"There is no future in it, but that's not ever been a must-have for Brandy." Jack had known her since they were young.

Her phone dinged. A message from Brandy, asking if she'd made it home okay.

Jack floated the phone to her.

She typed back a yes. Another message dinged, and Charlene turned the volume off so that she could relax with Jack and get to Brandy's texts in the morning.

"I like Grant, Trinity's dad, but his actions could be considered obsessive." The shrine, the childhood bedroom. The pictures and the scrapbooks. "He said I could come by anytime tomorrow to see the posters, so that's good. I sure hope that Mary gets hers back."

"Doubtful." Jack rubbed his jaw. "Somebody wanted it bad enough to harm her in a public place. Risky."

"I know. Wishful thinking." She placed Silva on her lap and patted the space next to her for Jack to sit, prepared for the cold from his essence.

"Are you sure?" Jack's brow rose.

"Yep! Check out this video with me. I made sure to use the panoramic view." Jack joined her, careful not to touch her body which would chill her to the bone. After the video, they went through the pictures.

Jack was properly impressed by the rich details, the lights, the clothes, the wine. The people. He stopped to enlarge a photo. "Who is that?"

"Grant Powers. He's a very handsome man."

Jack scrutinized the image Kass had taken of the three of them at the appetizer table. "Who is that?"

"That's me, the biographer, and Grant."

He leaned over the photos, returning to the ones of Grant. "Trinity must take after her mother. I don't see much of a resemblance."

Charlene zoomed in on the image. "Madeline was dark-haired with violet eyes, so I think you're right. But she got her love of mermaids and story-telling from him."

"That's sweet."

"Kass thinks she was helping me take pictures for the blog because she doesn't know about you." Charlene glanced at him with a half-smile. Jack missed life.

Jack brought the blanket around her shoulders when she shivered, then moved to the armchair. She was immediately warmer. "I like Kass. Do you think she could see me?"

"I don't want to take that chance. How would I explain it?" She peered closely at Jack to see if he would give her a hint. "Unless you want to try?"

"Right now, I'm content to keep things as they are." Jack changed the subject. "What were our guests fighting about?"

Charlene placed her tea on the table. "I overheard Barb whisper to Andrew that she lied to the police and covered for him. She asked him point-blank if he'd been with Cassie, the young woman at their table tonight, during that time."

"That's awful." Jack straightened in his chair.

"I know!" She tucked the blanket around her lap. "Andrew was at the Waterway and Mary confirmed it—with a blonde, not Barb. Unfortunately, he was having an affair. Or fortunately. He had no reason to kill Trinity and was too busy."

"What do we know about Cassie?" Jack asked.

"Cute, blond, and bubbly. No last name. If we hang on to the fan theory, then Cassie is Team Alannah, all the way."

"I don't know if we should rule Andrew out then," Jack said. "What if Cassie and Andrew were in on it together?"

CHAPTER 19

Charlene woke the next morning curious what Jack had discovered with his magical cyber skills, but her roommate was nowhere to be found. Not to her eyes or ears anyway.

Dressed for the day in lightweight jeans, sandals, and a powder-blue T-shirt with romantic ivory swirls, she headed to the kitchen, where Minnie had everything under control.

"I thought I'd make the girls mermaid pancakes since it's their last day," Minnie said.

"How thoughtful! And sweet—give them a pleasant memory to take with them back home to New Jersey."

The house phone rang, and Charlene answered cheerily, "Charlene's!"

"Why aren't you answering your cell phone?" asked a cranky detective.

"Sam!" She leaned her hip to the counter and accepted the mug of coffee with cream from Minnie, who traced a heart shape in the air.

Charlene laughed. Sam wasn't sounding at all besotted.

"Where have you been? I've been worried about you."

"Right here, Sam. Sorry about the phone." She blew on the brew, recalling turning off the ringer last night. It was probably in the cushions of her love seat somewhere.

"I asked you to text me this morning, remember?"

"I do—and that was before I discovered something that might help the investigation. But you go first."

Sam groaned.

Minnie rolled her eyes.

Charlene took the phone and her coffee to the front porch. Sun shone in a blue sky, a lovely late-summer day. There was a hint in the air of cooler weather to come, but for now, summer reigned.

Silva stalked a butterfly by the flowers, but the collar with the bell gave the birds and insects fair warning.

"What can you tell me?" Sam asked.

"A lot—but the most important thing was on the way home from the barbecue last night."

"I'm sorry I couldn't come. Something with a different case came up."

"It's okay—it was a toss-it-in-the-mix invite anyway."

"You didn't want me there?" Sam said in a low voice.

Charlene hurried to reassure him. "Not that! I thought we were being quiet about being together." She glanced around to make sure she was alone. No Jack. "In public. The barbecue was a party."

"Are you having second thoughts?" Sam demanded. "Should I take that promotion in Portland?"

Her stomach clenched. "Sam!"

He cursed under his breath, but she still heard it clearly over the phone. "Sorry. I don't know what to make of this, us. I don't like sneaking around."

Sneaking? That didn't sound as romantic. "It's a tryst. That's what we're supposed to do," Charlene said in a light tone. If Sam broke it off, she'd be devastated. She'd learned after Jared that she could survive, but Sam had helped. Jack had too.

A minute passed, then Sam said, "We need to talk about Portland. But not right now. I want to see you face-to-face for that conversation. What did you hear last night?"

For once, Charlene cut to the chase without any embellishments or extra words. "Barb whispered to Andrew that she'd lied for him to the police, and wondered if Cassie, the woman he was flirting with at their table, was who he'd been with at the Waterway. I also found out that Mary Clarkson can confirm that Andrew and Cassie were there. Together."

"Jeeeezus."

"I know."

"Cassie who?"

"I didn't get a last name. Serenity might have it. Or you could ask Andrew. Wasn't only his name on the room at the Waterway?"

"Yep. I appreciate your gift of gab, Charlene,

but Andrew could be dangerous. This was a crime of passion. Whoever did this to Trinity Powers was very angry."

She nodded, though Sam couldn't see her. "Mary said she saw Andrew and a blonde leave before she was attacked. Before two in the afternoon. They were occupied, for about an hour and a half. They were together . . . could there be more than one killer?"

Sam didn't answer. "I told Andrew not to leave town. Are they still at your B-and-B?"

"Yes."

"I'm tied up with something, but I'll have Jimenez come out and question the Martins."

Charlene froze at the idea of Officer Jimenez at her place, ruining the happy vibes with her cold gray stare. "Can I ask Barb and Andrew to come to the station instead? I don't want to disrupt the B-and-B any more than it already has been."

Sam paused. "If you drive them, then yes. Otherwise, there is a chance they might run."

"Sam . . ." She thought of her options and conceded. "Fine. After breakfast."

"Fine."

He hung up and she heard a dial tone. He hadn't ever told her what he'd wanted her to text him about. "Well!"

Silva meowed at her, a pink rose petal over her ear from hunting among the garden flowers.

Charlene blinked away tears of hurt. She didn't see any way to have everything she wanted. If Sam moved to Portland, then she would be here with a broken heart. Not shattered, but broken still.

She'd have Jack, her ghostly best friend, who

she could tell was getting restless. She had her friends in Salem because she'd made the effort after Jared, having learned her lesson to not be so focused on one person.

When they left, by choice or not, it was a lethal blow.

Minnie opened the door and stepped out to the porch next to her. "Everything okay?"

"Yes. It is. I mean, other than Trinity Powers's death, and one of our guests being a suspect." Charlene and Minnie exhaled simultaneously.

"Oh, that ol' song and dance." Minnie grasped Charlene's hands, facing her.

"What?"

"I just want you to take a minute for yourself and see what you've created at this bed-and-breakfast. The Southerns and the Wheatons are eating pancakes and making arrangements to meet one another in the winter for a mermaid festival. I bet they'll be lifelong friends, because of you."

Charlene sighed. "And your cooking."

Minnie released her hands. "What I want to say is that this is who you are, and you have grown so much since you first moved here. You'll take that strength with you no matter where you go."

"Are you trying to get rid of me?" Charlene lowered her voice. "Did Sam talk to you?"

Minnie laughed. "Never in a million years would I want you to leave Salem. I just sense maybe it's time to open your heart a little wider."

Jack appeared on the porch behind Minnie and Charlene's pulse fluttered. The phone in her hand rang and she dropped it, then picked it up. "Hello?"

How much had Jack heard?

"Why haven't you been answering your cell phone?" Brandy shouted.

"What's wrong?"

"I think Bobby skipped out on me last night."

"Bobby Rourke, the artist?" Charlene recalled him and Tina sitting thigh to thigh. "Is he not answering his phone or something? He and Tina looked pretty tight."

"I left a message with Tina. Mom's missing the diamond bracelet she was wearing last night and no, Bobby's not answering his phone."

Brandy's cool-as-ice demeanor was nowhere to be found and Charlene heard true panic in her friend's voice. "Listen, I'm in the middle of breakfast with the guests, but I'll call you as soon as they're out the door, all right? You should call the police! Maybe the bracelet is just missing."

"Too much of a coincidence for that expensive jewelry to be gone along with my temperamental artist." Brandy muttered something about Bobby and his descendants that sounded painful.

They exchanged goodbyes and Charlene hung up.

"What's wrong?" Minnie asked.

They stepped toward the door and Charlene opened it. Silva dashed in. Jack waited on the porch.

"Brandy can't find Bobby or her mom's diamond bracelet."

"Could he have stolen it?" Minnie asked, her fingers to her mouth.

"I hope not," Charlene said. They grouped together in the foyer. "Let's focus on giving the Southerns a nice meal, okay? We can deal with the rest later. Minnie, I'll be right back. Gotta get my cell phone!"

Minnie walked into the dining room where laughter abounded, while Charlene went to her suite. Her phone was on the couch cushion.

"Twenty missed calls!"

"It was vibrating like a rattler," Jack said, not meeting her eye.

"What?" Had he heard what Minnie said about her heart?

"I didn't mean to look."

"At what?" Could he have seen a text from Sam?

"Your phone." Jack shrugged. "Brandy texted, and Sam."

Charlene scrolled through the notifications. It was not a big deal that he'd seen a text from Sam, and no secret they were texting because of the recent case.

"I don't want you to think that I meant to see them, is all," Jack said. "I wasn't prying."

"It's okay! Jack, did you find out if Ariel was breaking the law by using Trinity's image without permission?"

"I'm on it now," he promised.

"Thank you!" She headed back toward the dining room, grateful that there was nothing to see on the messages, thank heaven. But what if Sam had texted her about a date or something?

She would need to be more careful.

Or . . . Sam sounded like he might want to move to Portland, in which case, the dates would be over and no longer relevant.

Charlene entered the dining room with a bright smile that was surely Hollywood-worthy, calling out, "Good morning!" She'd put down her coffee who knew where, so she poured a fresh cup, cream first to cool it just enough.

The twins were both in hyper mode and happy about going home to their bedrooms and their parakeets.

The Wheatons had selected several glamorous mermaid tails from the Southerns' website, Tida Wave's Creations, as family Christmas gifts. They'd get to pick them up in December in the Keys, when they met up again in person.

Andrew Martin came down and brought a tray of coffee and muffins upstairs. He didn't do more than nod at any of them. How was she supposed to convince them to go to the station? He'd left without looking at her, so she'd have to deal with it later.

The Wheatons planned a day trip to Boston.

After breakfast and hugs to the Southerns, along with the gift certificate for one night and an extra fifty dollars credit, Charlene went upstairs and knocked on the Martins' door.

Barb answered, her eyes red.

"Hi," Charlene said. She smiled softly at the young woman whose world was falling apart. "The police have some more questions for you both. I offered to drive you to the station."

"Why?" Andrew asked from his spot on the bed, where he sat, fully clothed, drinking his coffee.

"You know why." Barb leaned against the doorframe. "When?"

"I can take you in an hour. Okay?"

"Yeah." Barb closed the door, gently, but still in Charlene's face.

It wouldn't be pleasant to have a witness to the deterioration of your marriage. She tried not to take it personally.

Jack manifested by the stairs going down. "I wanted to make sure Andrew didn't give you any trouble."

She smiled at her protective ghost.

"Do you have time to look at something I found before you go?"

Charlene nodded.

Jack disappeared with a pop.

She walked down the stairs, taking much longer than simply disappearing and reappearing by actually having to move her legs.

Minnie hummed as she cleaned the dining room, where Silva batted at the housekeeper's apron strings as if they were toys—never mind that the cat had toys galore.

When she arrived at her suite, Jack was seated before the laptop.

"Hey, Jack." She closed the door and locked it. "Is this about Ariel?"

"No." Jack got up and she sat in the chair, the cushion cold from his essence. "This is an obituary for Trinity Powers. Her talent agent wrote an article in the *LA Star*. Charlene, this says that Lorianna Benjamin had accepted an offer for *Trinity* to do a sequel of *Sirena*—not Alannah."

Confused, she read the article and turned to Jack. "Was Alannah lying? According to this, the *Sirena* storyline would be forwarded ten years, though Trinity would have been twenty-five years older."

"Look at how beautiful Trinity still was." Jack scrolled to the farewell spread on Trinity, complete with a dozen photos. Her slender figure was toned, and she totally rocked the two-piece swimsuit she wore.

"Wow. She could hold her own against Alannah despite the age difference. These were taken just last month?" Pictures of Trinity in the ocean, on the shore, at the pool, her arms and legs sleek with lean muscle.

Whatever she'd been doing on her private estate seemed to agree with her.

Charlene hit the Print button on the computer.

"What are you thinking?" Jack asked.

"I'm going to Grant's after dropping the Martins at the police station to talk with Officer Jimenez to see the posters. I'll bring him this for his collection. He'll be so proud."

"Thoughtful."

"I'm running out of dessert ideas," Charlene said with a nose scrunch. "Mom taught me that you can't just drop by someone's home without a little gift."

"And how are your parents?"

Charlene immediately felt guilty for not calling more often. "I guess fine. When I'm busy, I tend to tune out after the first five minutes about the church potluck." Had it been over a week since their last family call?

Jack smiled and floated the pages to her when it was finished.

"Thanks." Charlene folded the article in the side pocket of her hobo bag, the pepper spray there but so far, untouched. "Wish me luck."

"You can find out who did this to Trinity," Jack said. "I believe in you."

She searched his gaze, her heart thundering. Had he overheard Minnie? She couldn't tell.

Minnie knocked on the door. "Charlene, the Martins are in the foyer waiting for you."

"Coming!" When she turned around to say goodbye to Jack, he was already gone.

The Martins were on the porch by the time Charlene left her suite. Barb wore a pretty sundress and Andrew a camp shirt tucked into shorts. They personified any young couple on vacation. This time when they hopped into the car, Barb took the front seat and Andrew sat in the middle of the rear bench. Barb wasn't wearing her wedding ring.

Charlene didn't force conversation during the ten-minute ride to the station, letting the radio fill the air, and parked before the brick police department.

"Gonna go in with us to make sure we don't run?" Andrew snapped before getting out.

Barb blushed but stayed seated. "I apologize for his rudeness, *our* rudeness. This hasn't been the vacation I'd hoped for."

Andrew walked toward the steps and then waited for Barb. He tapped his toe.

Barb looked at Charlene. "They think Andrew hurt Trinity Powers, don't they?"

Charlene shifted so that she faced Barb. "Right now, they're just asking questions. You should be honest with the officers."

"I lied for him. I know he's messing around, but

I don't think he's a killer. But," Barb sucked in a breath, "I never thought he'd be unfaithful, so I don't know what to believe."

Charlene squeezed Barb's fingers. "You call me if you need a ride back to the B-and-B, all right?"

Barb's skin flushed and she lowered her gaze, as if embarrassed or ashamed.

"You will be all right, no matter what happens." Charlene tilted Barb's chin so they were eye to eye. "It's okay to be alone—I never knew that until my husband died over three years ago, now."

"You were married?"

"I was." Charlene clasped the steering wheel. "To my soul mate. He was in a car accident, and I didn't think I could go on." She didn't go into the dirty details that had kept her up at night.

Andrew called, "Barb," impatiently.

Barb blinked tears from her eyes.

"I did go on, Barb. I moved to Salem and started my life over. It's possible. You are stronger than you know."

"Thanks, Charlene."

Barb exited with her chin high. Andrew opened the door of the police department and they both went in though Andrew tossed a last scowl at Charlene.

Sam hurried out to the top step of the station and searched the street. For her? Charlene gave a little honk, and he waved.

Her insides settled at his action. They cared for each other, but it was complicated. Sam went inside rather than talk with her. They were trying to be discreet and they were at the station, so she understood.

Charlene drove to Grant's house and knocked on the door.

Grant answered, his eyes sparkling with welcome. He was dressed for the day in jeans and a Henley, slippers on his feet. "Charlene! Come on in. Boy, that barbecue was something else. We didn't get home until after midnight."

"Brandy knows how to throw a party. I'm usually sound asleep by ten," she said.

"Me too. You wanted to see the posters?" Grant nodded to the thin staircase leading up to the bedrooms.

"I did." Charlene patted her purse. "I also brought you something I found online about Trinity this morning."

"Oh, great." Grant gestured with a thumb over his shoulder. "There's an office as well."

She followed the older man up the steep and narrow stairs. "I'm glad you had such a good time. Did you get a chance to sample the wines, or did you stick with the sangria?"

Grant gripped the railing. "I was very familiar with the Flints' merlot, but that cabernet winter grape is my new favorite. I already ordered several bottles."

"I order her wines by the case."

"You have a bed-and-breakfast," Grant said with a chuckle. "I might need to check myself in if I were getting cases for just me alone."

They reached the second floor. Grant released the railing and swung around to the hall.

"This way." He led the way to a room across from the shrine—both doors were open, but she hadn't seen his office before. Pictures on the wall of his accomplishments at the museum. While not as opulent as Trinity's, they were acknowledgments of a job well done.

Charlene pulled the printout from her purse and offered it to Grant. "I thought you might want this for your scrapbook. Trinity is, was, still so lovely. According to her talent agency, she'd accepted the offer to do a sequel to *Sirena* just last month."

Grant accepted the paper from Charlene with a bemused smile, scanned the photos, and fell backward into the wall. His eyelids fluttered.

"Grant!"

CHAPTER 20

Charlene helped Grant to a chair in his office. The small room, just bigger than a closet, had been converted to fit a desk, a chair, shelves, and a narrow recliner.

"Are you okay?"

"That's *my* Trinity?" Grant stared at the photos with pride.

"Yes."

"She's so lovely. Even lovelier than her mother. I was shocked, thinking it was my wife come to life." Grant lowered the article. "Now both Madeline and Trinity are dead and gone from me."

Charlene squeezed his shoulder, not liking the perspiration on his forehead or how pale he'd gotten. "Let me get you some water, okay?"

"There's a cup in the bathroom." Grant swiped the back of his hand across his face. "Tap water is fine."

Charlene exited the office and turned away

from the shrine and Trinity's bedroom to go left to the bathroom and Grant's master bedroom. She filled a paper cup from a dispenser on the wall with water from the faucet and returned it to Grant.

"Thank you." He sipped with his eyes closed, the printed article on his lap.

This was not the reaction she'd expected. "Should I call the doctor for you?" His pulse grew steadier.

"I'm fine. Heart's healthy. Just had my physical." Grant finished the paper cup of water and crumpled it. "It was a shock, though, don't mind saying."

"Well, just rest a while. There's no rush."

Grant, revived, perused the article again, more slowly this time. "I wonder if Michael's seen this yet? He's going back to LA on Sunday."

"If not, you can share it with him. It was online if he needs to verify the story."

"Why don't you check out Trinity's rooms for that poster while I read this? I don't want to miss a word." Grant smiled at Charlene tremulously. "My sweet girl was going to star in the sequel! I can't believe it. It's what should have happened before."

Now that his color had returned to normal, Charlene was glad that she'd brought it to him. "Did you know that there'd been several accidents when they'd tried to film *Sirena 2* back in the day? It's why she quit filming."

Grant shook his head. "No. My poor dear."

"She was too scared to continue with the water

movies," Charlene shared. "Well, that's what Alannah said anyway."

"What if they weren't accidents?" Grant stood, his hand braced on the chair, his balance shaken after the shock. "Did she realize that her life was in danger even then?"

Trinity's talent agency was listed in the article. "I don't know, but her agent might, or the film's producer. As her father, you've got a decent shot at them telling you the truth."

"I could call." Grant held on to the article, his voice shaky now too. "Will you help me find the phone number?"

"Sure, but I can't stay too long." Charlene read her phone—no messages from Barb. Or Brandy! Shoot. "I have my guests to take care of." Andrew could be in jail. He'd cheated on his wife, which required a layer of subterfuge that one couldn't ignore.

"I don't want to keep you." Grant left the office and crossed the hall. "What kind of poster were you looking for?"

"A movie poster with both stars from the original movie of equal prominence."

Grant entered the Trinity shrine room before Charlene and perused the walls, pointing at the stocked shelves. "Hmm. I have thirty-two standard-size movie posters. Any other details?"

"I'm not certain." Charlene smacked her palm to her forehead. He might know Mary's mother. "Do you recall a little girl who grew up with Trinity, last name of Clarkson?"

"Clarkson?" Grant tucked a hand into his denim

pocket and smiled. "Oh! Itty bit. What a sweet woman Nadia turned out to be. Taught elementary school. Had a daughter of her own. Nadia died several years back." His smile morphed into sadness.

"I met her daughter," Charlene said. "Trinity was staying at the Waterway when she was killed. Mary is a maid there. Trinity was very sweet to Mary and autographed a movie poster for her."

"That sounds nice." Grant glanced at the article he still held, probably relieved to hear that Trinity had been kind. "What is the connection?"

"Mary was attacked while leaving work the day of the parade, and someone stole her poster right from her hand."

"Oh, no! Why?"

"It seems the poster is unique." Charlene didn't see anything matching on the walls. "Maybe it was before the producers decided to focus less on the romance and more on Sirena, which makes it very collectible. Do you have that version?"

"I don't think I do." Grant touched Charlene's arm. "Is Mary okay?"

"Yes," Charlene assured him. "She is. I was wondering if, after this is all over, maybe you'd want to show her your memorabilia?"

"I would like that." Grant sighed and looked at the article, then Charlene. "I never meant for this house to be empty."

Charlene wished she could make Grant feel better, but all she could do was try. Putting two fans together, even if there was a big age difference, could be good for both of them. "Mary still wants that poster even if it's ripped—no monetary value, but I think it's because it was her mom's, so it's even more special."

"You could be right." Grant folded the news article and stuffed it in his back pocket. "You're welcome to look around. I have hundreds of things."

"Hundreds?"

"Maybe more. I was speaking with Michael about what to do with all of this memorabilia when I'm gone. Who else will want it? Or care for it, like me?"

Could Mary help? Charlene would introduce the pair and then butt out. She was curious and tended to act first and think later.

Most of the posters hanging up were Sirena on the conch shell, in various poses. Any of the ones with her costar showed the man very small in comparison. Lean, average height.

"In that case, I might need to come back," Charlene said, worried about Barb. "Let me help you find the number to her talent agency before I go."

They went into his office. Grant placed the now wrinkled article on the desk and got online via the older computer. Grant dialed the agency number, the phone on Speaker.

"I'm Grant Powers. My daughter is, was, Trinity Powers. May I speak to her agent?"

"I'm so sorry for your loss," a young man said. "I will ring Ms. Benjamin for you."

Grant tapped the article, his knee twitching.

"Lorianna Benjamin speaking."

Grant gulped and Charlene patted his arm. "Hello. I'm Grant Powers. Trinity Powers is my daughter. You did such a nice piece in the *LA Star* for her."

"My condolences." The agent's voice hardened. "Trinity was my client. A friend of sorts. She told me under no circumstances were you to get a dime—"

"What? That's not why I am calling!" Grant's skin flushed. "I saw that she'd been chosen for a sequel. I was so proud of her!"

"Your daughter cut you out of her life."

"I wanted to make amends," Grant said. "It's too late now."

"I'm sorry for your loss, Mr. Powers. Trinity suffered from severe, debilitating anxiety. She was taking a new medication that seemed to be helping. The trip to Salem was her first outside of California in over twenty-five years. I thought it would be good for her, but . . ."

"Do you know *why*?" Grant scrubbed his beard with shaking fingers.

A pause, then the agent said, "She believed she was being stalked."

Grant sobbed. "Stalked?"

"It was never proven. In this instance I believe that client confidentiality can be relaxed since Trinity is dead," the agent said. "She signed the prelim contracts last month. If you're serious that you didn't call about the money, I'll be frank— Trinity was flat broke. Another reason she was willing to seek help was so that she could work again. The studio she's with, Sunset and Vine, might have more information. Good day to you, Mr. Powers." The call ended in an instant.

Grant leaned back to study the ceiling. "My Trinity was being hunted like an animal!"

Charlene squeezed his forearm, but the motion was ineffectual to his grief. A pebble against a flood. "Is there anything I can do?"

Grant straightened, his eyes bleary with unshed tears. "Charlene, could you please go? I should have been there for my daughter. I need to get my bearings."

"Sure. It's okay." She stood and glanced over her shoulder at the threshold of the office. He hadn't moved. Was Grant a good guy or a bad guy? A bad guy who'd changed? She just didn't know.

She'd just stepped outside of Grant's townhome when her phone rang. It was Sam.

"Hey!" she said. Her heart lightened immediately knowing he was on the line.

"Hi." Sam gave a slight cough of discomfort. "I'm sorry about earlier."

"Me too." Charlene's nose stung with emotion. "This is a difficult position to be in."

"Can you talk?" Sam rumbled.

"I'm walking to my car from Grant's house."

"Grant Powers?"

"Yes. I dropped off the obituary for Trinity in the *LA Star*, a California gossip rag. She'd signed a contract to do the sequel. It seems that Trinity suffered from severe anxiety and had new medication that would allow her to work. Her agent is Lorianna Benjamin."

"How did you . . . you know what? It doesn't matter. People just talk to you."

"I'm nice, Sam. I care about them."

"I know." He paused. "Do you care about me?"

"I do." Charlene didn't hesitate at all. "You know I do."

Sam sighed heavily. "I wanted to let you know that Andrew's been seeing Cassie at the mermaid festivals for the last two years. Nobody suspected because he was Team Trinity and she was Team Alannah. They were together during the time of death for Trinity."

Charlene knew that already, but it still sucked to have it confirmed. "Poor Barb."

"Yeah. She said that you gave her a nice pep talk."

"Ah. Should I come to get her?"

"Barb is taking a walk to clear her head. Andrew can't be jailed for being a jerk and a cheat. He wasn't talking at all, but Jimenez had Cassie down at the station and she cracked right away."

"What does that mean regarding Trinity's killer?" Charlene held the phone to her ear, her grip tight.

"Still on the lamb." His voice lowered. "Any chance you can meet me for a cup of soup at our place?"

Her spirits soared. "Yes." She glanced around to make sure nobody was near. "Right now?"

"Meet you there." He sounded serious.

Charlene hurried to her SUV. Would this be the time he'd allotted for the Portland talk?

What did he care about a dreary state with bears and trees and . . . She didn't want him to go, plain and simple.

For being so nice, Charlene was discovering a very selfish part of herself when it came to Sam. And Jack.

* * *

Sam texted ten minutes after she'd gotten a table that he'd been called to a meeting. It was important and he hoped she'd understand.

Charlene said of course, laid a five on the table, and left. Her cheeks burned at being stood up so publicly.

Remembering that she'd promised to call Brandy back, she dialed her phone in the parking lot.

"Hello!" Brandy said.

"Hi. Did you find Bobby?"

"Bobby, no. Mom's bracelet, yes. Serenity performed a location spell. It had fallen off in the grass. I should know better than to overreact. I'm out of sorts and need to do a cleansing ritual to restore my mind and body. Murder does that to me." Brandy exhaled like a purebred filly at the starting line of a race. "Not just Trinity. I'm tempted to string Alannah up by her toes and add her to the body count."

Charlene gasped. "Why is that?"

"That *actress* slept with Tony. I know she did. He wasn't answering his phone." Brandy's tone held a hint of slyness. "I may or may not have gone to our apartment on the edge of town. I saw his car. I saw Alannah leave this morning, all that glorious hair mussed."

"Oh, Brandy."

"It took everything I had not to curse her and her descendants then and there." Brandy's voice returned to normal as she said, "But I didn't. Not even a little one—those things always backfire.

This could be my just reward for using magic to get Trinity here in Salem. I'll need a pound of sage, and moon magic, and . . ."

"I think you should calm down a little," Charlene interjected.

"You called me!"

"I did." Charlene remembered why. "I did. I'm glad you found the bracelet." Brandy's words gave her an idea. "Maybe you should drop by Tina's place to find Bobby?"

"Blessed be. Of course. They're probably shagging like crazy and don't hear the phone." Brandy paused, then launched into her favorite subject—the politician. "Do you think I should forgive Tony?"

"No!" Charlene's response was immediate. Any man who chose his career and other women wasn't worth Brandy's time. "I don't think you should."

Brandy's string of swear words made Charlene's ears burn. "Have they found the murderer yet?"

"No." Charlene rolled her eyes at the phone, glad that Brandy couldn't see it. "I would have mentioned it."

"Be careful," Brandy instructed. "I'll go pound on Tina's door and imagine that it's Alannah's cute nose."

Charlene never wanted a witch for an enemy. On the other hand, she was mostly certain that Brandy was blowing off steam and wouldn't hurt anyone.

She slowed down the driveway of her bed-and-breakfast, ready to unwind and talk over all that she'd learned with Jack.

Instead of a calm and tranquil scene, it was sheer chaos. Andrew was on the front lawn, knee bent while he serenaded Barb with music played from his cell phone. Dozens of red roses were in his arms as an offering for her, untaken, as he begged Barb to forgive him through song.

CHAPTER 21

Charlene exited her SUV in a state of surprise. Thankfully, the Wheatons were out for the day and the Southerns had gone home to New Jersey, so it was just Minnie, Charlene, and Jack who were witnesses to Andrew's desperate ploy to win Barb back.

Minnie took in the situation at once and climbed down the stairs to the grass. Barb's stoic expression and crossed arms made it clear she was not appeased by Andrew's too-late measures as he sang off-key.

"Stop this right now, Andrew," Minnie said brusquely.

Andrew tore his gaze from Barb, who wasn't moved in the least, and appealed to Minnie, then Charlene. Not one note of sympathy came from the three women. He sat slowly on his heels and turned the music off.

Minnie kept her firm, motherly tone. "I don't

know what's happening between you, but this is no way to behave, especially in public."

Charlene nodded at Minnie, who was an angel in more ways than one.

Minnie turned to Barb and asked gently, "Do you wish to talk with Andrew?"

"No." Barb lowered her hands to her sides. "Our marriage is over."

"No!" Andrew shouted.

Minnie skewered him with a look to behave. He remained on his heels, his head bowed.

Barb stepped toward Andrew in dazed disbelief. "You've cheated for *years*. I can't forgive that. I already told you that at the station. You're just upset because you got caught." The young woman faced Minnie and Charlene without a hint of doubt. "I'll be checking out today."

"You are welcome to use one of the other rooms if you'd like your own at no extra charge," Charlene said. Minnie hummed in agreement.

"It's okay." Barb sighed. "I did some thinking on my walk home and I'm going to visit my best friend from college. She's agreed to let me stay with her while I figure things out. I'll rent a car and hit the road." Hope shone from her eyes. "It's kind of exciting, actually, to think about a new future that I can create for myself." She hugged Charlene. "Thanks for your words of encouragement."

"That sounds wonderful." Charlene stepped back from the hug to study Barb's face. "Can I give you a ride to the car rental office?"

"No." Barb exuded more happiness than when she'd arrived. "I've already called for a taxi that will be here any minute. I'm going to dash inside and pack. Shouldn't take long. I'm only taking what I want."

Barb went inside without a backward look at Andrew.

Andrew scowled at Charlene and Minnie. He stepped toward them, but Jack intervened with a wall of cold. Andrew stopped in amazement and immediately backed up.

"I think you should go as well," Charlene said. "But wait out here with us until Barb is packed."

"You ruined my marriage," Andrew said.

"No sir. That was something you did all on your own." Charlene held his gaze firmly. If he budged out of line, she had her pepper spray and a ghost. And a housekeeper with matzo balls of steel.

"I'm not leaving until tomorrow," Andrew argued. "I paid through Friday."

"We will see about that," Jack said. He was not a happy ghost, and Charlene feared he could make Andrew's life miserable—in a visible way.

The taxi arrived and Barb rushed out. She didn't give Andrew a sideways glance as she thanked Charlene and Minnie, apologizing for the drama.

"It's not a problem," Charlene said. "Please, be good to yourself. If you ever come back to Salem, stop in at the B-and-B and let us know how you are."

"I will. Promise." Barb climbed into the taxi as the driver put her single suitcase into the trunk and then got behind the wheel.

Andrew fumed on the Adirondack chair on the porch as Barb escaped to her new life. "I should sue you."

"For what?" Charlene said, appalled.

"Destroying my life."

Charlene perched on the railing. Jack waited next to the chair for Andrew to make one wrong move. "I'll give you the same advice I gave Barb. Don't be afraid to start over. You owe it to yourself to be happy. Cheating in marriage signifies dissatisfaction. Let Barb go and give yourself a fresh beginning."

Andrew stood and studied Charlene. "You might be right. I'll grab my bag." He went inside to his empty suite.

Minnie and Charlene waited on the front porch. "What do you think he'll do?" Minnie asked. "That was good advice, and nicer than he deserves."

Jack said, "That's right. Can I trip him on the stairs?"

Charlene hated for anyone to be unhappy. She arched her brow at Jack, standing behind Minnie.

Jack disappeared.

Fifteen minutes later, a car arrived with a cute blonde driving. Charlene looked at Minnie with a shake of her head. "Well, that is Cassie. I guess he's going to avoid being alone."

Minnie clicked her tongue against her teeth. "Shame."

Jack returned with a pop of cold air. "Andrew is an idiot."

Andrew came out with his suitcase and an overnight bag. "I'm outta here." He glanced at Charlene and Minnie. "I love Cassie too—don't judge me, ladies."

"Team Alannah?" Minnie asked. Her question was a sly dig at his switched allegiance.

"Team Cassie," Andrew replied. "You can trash what Barb left. Sell it. Whatever. I'm officially checked out, Charlene." He climbed into the vehicle and leaned over to kiss the blonde on the lips.

Cassie backed up in her car without a peep at Charlene. What good could come from such a rough beginning of a relationship? What hope did Cassie have for something honest?

Jack shimmered on the steps. "Both of their wedding rings are on the bed. Sad. To make something positive from it you might donate the money to Felicity House."

"Smart idea."

Minnie looked at her. "What is?"

Jack laughed and disappeared.

He'd gotten her again. Charlene tapped her temple. "To donate any items she left behind to Felicity House. The orphanage can always use funds. I hope that Barb is happy now. *I'm* happy that Andrew is gone."

"Marriage is a beautiful thing when it works," Minnie said. "You had a lovely union with your Jared. I have one with my Will. It's not always wine and roses, but it shouldn't be toxic either."

"You're so wise," she said. They went into the foyer. Silva sprawled on the bottom step of the staircase. The energy was lighter with the Martins gone.

"This batch of guests has been an interesting mix." Minnie stepped toward the kitchen. "More of a challenge."

What a way with words. "And tomorrow we get a fresh batch of personalities. You gotta admit that it's impossible to get bored."

Minnie laughed. "So true. Can I interest you in some shrimp for lunch? We'll only have the Wheatons for happy hour, so we don't need all the food that I've prepped."

Charlene's stomach rumbled in agreement.

"I'll take that as a yes," Minnie said, smiling.

Minnie went home early when not even the Wheatons were there for happy hour since they'd decided to have dinner in Boston for their last night. Charlene caught up on her paperwork after she and Minnie cleaned the Martins' suite. As Jack had told her, their wedding rings were on the pillows. Barb had left all of her mermaid paraphernalia, not wanting to bring it into her new life. Charlene understood that.

Jack had discovered the Right of Publicity that provided a right to legal action which protected celebrities against misappropriation of their likeness. Because Ariel had agreed to take the fan page down once Trinity asked her, there was no more to do about it. She'd see if Ariel Glitter could sell the mermaid accoutrements on her website. Charlene was just looking up Ariel's contact information online when Jack appeared.

"Brandy's here," Jack said. "With Bobby Rourke. He's in the passenger seat of her Mercedes looking worn out, music blasting. Are they a thing now?"

"I don't think so." Charlene hoped Brandy had

broken things off with her cheating politician, but dating Bobby wouldn't be a step up. "Thanks."

She left her suite, walking through the kitchen and narrow hall to the foyer. Brandy knocked on the front door.

Charlene answered. "Hello, Brandy!" Bobby stood directly behind her.

Brandy swiped off her sunglasses and arched an auburn brow. Her long hair was in a loose braid. "That was fast." She peered into the foyer. "I know we're interrupting your happy hour, but I was hoping you could get the police off of Bobby's back. That Jimenez woman is a menace. She's like a terrier with a bone."

The artist, dressed in jeans and a T-shirt with one of his designs, appeared appropriately dejected, his curls mussed.

"Happy hour was a bust. All my guests are out, so come on in. Hungry? Minnie made shrimp tacos."

"We just ate, but that does sound nice. How about a glass of wine? I know you've got white and red in stock," Brandy teased. They were her house wines with a *Charlene's* label.

Bobby scratched his goatee. "Wine sounds good to me."

"Let's go to the living room." Charlene widened the front door and gestured them inside. "The bar is set up in there."

Once in the foyer, Silva meowed a curious hello from her hiding spot near the shell-shaped planter. Brandy and Bobby followed Charlene to the living room. She went behind the bar. "What can I get you?"

Bobby admired the craftsmanship of the piece. "This was made by a real artist."

"Parker Murdock," Charlene said. "I agree. I told him what I wanted, and he designed it from a few sketches I gave him. It's very functional for my happy hours and fits the aesthetic of the house."

Bobby turned around and studied the living room from the bar to the mantel and the mirror above it, the sideboard for the happy hours, and the antique furniture. "I can see why Alannah wanted to film something here."

How had he heard about that? "That was a ploy to see what I knew about the case," Charlene explained with heat. "I didn't appreciate her be-friending one of my guests and tricking them. Alannah can stay at the Hawthorne."

Bobby grinned and smoothed back his curls. "Gotcha."

Charlene lifted a white bottle and a red. "Which one?"

He studied the labels. "You did the design to match your *Charlene's* sign out front. Clever mar-keting."

"I was a marketing major before moving to Salem." Her education and experience had helped quite a bit in her bed-and-breakfast venture.

"White," Bobby decided.

"I'll have the same," Brandy said.

"Me three." Charlene poured out three glasses of chilled sauvignon blanc.

Jack appeared by the fireplace to find out why Brandy was there. Charlene was curious too. Was it really about getting the police to back off of Bobby?

"Have you heard anything more about the investigation?" Brandy asked as she and Bobby sat on the sofa.

"No." Charlene eased back onto the armchair. "You?"

"Yes. The more time that passes, the more Officer Jimenez wants Bobby to be the patsy," Brandy declared. "I heard that Andrew was cleared."

Charlene hid her surprise by taking a sip of wine.

"Cassie called Tina, who called Serenity," Brandy explained.

Bobby stretched out his legs. "I didn't do it. Even those tea leaves said I didn't."

A fact that Sam didn't deem logical. Charlene placed her wine on the side table. "Bobby, how did you know that Trinity had switched hotels? She must have mentioned her plans Saturday night at Ariel's party."

Bobby scowled into his glass. "Why?"

He hadn't directly answered. Interesting. "Ariel thinks it was because Alannah had moved into the Hawthorne on Friday with her fans . . . that it was too much for Trinity." Charlene bit her cheek to keep focused on the conversation as Silva's paw went through Jack's pants and his image wavered. "Ariel claims she didn't know Trinity left. Grant hadn't known either. How did you find out?"

Bobby's leg jittered. "One of the porters at the Hawthorne said they saw Trinity leave with her suitcase on Saturday night, but she didn't ask for a car. It was a matter of deduction. Not that many hotels within walkable distance. Then, I asked around in each one. Hit pay dirt at the Waterway and paid one of the kids in the kitchen to get her room number."

"That sounds very stalkerish," Jack commented. "Maybe the tea leaves are wrong?"

Charlene wondered that, too, and her stomach clenched.

"Not smart," Brandy chided. "What were you thinking?"

"He didn't give it to me, though he pocketed my cash. Anyway, I had to follow Trinity like a fool when she finished her breakfast." Bobby drank his wine. "I just wanted her to like me, and the new design."

Brandy swirled the liquid in her glass. "You've got to stop this neediness. Believe in yourself, and your talent."

Bobby pouted. Legit pouted. Charlene was borderline appalled at the grown man's reaction.

"Do you have an alibi? We saw you at the registration table. Were you there the entire morning?" Charlene hadn't been as she'd attended to various tasks.

Brandy scooted to the edge of the sofa and looked at Charlene. "I made the mistake of giving Bobby several breaks. I can't vouch for him the whole time."

"I was napping in my truck. It was a long night. I've been a Trinity fan my whole life!" Bobby said. "I would never hurt her."

"You must have been five," Charlene demurred. It might explain his overreaction.

"Does it matter?" Bobby straightened.

"He should be on the stage," Jack said.

Brandy appealed to Charlene with a bright gaze.

"So. We need to try a different angle and find out from that twit Alannah if she'd done something specific to make Trinity uncomfortable and leave. There might be answers there. If she did, great, and if she didn't, well, that is also information."

"How do we do that?" Charlene asked.

"She's staying at the Hawthorne," Brandy said, standing to drain her glass of wine. "I'll drive."

Charlene didn't have any guests to take care of, so she also rose. "Let me get my bag."

"To the Hawthorne!" Bobby cheered.

"Pack your pepper spray," Jack said.

Brandy was driving her sports car and Bobby folded himself into the small back seat, leaving the front for Charlene. Brandy messaged Serenity to set up a meeting with Alannah in the Hawthorne bar, if possible.

While Charlene often went around five miles, maybe ten, over the speed limit, if it was safe to do so, Brandy had a lead foot. She held on for dear life as Brandy sped toward downtown and the Hawthorne Hotel.

"We have got to clear your name," Brandy said. "I hope Serenity finds Alannah. Any other ideas?"

Bobby leaned between the front seats, holding his cell phone. "I have a friend who works in the kitchen at the Hawthorne."

"How is it that you have so many friends at restaurants?" Charlene asked, hand on the passenger side door.

"I used to work in them before devoting myself to my art. Not going to lie—they've hooked me up with a meal now and then."

"Makes sense." Charlene had more respect for

hardworking Bobby than pouty Bobby. "Who is this friend?"

"Margret Stevenson. She's a hot blonde from Sweden I used to date. Just texted her, and she's able to meet us for a quick break."

"Good." Charlene realized Bobby really wanted to clear his name if he was going to contact his lady friends.

"I caught her up with the situation so she can ask around." Bobby finger-tousled his curls.

Brandy flew into a parking lot with an abrupt halt at a spot. "We're here."

Charlene climbed out with a prayer of thanks and exhaled. She dug into her purse for a notepad and pen.

"What's that for?" Bobby asked.

"Notes," Charlene said.

"You have your phone." Bobby shrugged at her like she was old . . . well, maybe she was—over forty to his younger than thirty—but she didn't care. She couldn't doodle on her phone though there was probably an app for that.

They entered the hotel and went to the right. A statuesque blonde waved at Bobby and dragged them into a small room, minus customers but filled with tables.

"Hi, Margret." Bobby placed a sturdy kiss hello to her lips. "This is Brandy, my art sponsor, and Charlene—she owns a B-and-B."

"Hello," Charlene said.

"Hi!" Margret replied nervously.

"Did you discover anything about the morning Trinity left?" Bobby asked.

"I could get into trouble for talking to you. One

of the maids was fired earlier. We had an urgent meeting with the management, reminding us to honor our guests' privacy, but since Trinity is dead, and you are a suspect, well, yes." Margret glanced guiltily toward the partially closed door. "I did."

"What can you tell me, babe?" Bobby oozed charm like cheap cologne.

"Trinity Powers felt uncomfortable, as if she was being watched, and told the front desk not to give out her information. It wasn't the first time this had happened and why she didn't usually leave home. She was considering canceling her appearance at the parade."

"She was?" Brandy said, surprised. "Why didn't she tell me that? I could have helped her find somewhere safe."

"Did she call the police?" Charlene asked.

"I don't know. I just know that somehow, someone sent her a letter." Margret's eyes widened with fear. "On Hawthorne Hotel stationery. It was in her room when she returned from a party on Saturday. She left right after that and went to the Waterway."

"I can't believe it." Brandy wore a worried expression.

Margret checked her watch as she shuffled her feet.

"Can you find out why the maid was fired?" Charlene asked.

She scrunched her nose.

"Please, babe?" Bobby asked.

"I'll try." Margret stepped closer to Bobby. "For you."

"Thank you!" Bobby allowed their arms to brush.

"I have to go. Good luck." Margret kissed Bobby with full tongue and then hurried out of the meeting room.

"She's a doll," Brandy declared. "I just don't know what to do with that information." Her phone dinged and she read the text message. "Alannah, and Ned, will meet us at the bar."

"I could use a double," Bobby said. "Someone was stalking my idol. All I cared about when I was in Trinity's room at the Waterway was getting her to like the new design. I didn't hurt her!"

Charlene was chilled by what they'd learned just now. "Tell me again how you got in to speak with her?"

"I followed her after her breakfast. I kinda shouldered my way in." Bobby headed across the lobby to the bar. "I think she was already scared."

Of Alannah, or her fans? Bobby? Grant? Ariel?

Bottom line, Trinity had been right to be afraid, for her life.

CHAPTER 22

"I did not hurt Trinity. She crucified my new design, made snarky comments about Brandy, and kicked me out," Bobby said, repeating his story as they crossed into the bar.

Charlene recalled that Grant had also sent a note to Trinity here. She'd seen Hawthorne stationery beneath Trinity's body at the Waterway. His home was less than a mile from either hotel. Could Grant somehow have snuck into Trinity's room, desperate to make amends with his daughter? Had the idea of seeing her father again scared her into leaving recklessly?

It was a Thursday evening and hopping with summer tourists as well as locals.

Brandy beelined for a table by the window just as a few folks were departing. As they passed, Charlene saw Grant and Michael sharing a meal. They were intent on their dinners, so Charlene didn't interrupt them. Michael was staying at the

Hawthorne and would be leaving for LA on Sunday to continue writing his biography of Trinity. It would be a legacy project now for Grant.

She kept sneaking glances over her shoulder at the older gentleman waiting for some kind of sign that he was innocent. Why hadn't he gone to LA to bring back his family? Or stayed in California to be with them?

The table only had four chairs, so Brandy grabbed a fifth and stuck it at the end.

"Why is Ned coming?" Bobby asked with a sneer.

"Alannah insisted." Brandy tucked the chair close and scanned the bar. "We're having a predinner cocktail, my treat."

Charlene shared Bobby's scowl at Brandy. She wasn't looking forward to Alannah *and* Ned—one at a time she could probably handle more so than both. But it was why they'd arrived at the Hawthorne in the first place. They had to find out what Alannah knew about the note in Trinity's room on Saturday. Had it been the same one that Charlene had seen at the Waterway on Sunday? Who was the author of said note?

"What's the plan?" Bobby plopped down on a chair close to the wall, Brandy opposite him.

"Discover whether or not Alannah sent the letter to Trinity," Charlene said. She sat next to Brandy, leaving the other two seats for Alannah and Ned.

"Like she'd tell us if she did." Bobby's phone dinged a text. "Margret says that the maid was fired for talking about Trinity to one of Alannah's fans. The maid was Team Alannah. Also, the maid put the letter on the table—it was outside the door when she went in to clean, so now that mystery is solved."

Charlene nodded. "Part of it anyway. We still need to know if Alannah wrote it. And what it said."

"Right. Here she is now so we can ask her." Brandy lifted her fingers in a regal wave that would do any star proud.

Alannah turned heads in her sleek cocktail dress, which left little to the imagination. She was way out of Ned's league, but he was right there to pull out her chair and park himself next to her.

"Charlene! I didn't know I'd have the dubious pleasure of seeing *you* again," Alannah drawled.

Brandy placed her hand on Charlene's shoulder to keep Charlene from responding. How did Brandy keep her cool? She might need to try some of that sage too, to clear the negative energy.

A waiter came by as if summoned. "Are you ready to order?"

"Drinks all around," Brandy said. "I'll take the bill."

They ordered, Alannah, Bobby, and Ned all choosing top-shelf cocktails, and the waiter left.

"We can't stay long," Alannah said. "Our dinner reservation at Turner's Seafood is at seven and I want a tour beforehand to see if I can find a ghost."

Ned smacked his palm to his knee. "Ah, poor Bridget Bishop, unjustly executed for witchcraft. Unlike someone else at this table."

Brandy spoke before anyone could comment on the Flint family's religious beliefs. "Do you believe in ghosts, Alannah?"

"Absolutely." Alannah looked around with wide eyes. "You think Trinity will haunt this place?"

"Why here? She was killed at the Waterway," Ned said. "If that's how it works. I thought I saw Bridget once." He leaned in. "I smelled apples from the orchard she used to have."

Charlene hadn't smelled or seen anything when she'd eaten there—beyond the amazing seafood.

"Trinity left here because she felt like she was being stalked. This isn't the first time it's happened to her." Brandy rested her forearm on the table. "Did you leave her a note, threatening her?"

"Ah," Alannah said. "So, this is the reason for the drink. I'm glad I got top shelf."

The drinks arrived and the waiter passed them out.

"Alannah and I were with her fans all morning. Just like I told the cops," Ned said. "We have witnesses coming out the wazoo."

Ned did not appear the least bit worried. Neither did Alannah.

"Did you send her a note of any kind?" Charlene persisted. "Like a, 'hey, let's get together for drinks and settle the feud'?"

"I did not." Alannah batted those long lashes. "I had no hard feelings against Trinity." Her body thrummed with excitement. "My agent seriously just called me a half hour ago and I've got an appointment with the producer for *Sirena 2.*"

"Trinity's talent agency said that she had a contract," Charlene said. "I read an article in the *LA Star.*"

Alannah's brow rose. "Impressive dirt digging.

Actually, she did have the part over me, but now, well, the script is ready and so am I. It will be an easy million in the bank." She sat back and Ned hovered just right.

Charlene sipped her drink. The only reason Alannah had gotten the part was that Trinity was dead.

Alannah cradled her cocktail between her palms. "I might even forgive Salem for being so dull and come back for your parade next year, Brandy."

"How wonderful!" Brandy said. She kicked Charlene beneath the table, out of sight of Alannah. "And congratulations. To your new movie!" she cheered, as did Ned and Bobby. Charlene politely clapped.

Grant looked over at them in confusion and then got up. Michael held his arm, but Grant shook it off. His face was worn with grief as he joined them, accidentally bumping into Ned's chair. "What are you celebrating?"

Alannah braced herself, recognizing Trinity's dad from Sunday night.

"She's got the sequel to *Sirena*, old man," Ned said. "Sit down. Mind your own business."

At that, Michael rose quickly from his seat, as if to step between Ned and Grant. He reached the table out of breath. He was a large man, prepared to defend Grant.

Grant said, "That part will always be Trinity's, no matter how many times you try, Alannah."

"You have the sequel?" Michael asked.

"I do. You can add that to her biography," Ned said. " 'Trinity: Didn't get the role.' "

"Because someone killed her, idiot." Bobby shoved Ned's chair. Ned's face turned crimson, and he formed a fist.

Charlene's nape tingled as she realized that it was about to get ugly. Angry at the display, she remembered her pepper spray and stood to glare at Ned, Grant, and Bobby, her purse behind her if she needed it.

"Let's not make a scene. Trinity is an icon. Nothing will change that," Charlene told Grant. She nudged him toward Michael, who nodded and escorted the older man to their table. Grant had muscles. Large hands. And lots of guilt.

Ned and Bobby both took their seats, so Charlene did, too, her body shaking with adrenaline.

"Brandy, I didn't send Trinity a note. I wanted to mend the feud, but she ghosted me via email and phone calls." Alannah sipped her drink. "I'm willing to let this all be water under the bridge for next year and the parade."

Charlene didn't trust the actress as far as the front door. "Why?"

"I like your style, Charlene. Because my agent told me to be nice." Alannah drained her cocktail and placed it on the table. "Now, let's go, Ned. I'm ready for a good scare before our dinner."

They left. Charlene looked at Brandy with a question. Should they invite Alannah back to Salem? Would it boost the parade, which would help the town bring in tourist dollars? Alannah had slept with Tony Cortes, Brandy's politician boyfriend. It was obvious that Tony hadn't mentioned Brandy or Alannah wouldn't have been so smooth just now. That had to hurt Brandy, even if she and Tony were casual.

Bobby stood. "So, I'm gonna split too. Did we discover anything that will find the real killer?"

Before Charlene could answer, Grant was back, his expression as hangdog as they come. "I'm sorry to have intruded on your get-together. My emotions are all over the place."

"No worries," Bobby said. He took advantage of Brandy's distraction, nodded at them all, and left.

"Have a seat, Grant," Charlene said. "We suddenly have plenty." She looked to their table to invite Michael too, but he was gone.

"Michael had some work to do on Trinity's biography. He offered to pause the project, but I feel like it's more important to be written now than ever." Grant sat where Ned had been. "This whole fan thing is beyond me. I liked the Beatles *and* the Stones. I wouldn't take part in a deadly feud over it."

Charlene didn't want Grant to be a killer. She liked him. In the past, that hadn't always provided a clear lens.

Brandy wrapped a napkin around the base of her cocktail. "I agree with you, but we've witnessed firsthand how crazy people can be for their favorite."

A piece of paper slipped from Grant's pocket. It was a note, written on the Hawthorne Hotel stationery.

Charlene sucked in a breath and met his eyes. He put it back in his pocket without a show of alarm. Could he have been the reason the maid was fired?

She had to know. "Grant . . . did you come to the Hawthorne on Saturday?"

His cheeks flamed brick-red. "Yes. I just wanted to see my daughter. It's my fault she moved from here to the Waterway. My fault she was killed."

"Grant . . ." Charlene couldn't look away from his large hands. Trinity had been choked to death.

"I didn't do it, but I might as well have." Grant rose shakily and left the bar, passing through the lobby and knocking into people like a pinball.

Charlene murmured to Brandy, "He had the hotel stationery in his pocket."

Brandy hummed and stirred her ice with the small paper straw. "He lives just down the street from here. He might have picked it up anytime he stopped in for a coffee or a drink. Food. It doesn't mean anything."

"I like him." Charlene sighed.

"Me too. Either there is something wrong with both of our radar or he's innocent." Brandy wiped condensation from her now-empty glass.

"Let's go with that."

Charlene's phone dinged. A message from Sam, asking to meet for dinner at their place. Her body thrilled with excitement.

"Brandy, do you mind if I catch up with you later?"

A smile flickered around Brandy's full lips. "There is only one thing that puts the sparkle in your eye like that, and it's a certain detective."

"We're just friends." Charlene folded her hands demurely, her stomach fluttering with anticipation.

Brandy laughed. "Okay. You can be the mistress

of self-delusion all you like. I'm going to let Tony off the hook. He's been calling nonstop. If he's honest about Alannah, then we'll see. If he lies, then he's out, and we can scratch the parade from the New Business agenda."

She stood and the friends left the bar, saying goodbye on the sidewalk. Charlene caught an Uber to the tavern.

Her hunky detective waited for her outside, broad shoulders stretching a blue, button-up shirt rolled at the wrists. "You didn't drive?" Sam asked in confusion. Khakis, boots. Belt with a badge.

Charlene shouldered her purse, glad they were in the parking lot. She didn't want to ruin their romantic meal with the case. "I was with Brandy at the Hawthorne when I got your message. The police," Office Jimenez, "are hounding Bobby and she wants my help."

Sam studied her and gave a rueful chuckle. "How can I repay such honesty?"

"Leave Bobby alone?" Charlene suggested. "He didn't do it." She surveyed the pavement, not feeling good. "This is awkward, isn't it?"

He led her to a bench to the right of the restaurant, under a shady tree. It was private, secluded. Only the two of them. Her body warmed just being near Sam.

"Here's an idea. When we go inside, it's about you and me. Just personal stuff. If there are ever other things, then let's talk out here, okay?" Sam held out his arm as if he was the most accommodating man ever.

"That's fair." And it meant that he wanted to see her. Could that mean he'd decided to skip Portland, Oregon? They sat on either side of the wooden bench, facing each other.

Sam speculatively rubbed his mustache as she shared what she'd learned about Alannah, and Bobby, wondering if the letter beneath Trinity was the same as what was left at the Hawthorne. She didn't give up Margret's name.

When she finished, Charlene felt better. Sam gave a single nod and remained silent, as if thinking.

"Well?" She curled her fingers together, trying to be patient.

"Well . . . I can tell you that Bobby is less of a person of interest than he was. I'd love an alibi, but if he's telling the truth, then it's not likely he would have the time. Also, he's not on the security camera anymore that day."

Charlene nodded.

"Grant Powers as next of kin would inherit, but the property was in arrears," Sam said. "Trinity was in debt. Could be why she accepted the sequel. We've learned from several sources that she felt like she was being stalked, so there was a reason she didn't leave her home often."

"I heard that from her agency as well as our source at the Hawthorne Hotel." Charlene loved it when she and Sam could brainstorm together. "Did you talk to Lorianna Benjamin?"

"I did. The prescription bottle at the Waterway aligns with the new meds her agent said she was taking." Sam smoothed his mustache. "Now, this is public record, but let me add it to the mix. Mary Clarkson had a restraining order on file against her from a prior boyfriend."

"Sweet Mary!" Charlene was truly shocked because the maid at the Waterway had been soft-spoken, kind, and not at all violent.

"You can't like everybody, Charlene," Sam said with exasperation. "It expired a few years ago, but still . . ." He held her gaze. "Mary Clarkson is a super Trinity fan, and her poster was a collectible. It was found in a Dumpster behind the Waterway."

"It was? So, whoever stole it from her didn't want to keep it." Charlene considered that odd. "Does that make them a fan or not? Or maybe because it was ripped, they no longer considered it valuable?"

"It was ripped?" Sam straightened, as if jerked by a string.

"Yes. Mary said she heard a ripping sound that happened when she struggled to hang on to it. It was yanked from her grasp."

Sam pulled his phone out of his pocket and shot off a text. "I don't believe the one at the station has a tear. Mary was positive it was torn?"

Charlene nodded. "Mary still wants it back because of the relationship between her mom and Trinity, which makes the poster extraspecial."

Sam looked longingly at the tavern, which emitted savory beef smells, then hit the microphone on his phone so he could record the information. "Start from the beginning of what Mary told you, do you mind?"

Charlene did, speaking close to the phone.

"Thanks." Sam sent it off to Officer Jimenez.

"I hope that helps." Charlene reached for his hand and squeezed.

Sam rubbed his thumb over her knuckles. "It might. Investigations are about gathering threads."

"Sam?"

"Charlene," he said at the same time as she said his name.

"You first," Sam said.

Charlene knew she had to be honest with him about this at least. He would never understand about Jack. "What are your thoughts about the promotion? Is it something to talk about here or inside?" She watched him closely. Would he choose Oregon as business or personal?

"An outside topic." Sam raised his warm brown gaze to hers. "There are pros and cons for going, of course."

Business. "Like?" This was a list she wanted to hear with all of her heart.

"It would be something new," he rumbled, his gaze intent on hers. "New can be fun."

"It can be." Charlene remained on her side of the bench. "What else are you thinking?"

"More money would be nice." Sam shrugged. "It's a decent raise. Not necessary, because I've put quite a bit toward retirement already. I haven't had much in the way of expenses."

Was he talking about a wife and family? She bit her lip to stop a grin. "Nope. Just you and Rover."

"My dog understands me completely." Sam scuffed the grass with the sole of his boot. "Rover could live a life of luxury anywhere in the world." He didn't release Charlene's gaze as he leaned closer to her. "I think she prefers Salem."

Charlene swallowed, her mouth dry. "I like that about your pup."

Sam smiled, and her insides melted. Somehow, she managed to say, "What are some cons about Oregon?"

"My biggest reason for turning down this promotion is because of a certain tall brunette with hazel eyes and a big heart."

Charlene scooted closer to him on the bench, unable to stay out of his orbit. "I know it's selfish of me, but I want you to stay too."

Sam's jaw relaxed just the tiniest bit with relief. "Why is that selfish?"

"Because." Charlene searched for the words to be as authentic as possible without pushing him toward the promotion there. "I don't want my life to change too much. I love the bed-and-breakfast I've created. Living there is important."

"I understand that." He shifted to peer at her with sheer Sam sultriness. "But I have my house. It's big enough for two. You could even bring Silva."

Move! Her body tightened with anxiety. "I am not ready for that. That's why I feel so selfish, wanting you to stay in Salem because of me."

"You want a long, drawn out . . . what?" Sam was guarded, but he didn't release her hand.

"I'm not sure." Her cheeks heated. Charlene knew what she was ready to explore with Sam beside her heart—away from the bed-and-breakfast. She could get to know . . . Rover, and Sam, in their element.

"What?" Sam's question was heavy with caution. He sounded worried.

Charlene peeked at him from behind a fall of hair. She hadn't been with anyone since Jared. Times had changed in the last twenty years. "What would you say to monogamous friends with benefits?"

Sam sat back abruptly. "Charlene Morris."

She sucked in a breath and tried to pull her hand free from his. She hadn't meant to upset him. She thought the option was worth exploring.

"Where on earth did you get an idea like that?" Sam's question held disappointment but also interest. Was his pulse racing like hers?

Maybe she hadn't quite pushed him away. Charlene lifted their clasped hands. Her palm was damp, her body aware of Sam's every breath. "It's no secret that I am very, very attracted to you. But I don't know about getting married again, or—" Her eyes filled with tears. Jared had been her soul mate.

It would feel like a final goodbye to be married to someone else. She couldn't go there. But she was willing to have a relationship with Sam, to be open to love. And passion.

Sam scooped her on his lap, holding her in his arms. He kissed her deeply, taking her breath away. She was not a petite woman, but six-foot-six Sam made her feel dainty. She relaxed against his chest. His heart pounded solidly, a reassuring sound. His shirt was soft, his muscles hard.

Sam smoothed back her hair and caressed her cheek. "I will take you however I can get you, Charlene. I'll let the Portland office know tomorrow." He kissed her once more and peered into her eyes, her skin electric from his touch. "What type of benefits?"

* * *

The rest of the evening passed in a dream and ended with a kiss. She didn't let Sam walk her up to the door when he dropped her off after dinner but waved from the porch. They'd agreed to keep their relationship out of the public eye, and she hoped Jack's ghostly one. For now, Sam was staying in Salem and she couldn't ask for more.

CHAPTER 23

Charlene sang in the shower, her heart light. Last night Jack hadn't been around, as happened sometimes, and she hoped to see him today. Avery would be home for dinner tonight and she couldn't wait.

As she brushed her teeth and applied moisturizer, she noticed a little redness around her mouth from Sam's luxurious mustache. She dabbed on concealer—good as new. She was no teenager sneaking out but a grown woman and laughed at the butterflies in her tummy.

Sam had agreed with her that it would be difficult for him at the department if they were in a relationship because of their previous adventures. It would be odd for Avery. Minnie would sing alleluia from the widow's walk.

Jack. Her best friend—she'd have to keep it a secret from him so that he would not be hurt. That took a little of the song from her heart, but not all. She left her bedroom to the living room.

Jack, so handsome, so thoughtful, sat in his arm-chair, watching a documentary on the rainforest. His thirst for knowledge was unquenchable.

"Morning, beautiful Charlene. How did it go yesterday at the Hawthorne? Did you speak with Alannah?"

"Hello, Jack." Charlene compartmentalized Sam to focus on Jack and quickly caught him up with everything but the romantic dinner with Sam. "We did—her and Ned." She rested her hip against the love seat. "I want to know more about Mary Clark-son. Sam told me Mary had a restraining order filed against her by an ex-boyfriend. What if she's not so innocent?"

Jack opened the computer on the desk against the wall. "Was her job at the Waterway to get close to Trinity?"

"It couldn't be. It was only months ago that Trinity had agreed to headline the parade for us. The actress was supposed to be at the Hawthorne." Charlene tried her best to be fair. "Could Mary have clocked herself over the head to make it appear like she was attacked?"

"Hard enough to need stitches?" Jack let the words draw out. "Where?"

Charlene showed him a spot at the back of her nape, then pushed herself from the love seat to walk toward Jack.

"I've seen stranger things in my years of prac-tice. Under normal circumstances, I would say no, but we're talking about a murder. . . ." He turned to the computer and pressed some more keys. "Check this out!"

Charlene's stomach clenched at the booking mug shot of Mary Clarkson, her eye black, her face young but worried. The maid didn't even look twenty. "She was hit very hard. Why is the order against her? Seems like it should be the other way around."

"She's not a hardened criminal," Jack observed. "Nothing else on her popped up. The restraining order expired after a year."

"Should I ask her about it?" Charlene said. "I can't fathom how to bring it up."

"It might've been an argument between lovers that spiraled out of control—that is, unfortunately, something I saw in my office too often. If Sam and the Salem PD already know about it, then I think you should leave it be."

"You're probably right. Thanks, my friend." She moved away from Jack and the computer to her phone on the coffee table. "I have a full agenda today with new guests. They'll be trickling in today, not like last week."

"You and Minnie managed beautifully." Jack appeared in his armchair without a flutter of the curtain. "By next year's parade, it will be flawless."

The murderer caught, she hoped. Charlene picked up the phone. No new messages. "All right— let's go make these vacationers' dreams come true."

"Might not want to mention Trinity."

Charlene nodded and left her suite, closing and locking her door behind her. Minnie turned from the kitchen counter and poured Charlene a cup of coffee, making it the light-cream color she preferred.

"Here you are!"

"Thanks. Minnie, what smells so good?" Friday mornings were normally a light food day.

"Avery likes my cinnamon bread with pecans, so I thought I'd make some for breakfast tomorrow. When will she be here?"

"Last I heard, this afternoon."

Minnie bustled around the kitchen with a cloth, swiping crumbs into her palm, then the trash. "I can't wait to hear how her first week of school went."

"I think we're all excited," Jack said, manifesting by the small rectangular table.

"Me too." Charlene sipped her coffee and made sure the volume was up on her phone. A lot was being juggled today, with her B-and-B and the unsolved mermaid case.

"The Wheatons just came down," Minnie said.

"I think I'll join them." Charlene brought her coffee to the dining room and sat at the end of the table. She had yogurt with fruit, as did Lottie. Terry opted for a toasted bagel, and Dillon was on his second bowl of cereal. Dillon was very interested in the witches and vampires, so they were thinking of coming for Halloween.

"We really do it up," Charlene said. "I once rented a van for the guests. Now, I'm booked this October already, but maybe next year?"

"Cool!" Dillon said.

The Wheatons left at ten thirty. As usual, Charlene felt a little sad. She and Minnie cleaned their suite, the only one left to do, and prepared the other suites for the new guests. Each basket in the guest room would have wine, water, chocolate, and some of Minnie's cookies. Brochures of local places with discounts, lotions, and shampoos. Kass Fortune's teas. Another touch besides the basket was the small flower arrangements on each desk.

She wanted their guests to feel pampered in this home away from home.

At eleven, the doorbell rang. She was expecting the Joneses or the Binghams, but it was Seth Gamble, Avery's boyfriend. Brown wavy hair, blue eyes, lanky physique. He held a gift bag and a bud vase with a single red rose.

"Hi!" Charlene opened the door to let him in. "Avery isn't here yet."

"I know." His cheeks turned bright red. "I just wanted to leave her something for a welcome-home gift. Can I put it outside her door?"

"That's sweet—of course."

He dashed up the flights of stairs as if they were nothing, thanks to being nineteen.

"All right—that's a romantic gesture," Charlene said to her housekeeper and Jack. Both were in the foyer with her.

"Smart boy," Minnie observed with a smile. "Let her know she's appreciated while she's away."

"She needs to focus on her studies," Jack said.

Charlene didn't argue. He was right, in theory, but there was also room for fun. It was a balance, like life. Seth left, and the next two hours passed in a flurry of new guests.

Doug and Bonnie Jones, from Seattle, Washington—in their fifties, on their anniversary trip to where they got married twenty-five years before.

The boutique hotel was no longer there, so Charlene had won them with her blog posts and pictures. They were in the gold room.

The Binghams, Forrest and Malina, in their seventies, retired professors from New York wanting to check out places of interest that they hadn't had time for before. Blue anchor for them.

The Kingstons, a family of four. Lex and Deeanne both worked with computers, and their two boys were ten and twelve. They were home-schooled, so when school started didn't matter. They were in the green room.

And in the pink suite with the view of the oak were the Dooleys, newlyweds from New Hampshire. The two singles were open and, of course, Avery had her own room.

Charlene loved a full house.

She was having such a wonderful time organizing and suggesting dinners and spots to check out that she shouldn't have been surprised to see a missed call from her mother. After making sure everyone knew they were invited for happy hour—a fun thing, not an obligation—she hurried to her suite. It was only two and she had time to chat.

"Mom! Saw that you called." They'd texted but hadn't talked since the parade and possibly before.

"Just wanted to know if they nabbed the mermaid killer," her mom said. Brenda Woodbridge loved true crime, from novels to shows. "Are you too busy?"

"I've got a few minutes. It's been a little hectic getting the new guests settled." Charlene relaxed on the love seat. The air was warm in her suite, which meant Jack wasn't around. "They haven't found who is responsible yet."

"Sam will catch the murderer," her mother declared with all certainty. She liked Sam a lot.

"He will," Charlene agreed. "Did you ever see the movies?"

"Your dad and I watched the *Million Dollar Mermaid* with Esther Williams. She was incredible. Trinity Powers was just as lovely. Saw the remake too. Not sure I cared for that one as much, but your dad liked all the tail-shaking." Her mom sniffed. "I don't think shimmying your hips equals talent."

Mom could be a Team Trinity fan. "Well, it doesn't matter now. Alannah just got offered the sequel to *Sirena,* which they're finally doing. Trinity had accepted the part, but now she's dead, so Alannah wins by default."

"Hmm. Could Alannah be the knife?"

Charlene chuckled at her mom's use of slang. God knew where she'd picked it up. "I don't think so. She has an alibi for the time that Trinity was killed. I'd wondered too."

"Alannah's costar was much sexier than Trinity's, so it had that going too. Will he be in this next movie?"

"Mom!" What did her mother care about sexy? Charlene blocked it from her mind. "How is Dad?" He'd be Team Alannah.

"How would I know? He spends all his time with his nose in a book. We used to actually go to the movies and have dates. After seventy, the romance is gone."

Charlene's belly clenched. What was going on in Chicago? Last she'd heard, there had been an effort made toward having fun together. Come to think of it, in the last few conversations, her dad hadn't been around. "Are you playing cards with your group of ladies?"

"Sure am. Just because your dad wants to stay home doesn't mean I have to. Annabeth said that we aren't getting any younger."

Annabeth, a friend of her mother's from their church, had been behind Mom's changes toward kindness. Her mom wanted to move to Salem to be close, but her dad wasn't ready to leave Chicago. He was dragging his feet for Charlene's sake as well.

"Be nice to Dad, okay? Give him my love."

"Ha! And what about me?"

"I love you, Mom." Charlene ended the call.

Her senses were on high alert that something was not right in her parents' world. She put her feet up on the coffee table. What could be going on?

"Any update on the move?" Jack asked from behind her.

Charlene squealed and dropped her phone to the floor.

"Sorry. Let me." Jack levitated it to her in swoops and swirls.

"Thanks." Charlene snagged it from the air, much like Silva did when Jack played with her and her cat toys. "And no. I hope that Dad keeps distracting her. We're getting along so well that I'm terrified it will change if we're in the same zip code." She sighed. "Something sounds off."

"I don't blame you for being leery," Jack said. "Does a leopard change its spots?"

Charlene shot to her feet in alarm. "Mama Leopard better maintain. I can't go back to the way things were." Growing up, she'd developed a shield against her mom's criticisms of everything from her style in clothes to how she played soccer.

She stretched the crick in her neck from standing so fast, her mind returning to Grant and, of course, Trinity. "Jack, I keep thinking about Mary. Someone wanted Mary's signed poster. From her descriptions of it, it was different from the others. Maybe there's something to that?"

"Let's look online!" Jack said. "The more precise we can be in the search engine the better. Try marketing materials for *Sirena*."

She sat at her desk, opened her laptop, and typed in the phrase, followed by the year the original movie was released. The images that showed were what they'd already seen. "These are all the same, with Trinity as the focus. Poor guy."

"She's so lovely," Jack said with admiration. "It's a shame that her time on earth was cut so short."

Charlene studied the star's violet eyes and porcelain skin, her sable-dark hair. "Mom asked if Alannah could be the killer after I shared about her getting the sequel. With Trinity dead, she's the only option for the studio."

"She's sharp, your mother," Jack said.

"True." Charlene made a mental note to check

in with her dad without her mother on the line. "It's only two thirty. We should dig around for gossip regarding Trinity. I was thinking of the *LA Star,* which posted the article with her obituary."

"Okay." Jack rubbed his jaw. "Why?"

"The agency mentioned two accidents while they'd attempted the sequel and so Trinity stopped production."

"Were they accidents?" Jack mused.

"Exactly what Grant wondered." Charlene gazed at Jack in perfect accord. "Trinity was terrified to leave her home. Maybe gossip around that time will give us a direction. Social media wasn't a thing but mags like *LA Star* and the *National Enquirer* might have the scoop."

"Tabloids that paid for juicy details," Jack said. "Good thinking."

Charlene grabbed her notepad and pen, gesturing Jack toward the office chair and laptop as she resumed her position on the love seat. "You're faster than me."

"I have my ways." Jack flexed his fingers.

Smiling at his dramatic flair, Charlene said, "I'll write down the suspects. The police are focused on Bobby. He says he's innocent and the tea leaves back it up. I think so too." She jotted his name, then added Alannah, Dom, and Ned, sliding a line through them. "The fans vouch for seeing Alannah, Dom, and Ned during the morning."

Jack glanced at her over his shoulder. "Is Mary on the list?"

She grumbled but included the maid. "And Grant. Even though I don't think he did it."

"What about Ariel?"

"Maybe." She wrote down the fan club president/ wrestler's name. Who else?

"Bingo!" Jack called. She looked up from her pad. "I found this little tidbit—hang on, let me zoom in."

Charlene tossed her pad and pen to the cushion and stood to see the screen. "What?"

"Shall I read it?" Jack cleared his throat for effect. " 'Two accidents on the set of *Sirena 2* is enough for Trinity Powers. According to news around the water cooler, she's told her agent that she won't work with Mickey anymore.' "

"Mickey?"

"Must be her costar," Jack said. "I wonder if he was injured too?"

"Does it say more?"

"No."

"Dang it!" Charlene sighed. "Let me call the agency. Maybe they know exactly what happened on the set."

"Great idea," Jack said.

Charlene looked up the talent agency and asked for Ms. Benjamin.

"Lorianna Benjamin here!"

Charlene perched on the arm of the love seat, her phone on Speaker so Jack could hear. "Hi! I'm Charlene Morris. I'm the coordinator for the Mermaid Parade here in Salem."

"You sound official," Jack said approvingly.

"Yes?" Ms. Benjamin said.

"Could you tell me more about why Trinity quit

working in the water films? Specifically, *Sirena 2*, about twenty years ago."

"What does that have to do with the parade?" Ms. Benjamin replied.

"Well . . ."

Jack roared with laughter. "You got caught being nosy."

Charlene ignored her ghost and pivoted. "It doesn't. I'm wondering if it will affect the new *Sirena 2*, with Alannah Gomez? I've heard that the set is . . ."

"Cursed?" the agent filled in. "Oh, please, dear. If it is, so be it. I've made my money off the film. Alannah will too. It's a tragedy that Trinity died, but the show must go on."

Cursed? Goose bumps tickled her skin. "I read that Trinity refused to work with Mickey. Why was that?"

"Darling, I will tell you the same thing I've told other news folks about Trinity and Mickey. They had a love affair for the studio, and it didn't go beyond that. She didn't need his star power, and so the producers cut his part. Happens all the time in Hollywood."

The agent hung up as Charlene said, "Thank you for your time."

Jack laughed some more. "Well," he conceded, "we learned that the set might have been cursed or not, but the movie made money. Why was Trinity broke?"

"Her other two movies tanked, so she only had one that was generating income. Alannah being the star of the remake might be a threat to that money."

"But even twenty-five years later, Trinity's beauty and grace were such that the studio was going to star her in the sequel as their first choice," Jack said.

"Charlene?"

Charlene and Jack exchanged grins. "Avery!"

Avery being home was all that mattered for the rest of the evening.

CHAPTER 24

Charlene sat at the head of the dining table Saturday morning, very excited that Avery was at her right and *accepting* that Seth was on Avery's other side.

Jack was more alarmed about it than Charlene. Seth hadn't spent the night but had left late and then come back this morning. Nothing inappropriate was happening, and their ghostly protector needed to relax. Avery was an adult.

Charlene loved this part of getting to know her guests for the week and didn't imagine that it would ever get old. The Binghams were already out, but the other three families were enjoying their meals.

"More coffee?" Minnie asked, bringing the carafe around the table.

Seth and Avery both held out their cups. "Yes, please!"

College had changed Avery from drinking fancy

designer coffee to the hard stuff, sweetened and with cream.

"I'm going over to Seth's today to say hi to Dani, all right?" Avery said.

"Sure!" It wasn't like she was chained to the B&B. "Go out, have fun! When are you headed back to Boston?"

"Tomorrow afternoon. Can you believe we already have tests?" Avery shivered. Her caramel hair was in two braids on either side of her face, there was a delicate spider tattoo on her nape, and she had at least six bracelets on her wrist. Tank top and denim coveralls. Adorable.

"You will be fine. You're smart." Charlene smiled at Avery with encouragement. "And you have self-discipline, which a lot of kids lack. Gives you an edge."

"I also want to see Sam," Avery continued. "Will he be at the station today?"

"I don't know." Charlene could feel Jack's gaze on her and kept her expression neutral.

"Officer Bernard too. He's the coolest."

Avery was getting her degree in criminology to be a detective in Salem. Charlene had no doubt that her girl would kick ass and take names in whatever she wanted to do.

She was also a reason that Charlene wouldn't leave the bed-and-breakfast. It was Avery's home as well as hers, and Jack's.

They'd created a family of sorts—not a traditional one, but she didn't mind at all. It was perfect. If only Sam could be here too. Maybe someday in the future, but not a problem she was willing to tackle this beautiful late-summer morning.

"What are you doing today?" Avery asked.

"I'm going to see Grant Powers and check out his poster memorabilia for his daughter. I've sent a text to Mary Clarkson to meet me there around noon if she can." Charlene checked her watch. It was only nine.

"I'll make up a box of goodies for him," Minnie said.

"Thank you!"

"These blueberry muffins are the best," Bonnie Jones said. Her husband, Doug, had his mouth full, so he nodded.

"My favorite is this cinnamon pecan bread," Avery said. "Thanks, Minnie!"

The housekeeper smiled sweetly. "I'll make up a box for you too, love, before you go tomorrow. Studying is hard work."

"Do you any questions about activities for the day?" Charlene asked her guests. "Salem has so many options that it's hard to decide." She was proud of her adopted city. While property crime was high, violent crime was low, despite what had just happened to Trinity.

"We're going to the Peabody Essex Museum," Deeanne Kingston said. Her sons were on either side of her, carbon copies with blond hair and green eyes. "Is a morning long enough to schedule?"

"There is so much to do," Charlene said, "that I

still haven't managed it all. It depends on what your interests are."

"I want to see the ship at the wharf," Doug said after swallowing his bite of a blueberry muffin.

"The *Friendship* of Salem is great! It's a replica of a sloop from 1797 and also a museum," Charlene said. "I love that area. The Custom House Museum has a lot of information from Salem's glory days."

"That sounds fun!" Katya Dooley said. She and her husband, Emmet, were shoulder to shoulder next to each other. An aura of love pulsed around them.

"We want to see the House of the Seven Gables," Lex said as he drank his coffee. "Is it haunted?" The boys, twelve and fourteen, pumped their fists with excitement.

"I have a friend who believes that many buildings in Salem are haunted—just because the city is so old." *Many friends, actually,* Charlene silently amended.

"Scary ghosts?" Deeanne asked.

"None that I know of, but if you like that kind of thing, Kevin Hughes offers paranormal tours of the cemetery." The boys would eat it up. "His number is in the basket you were given upstairs."

"I definitely want to do that," Lex said.

"Have you seen a ghost at the cemetery?" Deeanne asked.

Jack laughed from his position by the sideboard. "Go ahead, Charlene. Have you seen a ghost?"

"At the cemetery? No," Charlene answered truthfully. She sipped her coffee and fielded questions about Salem. Jack danced behind the Joneses, the Dooleys, and the Kingstons, trying to make Charlene respond, but she was firm and didn't fall for his jokes.

At ten, everyone was out the door for their adventures, even Seth and Avery. Jack disappeared before she could scold him.

Charlene and Minnie cleaned the dining room, and Minnie made up a box for Grant with some of the leftover pastries.

"Thanks, Minnie. I'm about ready to go. Do you need anything while I'm out?"

"Nope. Did you see that Avery had two pieces of cinnamon pecan bread?" The housekeeper smoothed her apron over her round hip. "I just love to feed people."

"I'm glad! I just love to eat." Chuckling, Charlene brought a glass of water to her suite.

Jack sat at her computer, pictures of male movie stars on the screen.

"Don't be mad, Charlene," Jack said when he saw her expression. "I was just teasing. And I've been reading everything I can about Trinity Powers, curses, and her costars. None of them went on to great fame. Mickey Bee didn't do any more work in film."

She read the IMDb page. Mickey Bee, slim, with dark hair and a strong profile, white teeth, and a dimple, never did more after *Sirena*. Was that because of Trinity?

Her phone dinged a text from Mary that she could meet Charlene at Grant's. Officer Jimenez had dropped by Mary's apartment with the poster found in the Dumpster. It wasn't ripped and wasn't the right one.

"I think it's important." Charlene read the text to Jack. "Why steal it? It must hold a clue as to who the killer is. I hope Grant has a copy in his collection that Mary can identify."

Mary was downtown already and could be there in a few minutes. It was noon. She sent a text for a quarter after twelve.

"Be careful," Jack said. "You want Grant to be innocent, but the evidence doesn't necessarily support that."

"I know. I have my pepper spray." Charlene shouldered her purse. "Got my phone. I should be home in time for happy hour."

"Maybe you should ask Sam to join you?" Jack suggested.

That meant Jack was concerned, if he wanted her to bring Sam. She shook her head. "That would change the dynamic I've already established with Grant."

"You're right." Jack paced before the TV, restless that he couldn't go with her.

"I think you should keep digging about her costars and the curse. Mickey Bee was with her in *Sirena*, but what about the other two movies she did?" She had a hunch that they were connected somehow.

"There's not much to find, but I'll keep at it," Jack said. "I'll worry until you get back."

"See you later, Jack!"

She grabbed the box of treats on the way out, chatting with Minnie about the menu for the upcoming week. The housekeeper dusted the living room while Silva pretended to pounce on Minnie's shoelaces. What a cat.

Charlene was in the car when Sam called.

"Hey!"

"How are you?" Sam asked. "How's Avery?"

"Wonderful. It's great to have her home, but she's with Seth, saying hi to Dani this morning. I think she plans to stop at the station to see you and Officer Bernard too."

"Great. Just wanted to let you know that you were right about the poster. It wasn't the same one. Good recall on the tear."

Charlene warmed at his consideration—it hadn't always been this way. "Mary texted me. We're meeting at Grant's at quarter past. I'm running late, but not too bad considering we had a full house this morning."

"You're going to Grant Powers's home, a person of interest in his daughter's murder?" Sam's cordial tone disappeared.

"Since when?" Charlene's nape tingled. "I thought you guys were after Bobby."

"'You guys'?" Sam sounded offended.

"You know what I mean." She smiled to herself. *Them versus us.*

"Yeah. Any chance you can sneak away for a cup of chowder afterward?"

"At our place?" Her heart trilled with anticipation.

"Yes." Sam's voice rumbled. "I'd love to see you."

"I'll be there." She couldn't wait to look into his eyes, to taste his kiss, to feel his arms around her . . .

"Send me Grant's address, will you?"

She snapped out of her little daydream. "Okay, but don't show up. We get along very well, considering." He might be a killer. It didn't feel right.

"I'm glad that Mary will be there too. Let me know how it's going."

"I'll text you when I'm ready to leave. Are you at the station?" It was downtown, as Grant's town house was. All within walking distance of a mile or so.

"Yes," Sam said. "I don't like this."

He had an intuition of his own, though he denied it, Charlene thought. She rounded the Common. "I'm here. See you later—don't be such a worrier."

"It's my job to keep people safe. You, sweet Charlene, make that especially challenging. Why is that?"

"Because of my big heart?" She kept her words sassy.

Sam laughed. He'd told her more than once that she went with her feelings rather than her head.

They were figuring it out. She guessed they would never have a "normal" relationship, but that was all right. She'd had that before, and this with Sam would be something that couldn't compare with Jared. It was best that way.

Charlene parked on a side street and picked up the box of pastries for Grant that Minnie had packed. Slinging her purse over her shoulder, she breathed in the summer air. Three years ago, she never could have imagined being here and yet . . . taking a chance, she was happy.

She wished that for Barb Martin.

The Hawthorne Hotel was across the park, the hotel famous for many reasons. It was supposed to be haunted, but she'd never seen a ghost there. The oldest maritime business still operated on the top floor.

Grant, who had worked at the museum until his retirement, had been so enamored of the conch shell he'd found connected with the mermaid legend from an old sailor that he'd taught it to his daughter, who had become a famous mermaid through *Sirena*.

It was as magical in its own way as Brandy's witch powers.

What had happened to Trinity so long ago during filming that she'd pulled out of the movie and become a recluse? Were they accidents, or attempts on her life? Her agent said they'd never found proof.

Charlene crossed the sidewalk to Grant's town house, walked up the stairs, and knocked. She was fifteen minutes late. Where was Mary? She'd thought the young woman would wait for her outside. No reply.

She knocked again. Maybe Grant and Mary were catching up talking or upstairs and didn't hear her knock.

Charlene sent Mary a text.

No answer.

She pounded harder on the door, and at last Michael answered.

He was harried, his cheeks ruddy. "Charlene!"

"Hi! I'm here to see Grant," she said with a relieved smile. "I'd also arranged to meet a friend. Is Mary already here?"

"Uh . . . no," he said. "Don't know a Mary. Grant's out for a bit."

And he'd left Michael at home without him? Maybe they were closer friends than she'd thought.

A muffled sound from upstairs made her hair rise on her nape. She stepped back.

"You just couldn't listen." Michael roughly urged her into the hall and away from the door, then locked it behind her.

"Hey!" She almost dropped the pastries and juggled her purse and the box. She was alarmed by Michael's complexion. "Is everything all right? Who is upstairs?"

"Grant. He's fine." Michael walked her toward the kitchen the way Silva did a wayward mouse. Charlene didn't like it.

He grabbed the pastry box and tossed it on the table, on top of his manuscript papers. A pen. A Hawthorne Hotel stationery pad.

Charlene sucked in a breath and stared at Michael closely. She recalled the original *Sirena* movie, how beautiful Trinity had overshadowed her handsome costar, Mickey Bee.

He'd aged terribly and had gained a hundred pounds, which changed the shape of his face and body, but the nose was the same as in the IMDb photo.

"Mickey?"

He raked his hand through his hair. "Michael.

Mickey was a stupid stage name chosen by the producers. Michael Brown was "boring," so they changed it to Mickey Bee. I hated it then and still do. Michael Brown, they said, was dull. I couldn't compare to Trinity."

"You killed Trinity." Charlene's body hummed with adrenaline. She couldn't believe how close he'd been the whole time. If only she and Jack had spent more time following the thread of the co-stars, she might have recognized Michael sooner.

He didn't say anything—just stared at her with dislike. Her stomach clenched with fear as she heard more muffled noises coming from upstairs.

"Where is Grant? Is Mary here?" From the kitchen, Charlene looked toward the hall and the front door. The other exit was from the garage, not here. She sidestepped around the table.

Michael shoved it so she was pinned to the shelves behind her. Her purse slid down her shoulder and she tightened her grip on her cell phone.

"Let me go!"

"I can't do that, Charlene."

She pressed numbers on her cell, but the key-pad was locked. Michael reached across the table, grabbed her phone, and tossed it toward the stove.

There had to be an easier way! She plopped her purse onto the tabletop and searched her side pocket for the pepper spray. Michael overpowered her, flinging both purse and spray after the phone.

Well, she was far from defenseless. This was not her first rodeo. She could keep him talking and appeal to their shared humanity.

"Why hurt Grant?"

Michael didn't answer.

"Or Mary? Please, let us all go."

Michael ground his back teeth together. His gaze was intense, his tone as mesmerizing as a snake charmer's. "Just relax. You are going to die like the others." He leaned his considerable weight against the table, which cut into her thighs. "You have nobody to blame but yourself."

CHAPTER 25

Charlene twisted her body but couldn't free herself from Michael's weight pressed against the table. She reached to the shelves behind her and grabbed one of the photos, throwing it at Michael.

The wood frame hit him in the eye. Michael cursed and released the pressure enough that Charlene pushed the table and raced around it toward the hall. She was worried about Grant and Mary but knew she had to get outside and call for help.

Letting him take her upstairs would be a bad idea. Michael managed to clutch her hair, and she winced as it pulled her scalp. "Hey!"

Michael wound her hair around his hand to bring them face-to-face. Her eyes smarted with tears. "You're not going anywhere."

Charlene struggled for her life. He raised a fist. She tried to duck out of the way, but he clocked her in the temple. She smacked into the wall and slid down it.

* * *

When she came to, she was being tied to a chair in the Trinity shrine. She flexed her wrists and struggled against the rope. Sam would realize when she didn't text or meet him at their place that she was in trouble. He thought Grant was the murderer, so there was a better than high chance that he would come here looking for her.

Charlene had to buy time. She scanned the room and saw both Grant and Mary tied to chairs as well. Grant had partial tape over his mouth, but Mary didn't. Charlene must have interrupted him. "Why?" she asked, her head pounding.

Michael finished securing her wrists behind her, then stepped back as if to admire his handiwork, the three of them in a row on kitchen chairs he'd dragged upstairs.

Michael had taped the stolen, ripped movie poster, twenty-by-forty, over the center *Sirena* poster. To steal Trinity's spotlight? The image was of the couple sitting together on the conch shell, equals.

"Quiet. I need to think."

Grant spit the tape aside. "He fooled me. I had no idea who he was, but Mary—she'd paid attention to the Josh character. She recognized him despite his weight gain. Called him Mickey Bee."

"It was his profile." Mary's voice was thick with fear. "His dimple. I want to go home. I never want to see the movie *Sirena* again."

"Charlene, are you all right?" Grant asked.

She was glad that Grant wasn't a killer. "Yes. I was worried it was you who murdered Trinity. I didn't even consider that Michael might be guilty."

He'd been around to "help" Grant the entire time.

"I'm very good at blending in," Michael said. "It's an art, and part of why I would have made a great actor if Trinity hadn't accused me of causing the accidents on the set."

"Did you try to kill her back then?" Grant asked, horrified.

Michael gave a twisted grin. "It wasn't my intention to kill her. Not at first. I liked her fear, the power I had over her. She was right to be afraid. In LA, I've been Trinity's driver, her gardener, her checkout clerk at the grocery store."

Charlene shivered. "You were her stalker."

"No," Michael clarified. "I loved her. I was her number one fan."

Mary sniffled. "You weren't. If you loved her, you wouldn't have hurt her. Why did you do that?"

Michael paced the room. "It was vengeance for her dropping me like I didn't matter. I did matter. I was as good an actor as she was on land, but in the water, she was all things graceful. I had to keep her out of the water and show the world her true worth—she wasn't talented. I *was*."

"It's been twenty years," Grant said, struggling in his seat. "She lived in terror because of you for two decades. That's awful. I played into your hands! I shared her pictures and stories. I told you that she'd be at the Hawthorne Hotel."

"That's right, old man. You're a fool."

Charlene's head ached. Poor Grant! The man had compounded guilt to what he had already felt. She glared at Michael.

Michael wasn't impressed by her glare and pointed to the conch shell from Trinity's bedroom at the top of a box of memorabilia. "I have the magic conch shell. I'll be taking that with me to add to my own collection. This is paltry compared to what I have prepared for my love."

"What do you want?" Mary's body quaked in fear.

"You have to die." Michael shrugged, as if discussing the weather, not three people's lives. "It's the only way."

"Just go," Charlene said. "You don't have to hurt us."

Michael shook his head. "Charlene, stop sniveling. I'll take these things with me back to LA. I have the perfect plan! Grant will be found dead in his office, after killing you and Mary. I have his suicide note and confession written already." He pulled it from his pocket and waved it. "I've been practicing his handwriting. It worked on getting Trinity out of the Hawthorne like a charm."

"You're sick," Mary said. "Mentally ill. Why did you attack me for a poster?"

"Trinity and I were both on it." Michael traced Trinity's face on the thick paper hanging up, then the words, *with love.* "She'd signed it with love. I wanted it for myself. I'll take it with me when I leave. That poster has us both, sitting center conch shell. I don't want anybody to recognize me."

"Fat chance of that," Grant said snidely.

Michael waved the suicide letter. "I'll let you read it if you'd like. Grief-stricken and guilty for killing your daughter."

"Don't!" Grant said.

"Give me back my poster," Mary cried.

"Where you're going you won't need it." Michael folded the note and stuck it in a vest pocket.

Charlene had to keep him talking. How long had she been in the house? Sam would worry after an hour, surely! How long had she been unconscious?

"Why did you kill her after all this time?" Charlene asked. "Maybe you could have been friends again."

"I thought so." Michael tapped his chin. "I tried to talk to her, one on one."

"At the Hawthorne?" Charlene asked.

Michael shrugged. "Not there. She was careful. I couldn't get her alone."

Grant pulled and tugged against his restraints without relief. "So you scared her from the Hawthorne Hotel, where she might have been safer, to the Waterway."

"You got it," Michael said with an exaggerated clap. "I followed her when she left Saturday night. Even held the door open for her. She had no idea it was me." He pulled a beret from an interior vest pocket and a pair of glasses, putting them on with a slouch to his posture.

He was an actor. Charlene recognized the glasses as being on the man who had eaten lunch in the café at the Waterway on Sunday. He was a chameleon. "I saw you Sunday," Charlene said.

"Yeah? I had a room there too," Michael said.

Poor Trinity. Even if she'd been a diva, she didn't deserve to be stalked and killed by this man.

"My sweet daughter," Grant cried.

Michael clucked his tongue. "Stop with the

ruse, Grant. If you'd really loved her, you would have gone to LA, but you abandoned her."

"I told *you* that." Grant straightened his back against the chair like a rod was in his spine.

Michael pocketed the beret and glasses with a sneer. "You are entirely too trusting, old man."

Grant tried to lunge from his chair to reach Michael, but he was tied too tight.

"I've always loved Trinity. Always," Michael said in a matter-of-fact tone. "Even after she had me banned from the set. Blacklisted. Told the producers that I was trying to kill her career by my poor performance. Well, I decided to just kill her instead."

"And that's when you sabotaged the set for the sequel?" Charlene asked. *Hurry, Sam!*

"You bet. Tried to drown her in both water scenes, though she couldn't prove it—otherwise I wouldn't be here in Salem right now."

"That's not love. When you love someone, you want their happiness more than your own. Not want to kill them," Mary said.

"Like you'd know," Michael said.

"I do," Mary said. She didn't elaborate. Charlene wondered if she was thinking of her exboyfriend, who'd given her the black eye so many years ago.

Charlene wiggled her wrists against the rope. She had no plan on how to break free. She hoped to loosen them enough to pull out her hands and go from there.

If she could charge Michael and get downstairs, then she could find help. The station was a few blocks away. A main thoroughfare was just a block from here, the Common across the side street.

Her purse was in the kitchen, but it would do her no good—except slow her down while she searched for the keys to the Pilot.

No. Best just to go for the front door.

Charlene scooted her chair a little. Mary saw her and tilted her head to the table with the shells and the memorabilia. She squinted to identify the items. Was that a *Sirena* letter opener?

"The police will be here any minute. You don't have time to set your plan in motion," Charlene said, discarding the idea; it was plastic, and her hands were bound.

Best bet was to scare him into running away and leaving them alive.

"There will be no police." Michael opened the drawers of goodies, from keychains to magnets, fondling each item.

"You've already gone through everything," Grant said.

"Just want to make sure I don't miss anything of value." Michael's tone was too high, a man demented.

"Tell us again how you fooled everyone." Charlene scooted a little more toward the door. If she could get past him somehow to the hall, she could lock herself in the bathroom. Maybe there would be scissors or something in there. She could free her hands and then . . . do what?

A knock sounded at the front door downstairs. Michael lifted his head, a fox scenting a rabbit. "You never had this many visitors while I was here working on the manuscript, Grant. Whoever it is had better go away or they'll be next."

"It could be the police," Charlene said. "They know I'm here. It's the truth."

Michael cursed under his breath, then scowled with cold eyes at Charlene, Grant, Mary, and back at Charlene.

"Why would they be here?" Michael said, scoffing. "You are bluffing. You didn't know about me until you got here. I am too clever to get caught."

"The Salem PD are very good at their job." Charlene didn't share that Sam was taking her on a date. She wanted Michael to give up his plan to kill them and depart in a rush. "Grant, is there a way Michael can escape without being seen?"

"Yes," Grant said. "The garage is attached through the laundry room. Take my keys and car. Go!"

The knock sounded louder. Michael paced the room as he seemed to consider the idea, but he rejected it.

"I'll convince them to go," Michael said. He clambered down the stairs like a lumbering bear to see who it was. Charlene knew this was her chance to get help. She stood and hopped, the chair balanced on her back like a turtle's shell.

It was extremely uncomfortable, but she was almost to the open doorway as Michael puffed up the stairs to the hall and stood on the threshold, his skin flushed. "It's the police. It's really the police." The crazed man sounded jubilant. "They're really here. Let's have a shoot-out!"

He raced into the shrine room and Charlene used her body, awkwardly tied to the chair, to push into Michael.

He dropped something with a thud to the carpeted floor.

"Is that a gun?" Mary shouted.

Grant hopped to his feet as well, tripping and falling into Michael.

Michael scooped up the weapon and pointed it at Grant. Charlene ruined his aim by knocking into him with her body. The shot went into the ceiling.

That sound was enough for whoever was at the door to break it down. *Hurry, Sam*, Charlene thought. *Hurry*.

Officer Jimenez entered the shrine room first, tackling Michael and grabbing the gun. Sam, on Jimenez's heels, lifted Charlene, who'd fallen on her side. "Charlene!"

Her head swam, from the punch into the wall or from relief that Sam had arrived in time to catch Michael, she wasn't sure. "You came! I warned him that he should go. Grant told him to take the car. Michael is Mickey Bee, Trinity's costar from the first movie. He wouldn't listen."

Officer Bernard helped Jimenez subdue Michael. Jimenez handcuffed Michael and read him his rights.

Michael laughed maniacally. "Call me Michael. Boring Michael Brown."

Officer Bernard met Charlene's gaze with a steady one, nodding at her. Sam had a pocketknife and slit the rope tying her to the chair. He held her arm until she was standing on her own. She knew that he wanted to hold her closer, but he couldn't. He asked gruffly, "Better?"

"Yes." She rubbed her chafed wrists.

Sam freed Grant next, then Mary. Both thanked him profusely. But they didn't look like they wanted to kiss Sam, as Charlene did.

"How did you know to bring the cavalry?" Charlene asked.

"Officer Jimenez figured out from the letter found in Trinity Powers's room that she was being stalked. She'd interviewed Grant about the letter he'd sent to Trinity, but this letter was a threat to Trinity's life in Grant's handwriting. She contacted the LA police, who confirmed that Trinity had made several complaints, but they could never find the perpetrator. She thought it was Mickey but couldn't prove it."

"Michael!" Michael Brown said. "My name is Michael. It's one of the most popular names in the world."

"Why did you kill Trinity?" Grant asked again.

"I loved her. She laughed at me. Said I'd gotten fat—too fat for the sequel she'd just signed up for. She couldn't believe that I'd scared her so much that she hadn't left her house in years."

"So, you choked her," Charlene said, appalled.

"And stuffed that ugly T-shirt down her throat," Michael said. He didn't sound at all sorry.

Officer Jimenez escorted him out of the room and down the stairs. Officer Bernard followed.

Sam scowled in Michael's direction and then turned to Charlene. His exhalation was heartfelt.

Mary pointed to the poster on the wall. "This is mine."

"Take it," Grant said.

Charlene felt so bad for the man. He'd done so much out of love for his daughter.

Mary patted his arm to console him.

Charlene watched the pair and hoped they would find each other—Mary and Grant were both alone in the world but shared a healthy love for Trinity Powers.

"Can I give you a ride somewhere?" Sam brushed his knuckles softly across her cheek. "This will be a shiner."

"No!" She didn't tell him about hitting the wall downstairs out of fear that he'd make her go to the hospital. "My guests—what will they think?"

"That you're a hero," Mary said. "I couldn't think straight, but you—you saved us."

"It's true," Grant said. "Using that chair tied to your back like a wrecking ball to knock into him was brilliant."

"We heard the shot and broke the door down," Sam said. "Charlene?"

"I have my car, Sam. Rain check?"

"Fine." He sighed with disappointment. "I have to go to the station and fill out the paperwork anyway. I'm going to suggest that Jimenez get that promotion. She did good." He looked into her eyes. "So did you." Sam spread his arms to the side. "All of you did a great job today. An officer will be by later to take your statements."

"I'll stay here and help you clean up," Mary offered to Grant.

"Thanks." Grant looked like he needed a friend, and Mary would be there for now. "Okay."

Mary blew out a breath. "Where to start?"

Grant looked at the box and the contents, and then grinned when he saw the conch shell. He picked it up and showed it to Mary.

"Did you ever hear the story about the mermaid from Fiji?"

"No . . ." Mary righted the kitchen chairs and they each sat down.

"I'm going home." Charlene's cheek stung now that the adrenaline rush had passed. She left them to it and went with Sam to the kitchen to get her phone, screen cracked but fixable, and her purse and keys.

They walked out of the house together.

"Are you okay to drive?" Sam asked.

"Yep." She glanced at him. "You're welcome to stop by later if you'd like. I'm not sure what Avery is up to, but maybe we could have a barbecue or something."

"That sounds nice." Sam walked her to her car, but then seemed reluctant to leave her. She understood. It wasn't the right time or place to kiss him.

She opened the door and slid behind the wheel.

Sam glanced around to make sure that they were alone and then framed her face to kiss her deeply. She was glad that he'd taken the risk. She needed his touch to heat the cold tendrils fear had left behind.

"Sam." Charlene peered into his warm brown eyes and touched his cheek. "Thanks for coming to my rescue."

"I didn't do much." Sam leaned closer to her, his body against her hip. She turned to face him. "You are very capable, Mrs. Morris. I like that about you a lot."

She kissed him again but winced as he accidentally touched her bruise.

"Sorry," Sam said, leaning back.

"Don't be. I'm okay." A little sting was nothing compared to his warmth.

Sam kissed the tip of her nose. "I'll do my best not to give away my feelings for you if I come over, but it's going to be hard to do that." He placed his hand on his heart.

"I know what you mean." She thought of Avery. Jack. "But it's important." She straightened, already missing him. "All right—one more kiss for the road."

That kiss had to last her.

By the time it ended, they both were breathless.

"Bye."

"Bye."

He tapped the top of the car as she got in, and she checked the rearview to find that Sam was still watching her drive away. It took all of her will-power to keep going forward.

CHAPTER 26

Charlene arrived at the B-and-B to find Minnie sitting on the porch with a glass of iced tea and a magazine, taking a well-deserved break.

"Hi!" She saw Minnie begin to rise and said, "Don't get up."

"Hey yourself." Minnie sat back but rose in a hurry. "What happened to your face?"

"Is it that bad?" She touched it gingerly.

"Yes."

Jack arrived in a flurry of cold air, and she could feel it as he blew gently on her skin. She was surprised that Minnie didn't notice.

"You were punched!" Jack said indignantly. "Mickey Bee?"

"Michael Brown, the biographer, is the killer," Charlene confirmed. "He's in jail."

"Come inside." Minnie dragged her into the kitchen. "Sit."

Jack watched with his arms crossed as Minnie assembled an ice pack and handed it to Charlene.

"I dug into Mickey Bee, AKA Michael Brown, and saw that Trinity filed a restraining order against him twenty-five years ago. Nothing came of it. I can't believe he waited all this time," Jack said. "Do you know how many Michael Browns there are in the US alone?"

"Michael was a pretty sick man," Charlene said. "He liked torturing Trinity with the idea that if she left her compound, he'd be there. Somewhere. And then she took this new medicine and had a chance to take her life back with the sequel, and *bam*. He was able to reach her. Befriended Grant, who felt so guilty that he was easily fooled."

"Holy smokes," Minnie said.

"Michael saw that she would be in Salem and set up an elaborate scheme as Trinity Powers's biographer. He's an actor and conned her over and over. She'd said he couldn't act, and this was his way of getting her back. He wanted to show her 'true colors' to the world by making sure that her life was ruined. Her getting the sequel sent him over the edge."

"I can't imagine living that way." Minnie patted Charlene's shoulder. "What happened?"

She told Minnie, and Jack, welcoming Silva when the cat jumped up on her lap. "I was tied to the chair and there was nothing I could do." She felt Jack's cool essence over the rope burns that she'd forgotten about.

"I'll get some cream," Minnie said, darting out of the kitchen to the bathroom on the main floor.

"You could have been killed by that madman," Jack said. "What happened to your pepper spray?"

"It was in my purse, which he threw."

Jack raised his hands in the air. "Still! You are resourceful. I'm proud of you."

She smiled her thanks as Minnie returned and applied the cream.

"Ouch!"

"Sorry." Minnie blew on it, as if to take away the hurt. "So then what happened?"

Charlene continued, glossing over the danger of the gun and ending with Sam's arrival with the Salem PD. "Can you believe it? Officer Jimenez just might get a promotion."

"Maybe she can go to Portland, Oregon, instead of Sam," Minnie said cattily.

"That would be something." Charlene sighed and put the woman and her dislike aside. "So, what do you think about having a barbecue? I could invite Seth." But not his mom, because she saw ghosts. At least she saw the little girl in her own house.

Charlene retrieved her cell phone.

"The screen!" Minnie said.

"I can get it fixed tomorrow. For today, I'd like to hang out here." Relax in the safety of her home.

"I approve of that idea a lot." Minnie sighed. "Will Sam be coming by?"

"How would I know?"

This was normally Jack's cue to be jealous. Or upset. To disappear or comment on Sam.

Instead, he watched her carefully and she lowered her eyes. "Let me text Avery—she and Seth might already have plans."

She shot off the idea for a barbecue. Avery immediately replied with a thumbs-up emoji. "Good! We could have it in the backyard. I'm sure the guests will be out enjoying Salem's finest, but I'm ready to put my feet up. Invite Will, Minnie!"

"Okay." Minnie got up and opened the freezer, pulling out a package of burgers to defrost. "Buns . . . I might need to run to the store really quick. Are you okay?"

"Of course!"

The housekeeper left, and Charlene went into her suite with Silva and Jack, closing the door and locking it.

"Charlene," Jack said in a serious voice. "We need to talk."

That didn't sound good. It sounded heavy.

"About?"

"I heard what Minnie asked you a few days ago, about you being open to love."

She'd worried about that. She nibbled her lower lip. "Yes?"

"I keep asking if you're happy because I know that it's a safe question to ask." Jack studied her with compassion. With love.

Her stomach twirled. Knotted.

"I should be asking how you feel about Sam."

Charlene blinked. And blinked. She sat on the love seat. Jack stood before the TV, the images behind him slightly visible because he didn't keep his full form. He was upset too.

"Sam and I are friends."

"I know that. Do you care for him? Are you healed from your broken heart?" Jack stopped and kneeled before her in a gust of chilly air.

It was all she could do to keep her hands to herself at the angst in his turquoise eyes.

"I am healing, yes."

Jack reached for her, a human reaction, but pulled back so he didn't hurt her with his cold essence.

"I have been selfish," Jack said, taking the wind from her sails.

"What? Never!"

"Yes. I love you, Charlene."

Tears dripped from her eyes. "I love you. Jack, you are my best friend in the world."

"It can't be more—we both know that—but I have kept you from seeing Sam in a romantic light for too long." Jack stood.

Charlene scrambled to her feet. "I am the selfish one, Jack. I don't want to lose you. I don't. You helped me through the toughest, darkest patch of my life. You are my partner in this bed-and-breakfast. You take care of me, and Avery. Silva, Minnie. The guests—you care."

"How is that selfish?" Jack asked, shaking his head. "Because of you, I have a family. I never had that before. You have filled this home with laughter. Love."

"Jack!" Charlene sobbed, her body aching with pain.

"I don't want to go." Jack's essence blazed like gold. "I would rather be here, and see you flourish, than not be part of your life at all."

It was too much to hope for . . . this was true love in its purest form. "Is it too cruel to watch me . . . and Sam?"

Jack eyed the ceiling and rocked back on his heels.

Charlene was crying so hard she couldn't see through the thick tears. She gulped, her chest throbbing. She dropped to her knees and bowed her head. It hurt too much.

"No, Charlene." Jack was at her side, looking her in the eye. "What is cruel is not being able to hold you. What is cruel is not being a man. Human. I am dead. A ghost. You . . ." He searched her gaze and manifested a tissue to dab gently at her cheeks. "You are alive. You deserve to be held by a real, living man. The love I have for you is more than I ever knew as a man. It's different somehow."

After several moments, she dragged in a ragged breath. His turquoise gaze held the truth of his feelings. She sniffed. "Now what do we do?"

Jack whirled around the room in frenetic chaos and howled his frustration. She crumpled the tissue in her palm. Love sucked.

"I should go!" His tone entreated her to argue with him.

"No! Please, don't."

The curtains fluttered and the TV flickered. She was reminded of when she'd first seen him in his smoking jacket, so regal. It wasn't fair to keep him if he wanted to go. She dragged herself upright, using the love seat for balance.

"Don't go." Tears streamed down her cheeks, the pain anew. To not have Jack in her life? She needed him.

He stopped before her. "I don't want to leave you. I am selfish, I told you. I want to see you. *You* are my light, Charlene. I'm not jealous . . . my heart isn't like that anymore. I'm evolving too. But I might need some time before I see you with Sam."

Time? Of course. She nodded, her hand to her whirling belly.

With that, Jack was gone.

That night at the barbecue, Charlene couldn't stop the tears. She explained that she was over-wrought from the day of being threatened, but truthfully, it was fear that she would never see Jack again.

Sam arrived with Rover, his Irish setter. Silva watched the dog with golden eyes. Rover got too close to say hello and Silva popped his nose—no claws, so it was just a warning.

Sam laughed. "It's okay, girl. Silva will warm up to you."

Avery and Seth sat on a plaid blanket beneath the oak tree with the wooden swing.

There was so much that she was trying to process. Jack was in every thought—even the ones with Sam.

Sam didn't believe in the paranormal. She wished there was a way to open his mind to more beyond this world.

Will and Minnie sat together on foldout chairs, sharing a garden table. The barbecue emitted wonderful hamburger smells—a regular BBQ. Not a single lobster tail. Real potato salad. She searched the sky. No Jack.

"Summer is almost over," Avery lamented. "This is super nice."

"It is!" Charlene wadded a napkin with sandals printed on it and brought it to her eyes.

Avery lifted her glass of iced tea. "To home!" the young woman said.

Charlene blinked away more tears. Jack wasn't around that she could see. She had to trust that he would be back, if he could. She knew in her heart that if it was possible, he wouldn't leave without telling her goodbye.

Sam sat next to Charlene on the back porch steps and smiled at her. She gave a watery smile back. "To home."

Visit our website at
KensingtonBooks.com
to sign up for our newsletters, read
more from your favorite authors, see
books by series, view reading group
guides, and more!

Become a Part of Our
Between the Chapters Book Club
Community and Join the Conversation

Betweenthechapters.net

Submit your book review for a chance to win exclusive
Between the Chapters swag you can't get anywhere else!
https://www.kensingtonbooks.com/pages/review/